# DOUBLE MAGPIE MURDERS

## *Art of Murder Series*
## *Book 3*

## Pam Fox

Bright Fox Books

# ONE

She'd lost track of time. Night had fallen, and Kate Corliss was ravenous.

A drawing of two muskrats swimming in a creek had absorbed her, and she'd awakened from her work the way she did from sleep, slightly disoriented, her mind stilled. The window next to her, over the dinette in her truck camper, was black.

She'd gotten a quick dinner started, and now the omelet sizzling in the pan smelled like heaven. Chopped chives and crumbled Feta cheese—oh, dinner would be good. She flipped the eggy disc: golden brown, perfect. A minute more and—

The lights went out.

Rats.

Loss of AC power wouldn't usually be a problem, since the camper's battery kicked in automatically. But that afternoon Kate had pulled the battery to check its cells, then realized she was out of the distilled water she needed to top them off. No problem—she was plugged into the campground's "shore power," right?

She looked out the small window above the stove. The big Winnebago on the next site was still lit, of course, but the ankle-high, mushroom-shaped lights along the campground pathways had gone dark.

The house where the Roll and Rest RV Park owners lived must have power, though: its big back window was lit like a stage. Inside, a girl and the woman Kate had met when she'd paid for her site were stacking dishes at the dining room table. Then a light went on in the next room—the kitchen, Kate remembered—and the woman's face showed at the window over the sink.

The house lights were good news. Not a neighborhood blackout, then. Smaller problems get fixed faster.

A silhouette crossed the big window as someone slipped along the back of the house, turned the corner. A tingle of anxiety swept through Kate.

She must be getting paranoid, imagining malicious creeps everywhere because of her recent misadventures to the north, in Maine and upstate New York. Chill, she told herself. Whoever was out there was probably a campground employee trying to restore the power.

Ironic there was an outage: she'd needed to find a campground because the generator on the camper wouldn't start. Her plan had been to dry-camp, or boondock—which was free— as she worked her way south and west from Maine, with Tucson her eventual destination. Since she was living on savings she had to be frugal; campgrounds were normally a luxury. But she couldn't boondock without the generator to recharge her batteries every few days.

She caught her dinner before it was toast, snapped off the propane burner and slid the omelet onto the plate she'd set out.

Yum. Even in the dark, dinner tasted as good as she'd hoped.

\* \* \*

The domestic scene inside the house looked peaceful now, but when Kate had arrived at the Roll and Rest late that afternoon the woman had been distressed.

Her name was Yvonne. Frequent sniffling undermined the regal impression her long nose might have made; she dabbed at it with a series of tissues and dropped them into an overflowing wastebasket. "Sorry," she said. Her long hair was pulled into an old-fashioned bun, exposing a strained face. She sat at a small secretary-style desk tucked into the corner of the dining room and opened the lid, then bowed her head. Her shoulders shook.

"Is there anything I can do to help?" Kate had asked. "Or do you need some time? I could come back in half an hour."

Yvonne shook her head and collected herself. She took another tissue and blotted her face and then the papers in front of her. "It's my little girl," she said. "I don't know what's wrong with her. She's nine, but I'd swear she's getting Alzheimer's." She managed a smile. "Do you have children?"

"No, I don't." Kate had never wanted to start a family. She suspected her difficult relationship with her mother was a major reason.

"Being a parent is a total freak-out sometimes." Yvonne laughed. It was a hearty laugh, full-bodied, and Kate was startled it could come from a woman who'd been weeping a minute earlier.

Kate imagined being a mother wouldn't be difficult only "sometimes"—no, it would be one continuous freak-out a couple of decades long. She smiled at the woman, whose eyes were filling again. "I hope your daughter gets better soon."

Her credit card, when she got it back, was slippery with tears. The registration tag, which showed her name and reservation dates, was damp and splotched. She clipped it to the post at her site.

\* \* \*

Kate put her plate and fork in the sink. Maybe one of the other campers would let Yvonne know about the power failure.

She was too tired to deal with it. She'd driven the camper over a hundred miles south that day, crossing from New York into western Pennsylvania, then biked a trail she'd found in the Laurel Highlands near Greensburg. The foliage was starting to turn, with an occasional trend-setting maple flaring into full color. Flocks of blackbirds had swirled in the windy sky like the shadows of leaves.

As she climbed into the over-cab bunk, she congratulated herself for remembering to turn off the switch for the main cabin light. If the power came back on during the night she didn't want to wake up, blinky and crabby.

Usually she read for a half an hour before sleep, but tonight she closed the book after ten minutes when an enormous yawn squeezed her eyes shut. She tucked her headlamp under the pillow and snuggled into her down bag.

The trail came back to her in dreams, bike tires crackling over crushed limestone and rumbling across wooden bridges, the dusty smell of last year's fallen leaves rising from the dry earth.

\* \* \*

The leafy smell was still with her when she woke. Dark outside: the days were getting shorter. The earth had turned the round corner into October.

Yawning, she slid off the bunk and pulled on a T-shirt and jeans. Pushed the button on the five-cup coffee-maker. The orange light didn't come on.

Oh, right, the power problem.

She got out a battery-powered lantern, gave the coffee-maker a sad look and put the kettle on the stove, the burner's flame adding its blue light to the lantern's yellow. Her morning's necessary start-up hit of caffeine would take longer. She set the paper filter in its holder atop her favorite mug, the one with *La Brea Tar Pits* on the side, and scooped in ground coffee.

4

She could change campgrounds if she had to, but she liked this one. Rated four-point-eight out of five stars online, it backed onto a national recreation area along Loyalhanna Creek. The road it was on, Watkins Spur, had dirt shoulders wide enough to be safe for biking and didn't look like it got much traffic.

Hiking had always been important to Kate. These days she included a sketchbook and pencils in her pack and drew anything that caught her eye. She'd started working again seriously only a few months earlier, after a lapse of many years. In August, at an artists' colony, she'd met an older painter who'd both mentored and inspired her.

She'd been thrilled to rediscover such a vibrant connection to the physical world; she wondered how she'd lived without it. Drawing a bird was, for her, nearly becoming a bird. Landscapes she encountered opened her to landscapes within. Her mind became large, larger. Like a globe, her brain had two hemispheres. Its shape rhymed with planet Earth's.

As she waited for the water to boil she checked the house. Lights were on, and in the dining room a balding man and two children sat at the table, the man behind a newspaper opened wide. The girl was writing—doing homework?—and the boy was fiddling with something in his lap. Yvonne was in the kitchen, probably making breakfast.

Wait—what the heck? The boy was shooting rubber bands at the cat! A gray cat was rubbing itself against the kitchen door frame, probably hoping for a hand-out from Yvonne. The yellow eyes looked with interest at the bands hitting the wall near it, but the cat continued pushing the side of its face and then its shoulder against the door jamb. Kate could almost hear it purring.

When the boy landed one of his missiles square in the animal's ear, it shook its head and scampered away. His parents were apparently oblivious of both the campground's power outage and their son's unkind treatment of the cat.

Kate drank her coffee and watched. The man folded the newspaper and left the room; the children put on their jackets and backpacks and left too. They must be going out the front door. She waited a few minutes before stepping into the crisp fall air and crossing the patio to knock on the back door, its OFFICE sign bracketed by smiling cartoon cats. She was tempted to tell the boy's mother one of her cats wasn't smiling.

Yvonne was apologetic. Her hair was down, and she tucked it behind her ears nervously. "Oh, no, your lights are out? I'd better check the breakers. Just let me get a coat on."

Kate turned and looked at the campground. Only half a dozen sites were filled, not surprising on a Monday. Leaf-peepers might bring the place closer to capacity on weekends. Was she the first one up? The sky was brightening and a blue jay jeered. Then its cry was lost in the whinny of the generator starting up on the big motorhome next to her camper. The Winnebago shared its site with a small gray sedan, and Kate was happy her own rig was small enough that she didn't have to tow another vehicle.

Yvonne came out, shrugging her way into a lime-green parka that looked like overkill to Kate, who hadn't put anything on over her T-shirt. The coffee infusion must have turned her biological thermostat up. Of course, Yvonne had on a skirt, something Kate hadn't worn in years. Drafty things, skirts.

"The house has its own breaker box inside, so I didn't realize you'd lost your juice out here," Yvonne said, making her way around the chairs on the patio. Over her shoulder she added, "Thanks for being so understanding yesterday."

"No problem at all." Kate followed the campground manager toward the corner of the house and almost bumped into her when she stopped short.

Over the lime-green shoulder, Kate took it in: the door of the gray metal box mounted on the siding ajar, a piece of matching gray metal on the ground, short pieces of black wire scattered around like insects.

"No wonder there's no power," Yvonne said. "Damn." She took a few more steps and opened the box's door wide.

The panel looked like the one in the basement of the house where Kate used to live with her boyfriend: from fat cables at the top, wires ran down the sides to two columns of black plastic switches. The wires had been cut, their ends catching the light with coppery glints. Cut not once, but twice, so a piece was missing. Which meant they couldn't be reattached; they'd have to be replaced.

Yvonne put a hand to her forehead as she took in the damage. "I'll talk to John, our handyman." She poked at the bits of wire on the ground with a slippered toe. "But this is probably too much for him. That means an electrician." She shook her head. "I'll need to report this, and it'll cost us, since we tried to save money with a high deductible."

"Whoever did it had to unscrew the cover first," Kate said, pointing to the gray metal frame on the ground. "He must have come with tools. Not something done on impulse."

"You're right. Who would do such a thing?" Yvonne looked around as if she expected the culprit to appear. "I could talk to my husband about moving the box inside. This one got added to the house when the people who used to live here decided to put RVs in their back yard. First just a few sites, for friends. Then they turned it into a business."

"Has anything like this happened before?"

"No," Yvonne said. "This is usually such a quiet place. Ah, what a pain." She kicked at one of the wire bits and then brightened. "Or I could just ask John to put a padlock on the box after it's fixed." She turned to Kate. "Either way, it won't happen again."

Starting toward the door, she waved a hand at the back of the house. "The couple who sold us this place loved having a picture window back here, said it helped keep an eye on the campground. Didn't help this time, though. I didn't see a thing."

Kate had seen someone, probably the person responsible, but she didn't mention it. The silhouette hadn't given any identifying details. Instead she asked for a referral to a local shop that could repair her generator.

"Oh, John could help you with that," Yvonne said. "He's a whiz at RV repairs."

"Where can I find him?"

"Right behind you," Yvonne said.

# TWO

He was tall and thin, with a tangled beard and permanent squint. Neither his clothes nor his hands had seen soap and water in a while. He looked, in fact, a little scary, and he must have moved as silently as a cat.

Yvonne introduced them, and Kate was glad he didn't offer to shake hands.

"John can fix just about anything an RV can throw at you," Yvonne said. "And he's handy in another way, too—he lives in that big Chevy camper van over in the corner. Appointments are easy to get."

"Site thirteen," John said to Kate. "I'm not superstitious."

"Well, great," Kate said. "Could you have a look at my generator? It won't start."

"John, before you do that, would you take a look at this mess?" Yvonne tipped her head toward the open door of the breaker box.

He whistled. "Wow. How did this happen?"

"No idea," Yvonne said.

John blinked. "Vandalism," he said, "plain and simple." He leaned in, hands on knees, for a closer look. Nodded to himself a few times, then straightened and shrugged. "Sure, I can fix this puppy."

"You can?" Yvonne looked at Kate and grinned. "John saves the day. Not for the first time."

"I've got plenty of wire in the shed. Couple hours?"

"That's super." She twirled in a circle to celebrate, her skirt and long hair flaring. "He's all yours, Kate."

"Let me get some breakfast first, okay?" John said to Kate. "I came over as soon as I realized the power was out. I need a muffin before I do any heavy lifting."

"Sure," Kate said. "Whenever you're ready. I'm in the slide-in truck camper on the Ford. Site six."

"I'd like a lock on the box from now on, John," Yvonne said.

He'd already started toward his van; he turned and walked backwards a few steps. "No sweat," he said. "I've got a padlock I'll slap on there."

Yvonne smiled at Kate. "He uses my shed to store his tools and supplies, and it's a total zoo in there. I don't know how he finds a thing, especially something as small as a padlock."

\* \* \*

As the day warmed up, people came out of their RVs to drink coffee or read or just sit in the sun and enjoy the fresh autumn air. A big orange cat made the rounds, getting a few strokes from campers who held their hands out to him and made those peculiar squeaky noises cat-lovers everywhere use. For Kate, without a working camper battery, the power outage was a nuisance, but it had the pleasant side effect of drawing the temporary community of RVers together.

"Is your power out like ours?" An older couple sat in lawn chairs beside the Winnebago. The woman who'd called out the question was round and cheerful-looking, with a mass of tight gray curls. The man, taller, was slouched back with his eyes closed, but he sat up when his companion called out to Kate.

Curled up between their chairs, a border collie lifted its head and watched her approach.

Donna and Richard Miller, from Ohio. "Headed for Florida," he said, for "oranges and sunshine." His thick beard was gray even though the hair on his head was dark. "We've come here every summer for years on our way down to Florida—we visit our son in Pittsburgh and then head south. But this time we're going to find our retirement home. Maybe somewhere around St. Pete." Then he looked at their RV. "Too bad we aren't driving our old rig. Had it forever."

"We just bought this one, and the smallest car we could find to tow," Donna said. "Good thing we were close to home when the old motorhome bit the dust. The main seal failed, and before Richard could pull over the engine was fried. Oil all over the road." She was chewing gum, making small snapping noises.

"This one's good," Richard said. "Bought it from a guy who was giving up RVing after his wife passed away. It's newer than the one we had, which means a little more peace of mind, but it's too bad we had to buy it for just this one trip."

"We'll get our money back when we sell it, honey." Donna turned back to Kate and laughed. "He's been talking about Florida since the day I met him. Says you don't have to shovel sunshine out of your driveway."

Kate had heard that one growing up in Tucson, so she said what she always said. "No, but the heat is always up to here," holding her hand up over her head. "Snow stays on the ground."

The couple laughed. The dog stood and took a step toward Kate, then looked at Richard.

"Do you like dogs?" he asked Kate.

"Not all of them, but this guy looks like a sweetie."

"Okay, Juneau," Richard said to the dog, and it took a few more steps and sniffed the hand Kate offered, palm down.

"Border collies are so smart," she said. "If I had a dog, that would be the breed I'd go for. And this fella has such good manners. A lot of dogs jump all over people uninvited, stick their noses places they shouldn't. That's the kind of dog I don't like."

"Training Juneau was a piece of cake, and she's as gentle as they come," Donna said. "A lamb in dog's clothing." She picked up the mug beside her chair and took a sip.

Ugh, gum and coffee. But Donna somehow made the combination seem not just okay but upbeat. "Juneau's a pretty name," Kate said. "I'd love to go to Alaska. Is that where you got her?"

"No, she's a rescue who came with the name," Donna said. "I'd love to go to Alaska, too. Not sure we'll make it." She smiled at her husband. "What do you think, Richard?"

"Have to see," he said. "Bears and blizzards. Maybe you could go with a friend. You and Kate?"

"I'm not going anywhere without you, honey," Donna said. "Sorry, Kate."

Another camper joined the group and introduced herself. Annie had a small build and looked to be in her forties, with a red ponytail and green eyes. Her rig was a dark brown four-wheel-drive van. A classic, but in tough shape, with rust lacing the rocker panels. She was from Wisconsin, she said, and between jobs.

The side door of a pop-up camper a few sites from Annie's slid open and two young men got out, yawning and stretching. They gave the orange cat some attention and then meandered toward the group at the Winnebago. One of them looked like a bear, big and hairy. He scratched his belly through his T-shirt while he drank from a cardboard cup. More coordinated than I am, Kate thought. His friend, taller and thinner, hung back.

"Looks like a convention over here," the bear said. "Are we missing anything?"

"Don't think so," Richard said. "We're just out here enjoying the weather."

"Sorry we ran our generator for a few minutes," Donna said. "We needed it for our coffee-maker. I hope it didn't bother anybody."

"Oh, heck, no, it was time for us to be up anyway," the bear said. "We're here for the river." He waved a hand at the canoe beside their camper. "The Loyalhanna's so beautiful in the fall, and we want to paddle and fish. Water's low, though, on account of the drought." He looked at Kate's boat, which she'd turtled on the picnic table and locked with a cable. "Who's the lucky dude with the Hornbeck?"

"That would be me," Kate said.

"Those things weigh what, twenty pounds?"

"Sixteen."

The bear snorted and his friend rolled his eyes, both of them grinning.

"Yeah, it was a present from my boyfriend," she said, afraid the expensive boat made her look like she had a lot of money.

"Wow, what a great present. The boyfriend's a keeper."

"Nah, I dumped the guy, kept the boat," Kate said. Mike had ended their relationship, but nobody here needed to know that.

"Good move," the bear said, and the group laughed. He looked at her over the rim of his coffee, checking her out. Wait, he was way too young for her. Wasn't he?

"You know about the dam downstream about half a mile, don't you?" He lifted his cup toward the river.

"No," Kate said. "My first time here. Thanks for the warning."

"Those lowhead dams are hard to see from upstream—you almost have to hear them, hear the water going over. This one has a bunch of rocks beyond it, so it's pretty noisy. But no problem, good trails on both sides for portaging."

John walked by on his way to the shed, carrying a metal toolbox. He nodded at Kate and she raised a hand in return.

"You got boyfriends everywhere," the bear said.

Kate was pretty sure she didn't want a boyfriend whose beard was speckled with muffin crumbs.

* * *

The good news: John could fix the generator. The bad news: it would take a while. She was at her dinette, finishing a breakfast of cold cereal and soymilk, when he'd startled her by smacking the camper door with the flat of his hand—his style of knocking, apparently. He took an impressive multimeter out of his toolbag and in ten minutes had given her a diagnosis of a blown voltage regulator.

"This is a pretty old genset," he said. "I'll need to order the part, and it'll take a while to get here. I promised my brother I'd help him lay some flooring, so I won't be able to work on this for at least a week."

"How much you figure it'll cost?" Kate asked. They were standing outside her rig, the door to the generator compartment flipped open. She might be able to get it done faster if she went to a shop in Greensburg or even Pittsburgh, but she liked to stay away from cities and major routes. She was a back-roads traveler, out for scenery rather than speed.

"The regulator? That's a hundred. If you want a tune-up at the same time, plugs and filters and oil change, that'll go up to a hundred and fifty in parts," John said. "Labor, I charge twenty an hour. It'll take me an hour or two."

Kate was startled. RV shops charged over a hundred an hour.

John apparently misread her hesitation. "I guarantee you'll be happy with my work," he said. "Any problem, you know where I live."

He must be competent, or Yvonne wouldn't keep him on as a handyman. "Okay, John. Go ahead and order the parts. Repair and tune-up."

He nodded, headed for his camper, then did the walking-backwards thing again. "Check your stuff. Sometimes when people make the lights go out it's so's they can help themselves to something that isn't theirs."

"Thanks for the tip."

Her most vulnerable possession was the lightweight kayak. When she was on the move she strapped it to the camper's roof rack, but she'd brought it down to the picnic table so it would be handy for spontaneous paddles. A cable with looped ends that slipped over bow and stern met underneath the table with a lock—the boat was secure unless somebody took a chain saw to the table.

The other item she owned in the frequently stolen category was stowed safely inside her camper, on one side of the queen-sized bed over the cab: her bike. A cover kept chain oil and tires from messing up her sheet and sleeping bag. When she and her former partner went on trips together, they used to carry their bikes on a hitch rack, but the truck's rear wheels kicked up grit and Kate was unhappy with the condition of her bike afterwards, especially if the weather was rainy. After she and Mike broke up, when she'd first moved aboard the camper full-time, her friend Marjorie had made a joke about her sleeping with her bike.

"It works for me," Kate had said.

"Whatever floats your boat," Marjorie said. "Or likes your bike."

As she looked at John's retreating back, another warning came to her. Sometimes people who thought of theft did so because they were thieves themselves.

Yvonne trusts him, she reminded herself.

\* \* \*

15

By the time she came back from exploring one of the trails in the conservation area, power had been restored. As soon as she climbed on board her camper she hit the button on the coffee-maker.

The orange light came on and the little machine chugged and gurgled, on its way to producing the magic black liquid.

Life was good.

She worked on a drawing for a few hours, ate a quick lunch and got back to work. Eventually she surfaced from the peaceful trance, stretched, dropped from the camper and knocked on the office door. Painful as it was to pay for a full week at Roll and Rest, it made sense: she'd save a lot by having John fix her generator, and the weekly rate was discounted well below what seven individual days would cost. The sites weren't too close together, and the abutting river and conservation land offered plenty of opportunities to paddle and hike. Maybe Kate shouldn't be sorry her generator had quit, since that had brought her to such a pleasant place.

In the dining room, Yvonne opened the lid of the secretary and pulled a form from one of the cubbyholes. This time the papers stayed dry. After giving Kate her receipt and a new tag for the post at her site, the campground owner suggested coffee, an offer Kate rarely refused.

Yvonne went to the kitchen and opened a cupboard. "What do you take in it?"

"All I want in my coffee is coffee," Kate called back.

At the table, Yvonne added cream to her cup. "I wish I could take it black, too, on account of the calories. I don't know how you can drink the stuff straight, though. Curls my tongue." She had a serious, aristocratic face but eyes that sparkled with humor. If she carried a bit extra around the middle Kate couldn't tell, especially under the big pullover. Sometimes people were their own worst enemies, calling attention to small faults nobody would otherwise notice.

"Sorry about the power failure," Yvonne said. "I don't know who would want to hurt Roll and Rest's business." She picked up a pile of magenta yarn from the table and somehow organized it into a coherent piece of knitting. "Shawl," she said. "I always knit for the crafts fair." The needles snicked in the quiet house.

"Have you had any unhappy customers recently? Your online reviews are really good, but all it takes is one turkey in the flock to pull a stunt like this."

"Can't think of any campers," Yvonne said slowly. "But now that you mention it—" She laughed. "You said 'turkey,' and that's what I've started calling my brother-in-law Gaston. He was a business partner with me and my husband Duval until last August. Then he pulled out all of a sudden for no good reason, and hasn't been in touch. So now I call him a turkey."

"Real turkeys might take offense."

"I don't want to call him something worse with the children around." The knitting was lacy, fine, and Yvonne's fingers knew exactly where to pick it up again after a coffee-drinking foray. She barely looked at her work.

Gaston? Duval? "Sounds like there's a big French influence in your husband's family."

"Yes, our last name's Chouinard, about as French as you can get. Duval's parents still live in Quebec." She was looking at the ceiling, her mind still apparently on her brother-in-law. "Gaston." She giggled. "The children call him Uncle Gassy."

"I bet when he was a kid he got called Gassy, too," Kate said. "Not the easiest name to grow up with. I had a friend with the last name Woodcock who told me about the awful teasing he had to deal with."

"Oh, Gaston could always take care of himself," Yvonne said. "He moved down here before we did, said he could make more money in the States. We were visiting him, staying at this campground when the kids were little—let's see, five years ago, so Savvy was four and Carson was seven. And the place came up for sale. When Duval said we should buy it I was stunned." She raised her eyebrows. "I don't know if it was the best thing, but here we are. He left the insurance company and I left my fourth-graders."

"You're living in a gorgeous area, right next to a lot of conservation land. That's one of the reasons I chose this campground."

"Yes, the protected land along the river is beautiful. I have maps if you want them, but it's hard to get lost with Loyalhanna Creek running right up the middle. When you paddle, be careful about the little dam between here and the lake. There are take-outs on both banks and the carry's short."

Her face dimmed. "We're too busy now to get outside much. Since Gaston isn't here to help with the business, Duval's back in insurance. A town job. Running this place ties us down, and he doesn't even get to talk to the campers coming through. He used to enjoy that. Now he works too darn hard."

The gray cat meandered into the room and Kate felt it rub against her leg. She reached down and stroked its sleek back, felt it purr under her hand. "Hi, sweetie."

"Cats are so different, just like kids," Yvonne said. "This one's usually shy, although she seems to like you. I keep her indoors. We have another one, a big orange kitty you've probably seen around, Rusty. He's so social he's practically human—goes right up to strangers to see if he can cadge a treat."

"I've seen him already, working the crowd. Exactly as advertised," Kate said. "He's a big success as a furry pan-handler."

Yvonne smiled. "My two kids are way different, too. Savvy—Savannah—she's smart as a whip but shy, like Shadow here. All of a sudden she's getting headaches, and forgetting things—that's why I was so upset yesterday. She got lost walking home from school, which is ridiculous, and a neighbor had to bring her home."

"Oh, dear," Kate said.

"Until now my son Carson was the one keeping me up at night. He's smart too, but quiet. Too quiet. The last time he was tested, his social development wasn't up to speed for his age group.

Kate had no experience raising children, so she went back to the vandalism thread. Maybe she could help with that. "Did your brother-in-law pull out of the campground because he was angry about something? Do you think he might be responsible for the damage to the breaker box?"

Yvonne looked startled. "He didn't say he was upset about anything. If anybody was angry it was Duval, because we had to get a loan and he had to go back to work. But he was hurt more than angry. Hurt and puzzled." She sighed. "Gaston's always been full of schemes and oddball ways of making a living. I suppose he wanted the money for his latest project, whatever it is."

Shadow jumped into her lap, right on top of the magenta yarn, but Yvonne's expression was affectionate instead of annoyed. Looking into her owner's face, the cat cocked her head, then her shoulders, and kept turning until she fell over.

Kate laughed, and Yvonne looked up with a smile. "Isn't that cute? She does it a lot, falls over with love. I always tell her it's okay to lie on my knitting as long as she doesn't drop any stitches." She rubbed the side of the cat's face. "She's so relaxed now. She was a rescue cat, and so jumpy at first we disconnected the doorbell because it terrified her."

Kate liked this woman. Her priorities were in the right order.

"After we moved here I home-schooled the children, but this year, with Duval working, I couldn't do that and keep up with running the place. It's crazy busy earlier in the fall, and in the spring, too, even before school's out. Full every night for months. I'm glad it's late enough in the year now that I get some quiet time to knit and hang out with Shadow, meet some of my new customers, like you. And chat with the ones I know from earlier years, like the Millers. They're old friends."

"Busy means you must be doing things right," Kate said. "Hey, maybe Savvy got lost because she's not used to going to school outside the house."

"I wish," Yvonne said. "But there's just one turn, and it's less than a mile. Over a mile and the two of them would qualify to ride the bus."

"Rats."

Yvonne looked around as if worried her children might be listening. "You know what? I feel like somebody just let *me* out of school! I'm so glad I'm not their teacher any more. It was hard to keep them interested, to come up with creative ways of getting them to eat their intellectual vegetables. Especially Carson. Savvy's curious, so it was easier with her."

Kate emptied her cup, about to say thanks and leave, when Yvonne apologized. "I've been talking your ear off. Tell me about you. You're kind of young to be on the road. Are you on vacation?"

"I'm taking a break," Kate said. The flicker of judgment she'd seen on other faces when she said that didn't show on Yvonne's. "I've worked as a newspaper reporter, and before that as an EMT—a medical tech on an ambulance. I'm taking about a year off, making up my route as I go along. When I get to Tucson, where my mother lives, I'll have to think about the next step."

"Tucson! That's quite a trip."

"I've lived in Arizona and Massachusetts, but there's a whole lot of the country I haven't seen."

"I think it's wonderful you're able to travel while you're young," Yvonne said. "You'll never regret taking some time off. And it's so brave of you to travel alone."

"It isn't, really. But thanks." Other people, both friends and strangers, had said similar things, but she didn't think her lifestyle was such a big deal. Why was a woman traveling alone called brave while a man traveling alone was called a man traveling alone?

"At least you don't have children to worry about," Yvonne said. "It's tough to be a mother sometimes. It's a scary world these days, isn't it?"

"Yes," Kate said. She thought of the figure she'd seen slipping along the back of the house shortly after the power failure. She'd calmed herself by guessing it was a campground worker. But the only employee was John, who'd whistled in surprise when he'd seen the cut wires.

She must have seen the criminal leaving the scene. A shiver went through her. But at least the crime was only vandalism.

# THREE

Kate leaned her daypack against the high bank and sat down, sketchbook on knees, pouch of pencils open beside her. Yvonne had told her about this sandy area at the end of the path from the campground to Loyalhanna Creek. "The kids call it a beach, but it's just a patch of sand," she'd said. "Smaller than it sounds, but then our creek is bigger than it sounds."

She was right. In Kate's mind creeks meandered, slow and narrow, their dark water sometimes wide enough for only one kayak. Here, the far bank was at least fifty feet away, the water bright and purposeful with current. This creek was a river.

Kate was pleased with herself for having walked the mile to the village of Union Hill that morning to buy a plastic jug of distilled water for her battery. She could have gone in her truck, but walking felt much better; exercise balanced the nearly motionless hours she spent on her artwork, indoors and out. On the way back to Roll and Rest she'd used the gallon jug for curls and extensions.

Two of the cells had been low. She'd used an eyedropper so no dirt got washed into the ports, then snapped on the plastic covers. As she lifted the battery from the picnic table and slid it into its compartment on the camper, her arms tingled and she hoped she hadn't overdone the exercise bit with the water jug.

Clouds had moved in while she'd worked on the battery, but the sand under her legs was still warm from the sun earlier in the day. She felt calm, anticipating the pressure of a pencil in her hand, the small noises the point made against paper. A distant crow cawed, and a clean-laundry smell rose from her shirt.

Water. An impossible subject. You could never draw a river, because it was never really there. It was always just leaving.

Wasn't everything in motion? Light, even. Color was light moving in a wave at a certain frequency. Kate knew that, but she couldn't see it. What she could see was a pewter surface with silver highlights, the river's revision of the overcast sky.

Ten feet from shore, the river roiled and bulged around a slate-gray rock with a flaky toupee of lichen. The water was clear enough that she could see the dark shape of the boulder almost to the bottom, darker and less detailed than the part above the surface. Her view of the submerged portion was distorted by light bending through the water, of course, as if she were looking through a lens. A lens of moving water.

Even the rock was in motion, a physicist would tell her. Not as much as the river, but it was home to electrons swarming in clouds. Its molecules packed tight, the rock held its shape, but on the inside it was a busy place.

An eddy near the shoreline attracted her eye: red and yellow leaves spun slowly, their contrast with the black water sharp. She drew for a while, gradually losing her sense of where she was, becoming a red leaf, floating—

Something shoved at her elbow and she yelped with surprise. Her hand jerked across the page and the pencil left an ugly scratch.

The eyes gleamed yellow, their pupils slits of blackness. Kate took a deep breath and scolded the orange cat.

"You're not helping, Rusty," Kate said. "In fact you just wrecked my drawing." She got out her kneaded eraser. She had a new one, but she liked the old—soft and gray from use. Good for a while yet.

The big cat didn't look the slightest bit guilty. He rubbed his face on her arm and purred, and she relented and stroked the rough fur. Definitely an outdoor cat. A lucky outdoor cat, with the thousands of acres of the Loyalhanna Recreation Area to play in. Or likely half that, since Rusty probably wasn't a swimmer and would stay on this western side of the creek.

"You look like a tough kitty," she said. "But you can't fool me. You're just a pussycat inside."

She pushed him gently away and got back to work. First job was to repair the pencil slash.

Perhaps two hours passed as she filled pages of her sketchbook with leaves floating on water and then a branch above the river, its calligraphic shape black against the pearly sky. Finally she chose the boulder as a subject, considering its shades of gray, the shape of the water piling against it on the upstream side, the shiny spillway beside it, the dark dent it caused in the river just downstream.

She was observing it closely, and then she stopped seeing it at all. Her scalp prickled with the sensation of being watched. Without moving her head, she looked around as much as possible.

Not another creature nearby, not even a certain yellow tomcat.

She looked across the river. Unlike this side, with a high bank over a sandy stretch, the far bank was solidly forested right down to the water. She stared at the dimness under the trees until her eyes watered. Was somebody over there watching her?

The boulder could wait for another day. She couldn't work until she shook off the ominous feeling. Kate hated being watched, even when she knew who was doing the watching. It was one of the reasons she'd majored in biology instead of art in college: studio classes meant a professor was looking over your shoulder all the time.

That had been unpleasant. An anonymous watcher was intolerable.

Standing, she looked around, then stretched, arms wide to the sky. Knelt to pack up her supplies, the pencils and charcoal, the sketchbook, the spray can of workable fixative.

Because she was tense, the commotion in the leaves on the bank above her sounded like an explosion. She jumped to her feet. She couldn't see over the wall of soil and roots, but something large was running away through the woods, the crackling of leaves that marked its progress fading with distance.

Kate scrambled to the top of the bank. The path she'd taken down to the beach was empty, the woods on either side of it still.

Animal or person, it was gone.

Dropping back onto the sand to get her pack, Kate told herself to relax. It could have been a deer that had been napping, the way deer do between their favorite foraging periods of dawn and dusk, and some eddy of air had brought it her scent and spooked it. She'd been startled before on hikes when she accidentally flushed deer.

She did such a good job convincing herself it was a deer that she looked along the top of the bank for the animal's bed, the flattened foliage where it would have been lying.

No bed. A bent tuft of grass, an overturned pebble, but no impression of a deer's body. In fact, no area free enough of bushes and saplings to leave room for a deer to lie down. Kate ran the sound through her mind again. Did the steps have the rhythm of four feet, or two? Were they loud enough carry the weight of a deer, or a person?

She didn't like her conclusion.

She stood a moment, unnerved. Was trouble following her? She hadn't completely recovered from her paddling trip in the

Adirondack region of upstate New York, where a friend had been arrested for murder. Finding the truth had been frightening and dangerous.

Taking a deep breath, she talked herself down. Things had turned out all right, her friend had been cleared and released. And what had just happened was nothing more than another hiker passing by, perhaps startled by an unexpected *plein air* artist. She didn't own the woods, she told herself.

Moving back toward the path, she saw something blue and shiny among low leaves. A candy bar wrapper? She hated litter and reached for the bright object before realizing what it was.

Solid in her hand, it wasn't the wrapper she'd taken it for.

A cell phone.

Well, she knew one thing. White-tailed deer didn't carry phones.

\* \* \*

Back home in the camper, she examined her find. It was a flip phone, the kind that folds in half and fits in a pocket. Some brand she'd never heard of. Its blue was a dazzling azure, with embedded glitter that made the phone sparkle as she handled it.

She opened it and the screen glowed blue. She touched a button that had the silhouette of a person's head on it. The screen went blank for a second, then lit up again with CONTACTS at the top.

It was a short list. Only three items, and they weren't names but single letters: S, W, and C. She arrowed to S and hit the green button again. Seven rings, eight. She touched the red button. Roll and Rest must have a lost-and-found box; she'd give the phone to Yvonne. Whoever claimed it would be a strong candidate for the sneaky watcher in the woods.

Or the innocuous hiker, she reminded herself.

She worked on drawings the rest of the day, the best way she knew to banish the uneasiness she felt. If the person in the woods was simply a fellow hiker, why had he run away?

* * *

Insomnia was a bitch. At midnight she boiled water for chamomile tea, let it steep while she pulled on jeans and her leather jacket, then took her mug outside and sat at the picnic table. Her sleeping bag would feel cozier after she'd spent a few minutes in the cool night air.

The moon was full and high. A great-horned owl hooted from the woods near the river. Such a peaceful sound. She wondered why superstition said an owl's call meant someone was about to die.

Maybe because the belief had been formed hundreds of years ago, before electric lights changed humankind's relationship to the night, pushing darkness farther from the dinner table, the book, the bedside chair. Avian populations were higher then, the habitat that supported owls and their prey not as ravaged as today's. Hoots would be heard by those unfortunate souls sitting up to comfort sick or dying family members and not, of course, by their carefree, sleeping neighbors.

Still common, to assume cause where there was only correlation.

And if you considered the seven billion people on the planet these days, you could say with confidence that people were dying all the time. No matter when the owls hooted, the superstition was correct.

She shivered, stood. The last swallow of tea was cold. Time to go in.

What was that noise? The dry scrape sounded loud in the quiet night.

The pathway lights, at ankle height, weren't any help, but the moon's white glow flooded the night. Kate scanned the campground.

She wasn't sure which direction the sound had come from. She wished she had the ears of an owl, those huge openings at offset positions on the head, configured to triangulate a source, pinpoint a tiny noise like the scratch of a mouse claw on a leaf.

No, "pinpoint" is what the owl did after it knew where the mouse was. She imagined sharp talons sinking through fur and skin and muscle.

But what she'd heard was too loud to have been made by a mouse.

While she was drinking tea, had someone been out here in the night with her, watching?

Don't be so jumpy, she told herself. There was some simple, innocent reason. Maybe someone in an RV had opened a window for a dose of fresh air. Or some nocturnal animal like a raccoon had squeezed its way into a tight space to score a tasty tidbit. That rascal Rusty could be roaming the night, up to one of his tricks.

Hard not to connect the dots, though. She tried to empty her mind of the scraping noise and the sound that afternoon of footsteps running away through the woods. Was one of Yvonne's kids sneaking around, watching her? She went inside and locked the door, her mind shouting Go to sleep, Kate!

Eventually, she did.

* * *

In the morning she hiked, but the light didn't look right and something in her head buzzed like a cicada. Insomnia's after-effects. She went home and climbed up to her bunk for a good long nap.

Knocking awakened her. She dropped from the bunk to the camper floor, slipped into jeans, and unlocked the door.

Yvonne, paper plate in hand. "I just made some cinnamon rolls," she said. "I wanted to bring you some."

The scent of hot butter and cinnamon rose through the open door. "Oh, they smell so good." What time was it? She was still half asleep.

Yvonne must have read the confusion on Kate's face. "Oh, I'm sorry. I thought it would be okay to come now. While they were still hot."

Kate shook herself alert. "That's really nice of you, Yvonne. C'mon in. I'll put on some coffee." She took the plate so Yvonne could use the handrail. The camper had a step that dropped down from the bumper, but the entry angle was steep. Kate was used to it and popped into her camper without thinking, but her visitors sometimes had trouble.

"Give me a minute to clear the table," Kate said. "Between meals, it's my work space." She scooped the pencils and erasers into their pouch and blew eraser crumbs off her drawing of the eddy with leaves she'd started the day before.

Yvonne looked over her shoulder. "You're an artist, how cool. Oh! I like that one." She pointed to a half-finished drawing of Rusty. "May I take a picture of it to show Savvy? She draws sometimes. She'll be excited to know you're a real artist."

Kate blushed. "Sure. As long as you tell her it isn't finished."

"A traveling artist," Yvonne said. "I don't know any other artists, unless I count my quilting friend." She held her cell phone level above the drawing and touched the screen.

"It keeps me out of trouble." As she said it, she realized it wasn't true.

# FOUR

Somehow Yvonne's personality came across as sunny even though she worried about everything—her aging parents in Maine, Duval's parents in Quebec, Duval's health, and the campground business. But at the top of her worry list were her children.

"Sending my kids to public school here was huge," Yvonne said. "I was concerned about Carson especially, because he's small for his age and wears glasses. And he did seem really unhappy at first. But here we are, a month later, and he has friends and stays after school with them on Wednesdays. He's in some kind of computer club. Which is good, because we don't have computers at home for the kids yet."

"That's unusual," Kate said. "I thought kids these days were born with computers in their laps. Cell phones in their hands."

"I know. We've got to get more electronics soon, so the children won't be left behind. Duval and I have a computer for Roll and Rest, a desktop—he put up a website, with a place where people can make reservations. And now he uses it for his insurance job, too. But he doesn't want the kids playing games on the same machine his spreadsheets are on."

"Is Savvy making friends?"

"That's what's odd. She's having trouble, both socially and with her schoolwork. I've told you she's forgetting things?" Yvonne sighed. "Yesterday she came running back, saying she'd forgotten her spelling workbook. I helped her look in her room, then all over the house. It was in her pack the whole time. And she wakes up with headaches. She never used to get them."

"How old is she? Maybe she's turning into a teenager."

Yvonne laughed that hearty laugh of hers. "Oh, what a thought—she's only nine. I sure hope she isn't going to be a teenager this soon. The Terrible Twos were tough sledding, and I'm not over them yet."

Kate's glance fell on the phone she'd found it in the woods. "Oh, I have something for your lost and found box."

Yvonne took the sparkly blue cell, flipped it open. "Maybe we can find the owner. Or at least call him. Isn't there a way to find a phone's own number?"

"Good idea," Kate said, "but I don't know how to do it. I called one of the contacts. See? Only three, all initials. It rang a bunch of times with no answer."

"That's odd. Who doesn't have voicemail these days?" The phone chirped in Yvonne's hand and she jumped, then laughed at herself. As she looked at the screen her face sobered, and she handed the phone to Kate.

A text message hung on the glowing blue screen. *She's easy pickings. You ready?*

"Weird," Kate said.

"Sounds like something bad's going to happen to her, whoever she is."

"I'll try to get a lead," Kate said. Safe to answer, since the phone wasn't hers. She texted *Where?* If she knew the place, she'd call the police on her own cell phone so they could stop the attack, or whatever it was.

31

The screen glowed in her hand. Eventually its color faded as it went to standby. "Darn," Kate said. "I guess the guy at the other end figured out I wasn't who he thought I was."

"Right. You were supposed to already know where."

"Well, it was worth a shot."

"If somebody asks for this at the office, I'll get his name," Yvonne said. "And a license plate number, if I can. In case he really is up to no good."

"Why don't we take it to the police station? Maybe somebody there can trace the numbers, find out what's going on," Kate said.

"Oh, of course," Yvonne said. "That's the best thing. I'll drop it off the next time I go downtown." She made a face. "I'm going to get a reputation. The cops were here yesterday because of the breaker box. They looked at it and kind of shrugged, but I thought it was smart to report it."

"Yes," Kate said. Restless, disturbed by the text message, she got the pot and topped off their mugs.

"Have another roll," Yvonne said. "There are two left; they're for you."

"No, thanks. It was yummy, but I couldn't eat two in a row."

Yvonne's cell buzzed in her pocket, and she rolled her eyes. "Sorry," she said. "Might be a customer." She touched the screen. "Roll and Rest RV Park, how can I help you?"

She frowned. "Oh, no, what?" A pause. "I'll be right there." She got to her feet, clutching her phone. "Savvy, she—" Her voice was tight.

"What?" Kate asked. Was the girl sick? Hurt?

"Savvy got lost. Again." Yvonne's eyes filled. "I can't believe it. Just one turn. She's been doing it for weeks. How could she get lost? Thank God for the neighbor." She started for the door.

"Go out backwards, like a ladder," Kate said quickly. "It's easier, trust me. And hold on."

A minute later Yvonne's old car rattled down the driveway beside the house.

Darn, she'd been too distracted to take the blue cell with her.

Kate went outside with the plate of rolls—she didn't want to tempt herself to eat another one. Rusty materialized at her feet and pressed himself against her ankles. She bent to give him some good scritches behind one ear, and he rubbed his whiskers on her hand and purred loudly. Like a mountain lion, Kate decided, though she'd never been close enough to a mountain lion to hear it purr.

That was probably a good thing.

Donna and Richard were in their lawn chairs, facing the sun, with Juneau alert between them; Richard was reading a paperback. Donna waved, and Kate headed her way. Rusty followed her like a dog. The border collie sat up and stared at Rusty.

"Stay, Juneau," Donna said. "Kate! How goes it?"

"Fine, thanks. Don't suppose I could interest you in some home-baked cinnamon rolls, could I? I just ate one, and it was really good, but I can't eat any more before they go stale."

"Are you kidding? Fork 'em over," Donna said. To her husband, "Hands off. They're mine."

Richard groaned. "I don't get one little bite?" He looked at Kate. "I'm supposed to be watching my blood sugar. Have to be careful with bread, pizza, all the good stuff. I don't suppose they're made with whole-wheat flour, are they?"

"I don't think so," Kate said. "And they're frosted."

"Oh, forget it," Richard said.

"I win," Donna said, taking the plate onto her lap. "Thanks." Then she looked past Kate's shoulder and smiled. "There's my girl. Hi, Savvy."

Kate turned. A girl had come around the corner of the house. Her backpack sagged, and so did her posture. She was headed for the back door but saw the three adults and changed course. Yvonne, behind her, gave the Millers a wave and went inside.

"Hello, Mrs. Miller," Savvy said. "Hello, Mr. Miller." She let the pink backpack slide off her shoulders, and it hit the ground with a thump.

"Hi, Savvy. I'm Kate."

"How's it going, sweetie?" Donna said.

The girl shrugged. "Okay." Her voice was flat. Even if Kate hadn't heard Yvonne answer the neighbor's phone call, she'd have known Savvy was having a bad day.

Rusty rubbed himself against Savvy's leg, and she knelt down to pet him. "I think Mum's mad at me. Usually we walk home. Today she had to pick me up, and then we got Carson." Maybe it was easier to talk when she wasn't looking at the adults. Or maybe she needed a therapy cat. In that case, Rusty was an excellent choice. He leaned into her strokes.

The girl looked behind her, apparently for her brother, who came around the corner of the house head down, kicking a stone in front of him. His backpack sagged, empty.

"Carson," Savvy said.

He looked up, and a shadow went across his face. Groups must not be his thing. Or maybe adults weren't. But he trudged toward his sister and stood slightly behind her, poking at the gravel with the toe of his sneaker.

Rusty bolted to the shed and disappeared behind it.

Savvy hip-checked her brother and he looked up. Each of the adults got half a second of his attention.

"Hello. 'Lo. 'Lo." He sounded like an echo of himself. His glasses slipped down and he scrunched his nose to push them back up. Juneau barked.

"Mum says not to do that. Push your glasses up with your finger," his sister whispered.

"No, Juneau," Richard said. "No barking."

The border collie barked again.

"Juneau, no!" Richard said sharply. The dog sat, whined once. Her nose was pointed at Carson, who went to the other side of his sister. The dog's nose tracked him. A bruise smudged the boy's left cheekbone.

"What happened to you, Carson?" Donna asked, tapping her own face.

He looked up and shrugged. "I fell." He looked back at the gravel, poked it some more. Puffs of dust rose.

"Carson, stop that," Savvy said, but he ignored her.

"I'm sorry I don't have any cookies for you today," Donna said to Savvy. "But your mother made cinnamon rolls. They're even better than cookies. Would you like one?"

"No, thank you. But cinnamon rolls are very good." The girl's tone of voice was so serious, and she was so obviously being polite instead of honest, that Kate almost laughed.

Carson had plowed up so much gravel with his toe that his blue and lime-green sneakers no longer matched, one of them dimmed by dust. "It was your turn to take the trash out last night," he said under his breath to his sister. "And you forgot."

Savvy hung her head.

"That's twice," he hissed.

"How was school today, Carson?" Richard asked. Yes, a change of subject was a good idea.

"It was okay," he said. "I like science. I want to be an astronaut."

"That's not easy," Richard said.

"You can do whatever you set your mind to, Carson," Donna said quickly, giving her husband a look.

"I like stories," Savvy said. "The teacher's reading us a book about a mouse named Stuart Little."

"I know Stuart," Donna said. "I liked him when I was your age. I still do."

"That's stupid. Mice don't have names," Carson said, and ran off.

"He's a boy," Savvy said, as if that explained everything. She had a seriousness Kate found both funny and sad. As if the girl had been miscast in a play and given the role of a thirty-year-old.

"You're getting to be a such a grown-up," Donna said. "The first time I saw you, you'd just learned to skip and you were skipping all over the campground singing the Itsy Bitsy Spider song. Do you remember that?"

"You used to come in the summer," Savvy said. "You taught me how to float."

"Yes. We went down to your little beach. It was hot that year, wasn't it? Now we're coming in the fall because we spent all summer selling things and giving things away and packing up. We even sold our house."

Savvy looked alarmed. "Where are you going to live? In your RV?" She must have inherited the maternal worry gene.

"Until we get to Florida. And then we're going to buy a house there."

"Or a condo. Like an apartment," Richard said. "We're finally moving to Florida. Orange juice and alligators. Sunshine and mosquitos."

"Oh. Aren't you going to come back here anymore?"

A pause. Then Donna said, "That would be nice, wouldn't it? But you'll always be our special girl."

"That's right, we'll always be friends," Richard said, but Savvy had turned toward the house, head down.

"Don't forget your cooking lesson!" Donna called as the girl went inside. "She's such a sweet kid," she said to Kate.

From behind the shed, Rusty shot across the gravel and crawled under the front end of Annie's dark brown van. Carson pelted after the cat, his arm cocked.

"Hey!" Kate sprinted to the boy, who had gotten on his knees to peer at Rusty. The cat had taken shelter behind a front tire and gave Carson an impressive hiss that displayed a nasty set of teeth.

"You leave that cat alone."

He didn't take his eyes off Rusty. "You're not my Mum."

Kate grabbed him by his shirt collar and pulled him to his feet. He was surprisingly light.

"Being mean to animals is—" She was going to say "despicable," but he might not know the word. "A very bad thing to do." She was so angry she was shaking.

"I'm not hurting him. Just chasing him."

His right fist was clenched. "What have you got in your hand?"

"Nothing."

"Show me."

He opened his hand and a rock fell out. It was a small rock, but it was big enough to hurt a cat. Even a cat as big as Rusty.

Kate still had Carson by the collar. She marched him to Yvonne's back door and rapped on it. When Savvy answered the door, her eyes got wide.

"I need to speak to your mother," Kate said.

# FIVE

After talking with Yvonne, Kate rejoined the Millers. Annie had apparently been roused by the commotion under her van. She was perched on the wooden picnic table near Donna, eating the last cinnamon roll.

"Way to go," Annie said. "That kid's weird."

"Oh, he's all right," Donna said. "Boys will be—"

"Will be little monsters sometimes," Annie said, and laughed. "I saw him chasing the cat a few days ago but it didn't cross my mind to stop him. Thanks, Kate."

"Maybe I shouldn't have," Kate said. "He's not my kid. Heck, I don't even have kids. But I like cats, and he was being mean to Rusty right under my nose." She'd told Yvonne about Carson's shooting rubber bands at Shadow the morning of the power outage, too, but she didn't tell the other campers. The Millers seemed to like him, and she wanted that to continue. Losing friends would make the boy act out even more.

"Acting out" was a phrase she knew from her friend Marjorie, who was taking courses toward a master's degree in psychology back in Massachusetts, where Kate had lived until last summer. Less judgmental than Annie's language, the phrase suggested the boy had reasons to commit his small acts of violence. Kate wondered briefly what those reasons might be.

Yvonne had been thoroughly outraged; Carson would have gotten no encouragement to mistreat animals from her.

"Donna and I raised a boy and a girl, just like the Chouinards are doing," Richard said. "But it takes a village, as they say. You did the right thing, Kate."

"I missed the whole show, " Donna said. "My chair's at the wrong angle. All I knew was Kate took off like she was in some race nobody told me about, or trying to catch the last bus. It wasn't until you came over, Annie, that I heard what Carson was up to." She shook her head. "He's gotten to be a handful since last year."

"Our boy wasn't anything like Carson, at twelve or thirteen," Richard said. "Or any age. I don't envy Yvonne. Or Duval." He looked at Donna. "You said once you thought Duval was too strict. Maybe this is what happens. Maybe the kid's rebelling."

"Gosh, do you suppose—" Kate's mouth had gotten ahead of her mind, but now the other three were looking at her, so she finished the thought. "I was just wondering if maybe Carson was the one who vandalized the electrical box."

"Oh, no, he wouldn't do *that,*" Donna said. "Besides, he's not strong enough."

They all looked at the gray box with its new padlock.

"He's not tall enough," Richard said.

Yes, he was small for his age, and it had been easy for Kate to propel him to the door. The Millers were right.

"Maybe the Loyalhanna Hermit did it," Donna said.

"A hermit? Around here? For real?" Kate asked. For a moment she thought of the person who'd run away from her through the woods the previous afternoon, and the stealthy sound at the campground when she'd been treating her insomnia with chamomile tea. But hermits were usually myths, like Bigfoot.

"Nobody knows for sure, but—" Donna began.

"That's ridiculous. There's no hermit," Annie said, startling Kate with her vehemence. Donna wasn't serious, was she?

"Oh, Annie, I was just horsing around."

"It's nothing to joke about." Annie jumped off the picnic table and stalked back to her van.

"Wow," Donna said. "Touchy."

"Really," Richard said. "I'm surprised. She didn't seem like the huffy type. Until now."

"Is the hermit some kind of local fable?" Kate asked.

"Some people say there's somebody living in the woods," Donna said. "We first heard about him last year. Little things go missing, especially from houses near the conservation land. Canned food, a flashlight or two, maybe a shirt. Yvonne swears a pair of her husband's jeans disappeared off her clothesline. A loaf of bread, a few days later. She was talking about it last summer, but she hasn't mentioned anything happening this year."

"Did you hear about that guy in Maine?" Richard asked. "The Hermit of North Pond? He lived in the woods for almost thirty years. Our hermit is just a beginner. And he doesn't have to deal with temperatures like the ones Maine dishes out in the winter."

"It gets cold enough around here for me." Donna shivered. "I'm glad I don't have to sleep in the woods like the Loyalhanna Hermit."

"If he even exists," Richard said.

"Right. People misplace things, or think they brought stuff to the cabin when they didn't. They go home and find what they thought was stolen, but the rumors have already spread."

"A burglar broke in and stole my scissors!" Richard said.

Donna laughed and said to Kate, "He's teasing me. I used to say things like that when we lived in a house. 'Where are the scissors? I can't find them anywhere. Somebody stole them!' Now I live in this rig," she tilted her head at the Winnebago. "I have to know where everything is. All the time."

40

"But at least there aren't as many places for things to hide," Kate said.

"You looked for your sunglasses for an hour one time, all over the house, and they were on your head," Richard said.

Donna groaned. "Don't remind me. That could still happen."

"Funny, you know where everything is in the kitchen, all clean and tidy, and you're a super cook. So organized you won't let me put anything away because I might put it in the wrong place. That's in the kitchen. Everywhere else? A different story."

"So pretend the Winnebago is one big kitchen," Kate said.

Donna laughed. "A kitchen with a couch? Queen-sized bed? Engine and transmission?" She snapped her gum. "And a back-up camera?"

"Hey! I'll stay out of the kitchen," Richard said, "if you won't go under the hood."

"Deal, honey. Tell you what, you can have the whole outside of the rig. It's so dusty around here, every time I open a window I get a pound of dirt."

True, it was a dry fall in this corner of Pennsylvania, but Donna apparently had high standards when it came to dust. She must not have spent any time in a desert. Yellow clouds in Tucson could blur the ridgeline of the Catalina mountains and close I-10. On calm July days, dust devils sprang up like mobile weeds. But Donna didn't need to hear such horrors.

Richard looked toward Annie's van. "I really don't think there's a hermit," he said. "People love a good story, even if it's not true."

"I think Annie would agree with you," Kate said.

* * *

After lunch she got into the passenger seat of an aging Dodge, happy to go to the library. Yvonne had offered to take out books for Kate so she could save the e-books on her tablet for later on. Without books to read after dinner, an evening could be a long time.

Yvonne's car was a beater, which must have embarrassed her, because the first thing she said to Kate was that she and Duval were planning to replace it as soon as they got ahead of their bills a bit. "He's only had his town job a month," she said. "So we have to wait a while. He has a pick-up truck he takes to work— Union Hill is close by, but he needs a vehicle to visit clients all over the county."

"This ride gets the job done," Kate said. The paint on the green sedan was blistered and a crack ran across the windshield, but the engine had started right up and it ran smoothly and shifted well. Give it a paint job and call it new.

Except it rattled. Yvonne had to raise her voice. "You're going to love Edna, our librarian. She's friendly and full of good ideas. Started a story hour for kids and a book discussion group for adults I usually go to. She knows everybody in town and remembers what they like to read. And makes suggestions. The most energetic and organized person I know."

"Great," Kate said. She loved libraries, always had. As a kid she'd spent hours at the one near her house, looking at picture books and making her own crayon drawings for the stories. It had been one of her favorite places to go, second only to a hike in the desert with her father.

The Union Hill Library was in a strip mall, between a tax accountant's office and an insurance company. Open only a few hours a day, according to the sign on the door; the budget must be tight. Kate would bet Edna was the sole librarian.

A sign on the counter read QUIET, PLEASE. OR ELSE. Yvonne leaned past it and introduced Kate in a low voice to a woman at a computer. She was large and wore a dress with frills on top and a billowing skirt below that hid the chair she was sitting on, so she seemed to float like the Cheshire Cat in *Alice in*

*Wonderland.* Edna completed the resemblance by smiling and nodding enthusiastically at Kate, who smiled back.

"Browse away," Yvonne whispered to Kate. "I'm going to chat for a bit." She went behind the counter and turned a chair to face Edna's.

Kate sampled her way along the shelves in the fiction section, pulling out a book here and there with an attractive title and reading the front flap or the synopsis on the back. Half a dozen intrigued her enough to open and read a page at random. Eventually she kept two, one set in Alaska and the other in Maine, the Mickey Mouse ears of the continental U.S. She often chose novels based on setting, because landscapes were important to her.

Since Yvonne and Edna were still sitting behind the counter, heads together, voices inaudible, Kate found the nonfiction section and a shelf with a STAFF CHOICES sign. Edna's choices, most likely. Skipping the latest in cooking, parenting and investing, she added a book about the plants and animals of Pennsylvania to the novels.

By then Yvonne had moved to the patron side of the counter. She checked out the books, then she and Kate waved their silent goodbyes to Edna and went out to the car. Yvonne had taken out a single book, one the librarian had saved for her. *The Quality of Silence* was a suspense novel, up for discussion at the book group's next meeting.

"Edna raved about it, and her taste is usually pretty close to mine," Yvonne said. "She alternates fiction and nonfiction. I'm glad she organized the group, because I never know what to read."

"Getting told about a good book is such a gift," Kate said. "Edna's a terrific librarian."

"A community asset," Yvonne agreed. "Poor Duval used to read and go to her discussion group with me, but he can't touch a book any more, he's up to his ears in the paperwork he brings home. I worry he doesn't get enough exercise. Of course I don't either, but at least I bend and stretch when I'm doing housework." She sighed. "Having a meeting—and a deadline— helps me get around to the book. And reading's good for my brain."

She turned the wheel sharply to avoid a pothole. A good thing, too, given the amount of rattling the car was already doing. Hitting a pothole might disassemble the old Dodge: Kate imagined it airborne, she and Yvonne surrounded by a cloud of parts like one of those exploded views in a maintenance manual.

"I really go just to get out of the house and see some friends," Yvonne confessed. "Reading the book is the price of admission."

A different reading philosophy from Kate's. She gobbled books down like cookies and would have taken out more novels if she hadn't seen a sign limiting borrowers to six books. She'd figured three for Yvonne and three for her.

"I told Edna you're an artist, and she suggested you might want to take some of your work to the county's Fall Crafts Fair at the end of the month. I'm taking some sweaters—I always sell a bunch."

Kate didn't respond right away, and Yvonne glanced at her. "Your work's great—I bet you'd make some money. Pay for your generator?"

"Sounds like a good idea," Kate said. She didn't think she'd be good at selling her work, but she'd accumulated so many finished pieces that space in the locker where she was storing them was getting tight. A little cash wouldn't hurt, either. "Generator, right. Thanks, Yvonne."

"You can thank Edna for the idea. And for something else, too—she offered to let you put a few of your drawings up in the library. That's quite a compliment. She has a section of wall dedicated to local artists. I showed her your drawing of Rusty, that picture I took on my cell phone."

"Oh, no, it wasn't finished."

Yvonne waved a hand. "Close enough. We'll both share her table at the fair, like I do every year. Edna sells her quilts. They're incredible works of art. You're both artists."

"You are, too," Kate said, thinking of the elegant shawl taking shape between Yvonne's knitting needles during their morning coffee.

Yvonne hadn't kept her eyes on the road. The old car hit a pothole that rattled its bones.

And Kate's brain. "Oh, rats," she said, and Yvonne looked a question at her. "I forgot to bring the darn phone."

\* \* \*

The next morning, Kate got up early, pulled out her stack of finished drawings and counted them. Eight. Not too bad, but she'd need more if she wanted to attract customers at the fair. She'd never exhibited her work, and the prospect made her nervous.

Something chirped. The blue phone she'd found, the one Yvonne and she were taking turns forgetting to deliver to the police.

She opened it. A text message glowed. *Who are you?*

A good question not to answer, considering there might be a predator on the other end. She watched the screen.

After a minute, another message. *I want the phone back.*

Kate thought about it. She could set up a meeting and let the cops know about it. They could meet the texter—she wouldn't—and ask questions about what had happened to the woman who was "easy pickings." Without exposing herself, she could do something to bring a possibly dangerous person to the attention of the police.

*OK,* she texted back. *Tomorrow. Where?*

The answer came quickly, and a jolt of fear went through her. *Tonight. I'll come to you.*

Oh, damn. He must be able to trace the phone's location, something she'd thought only the phone company or the cops could do. She wasn't as good with phones as she should be—it was the twenty-first century, after all.

Wait, all she had to do was turn it off. Then nobody could trace it, right? She held the red button down, and the screen—its blue a penetrating shade that was beginning to look evil to her—went dark.

Perfect.

She sat for a minute, letting her heart rate fall back to normal. Then she put the disturbing message out of her mind and propped the drawing of Rusty against the window. It had come out well: the cat was sitting on the picnic table next to her kayak, his gaze direct and full of feline intelligence and dignity. While working on it, she'd decided to give it to Yvonne. She sprayed the piece with fixative and waved it around a bit, then laid it on the table and looked out the dinette window. Drought had kept the fall colors from reaching their usual brilliance, but the sky was pearly with clouds. Maybe rain was on the way.

She touched the drawing lightly with the tip of her finger. Dry. Done. She dropped it into a cardboard portfolio, set it aside and got back to work on a drawing of her bike. She used her hardest pencils and found herself frowning in concentration. A bicycle was a different proposition entirely from a leaf or a landscape. Or Rusty's fur.

A couple of hours later, Kate slipped the cell phone into the pocket of her leather jacket, picked up the portfolio and knocked under the sign with the cartoon cats. She and Yvonne had gotten into the habit of having coffee together after the children had left, and today Kate had a gift. And a favor to ask.

Yvonne was thrilled. "It's wonderful—it looks just like him. So real that I'm waiting for him to move. And yet so not like a photo. Oh, thank you!"

After they'd settled at the table, Kate said, "So I'm wondering if you'd be willing to be a model for me. I'd like to have some variety in what I take to the fair. So far I've mostly got landscapes. Would you pose?"

"Sure," Yvonne laughed, "as long as I don't have to take off my clothes."

"Don't worry, none of my work is X rated."

She'd tried to draw Yvonne once before, during morning coffee, but Kate's new friend complained their conversation suffered too much. "I can knit and talk, but you can't draw and talk," she'd said. "Besides, you didn't drink as much coffee and I had to throw some out." It was the first time anyone had accused Kate of not drinking enough coffee.

"Will this afternoon work? I just have one errand, and then I'll be ready." She skipped telling Yvonne about the latest in disturbing texts, since the woman worried too much already.

* * *

Kate rode her bike to the village of Union Hill and found the police station, a one-story brick building with wilted forsythia bushes next to the steps. She turned the blue phone over to an officer at the front desk, who gave her a lost-and-found form the size of a playing card. Filling it out with the location where she'd found the cell and her own name and number, she squeezed a message into the margin: "Check out creepy texts. Sender sounds dangerous." She hedged her bets by telling the cop on duty the same thing.

"Will do," he said, turning back to the screen on his desk.

There. Let the person who texted her track the phone's location and show up to claim it. He'd be in for a surprise.

At the edge of town she stopped to look out over the wooded hills. Not high enough to see the Loyalhanna, but a pretty view. The trees were piebald, mixed green and prophetic reds.

\* \* \*

She'd just covered her bike and lifted it onto the bunk when she heard a knock on her door. A timid one, not John's resounding slap. She opened the door a crack.

Annie's red hair caught the sun with glints of gold; her eyes were green and gold. Heavens, she was pretty. Kate invited her in, and she climbed aboard as easily as if she did it every day.

Oh, she did, of course. Her four-by-four van must have a similar bumper-step entry.

"So, like, I found something." Annie's voice was soft. Outside the door, her face bright with afternoon light, she'd looked angelic. Inside, she looked nervous, tremulous, as if her heart beat faster than most people's. "In the woods, you know, by the river." Her green fleece was old, pilled, the cuffs of her faded jeans frayed and tan with dust.

"Have a seat. Want some coffee? Hey, relax." Kate remembered too late that *relax* wasn't a good choice. It tells nervous people you've noticed they're nervous, which only makes things worse. Her back to Annie, she put a filter in the coffee machine and scooped. "What did you find, a cell phone?" Pushed the button.

"No, I found this."

Something heavy thunked onto the table, and Kate turned. A necklace. It had three strands of square beads, a lustrous green so deep it was almost black.

"Under a bush." Annie stroked the beads, her face almost reverent. "Do you think I could keep it?"

Maybe the light touch was best. "Gosh, Annie, I'm really bad at decisions. Besides, I'm not into jewelry. I have two pairs of earrings to choose from when I dress up—and dressing up means I'm wearing my best black jeans." She put a second cup on the table.

Annie's smile was subdued. "I feel like one of those birds, like a magpie? They collect shiny things." She gave the necklace another stroke.

"Actually, they don't," Kate said. "They're smart, like all members of the crow family, and curious. So they scope things out, especially things that look unusual. But they're not collectors." She got the pot and poured. "Bower-birds, now, they're the real deal. They live in Australia, and the males make nests and decorate them with blue objects to impress females during courtship. Only blue, isn't that strange? And the birds are blue, with blue eyes."

The small smile was gone. Annie looked defeated.

Kate wished she hadn't said so much. She slipped into the dinette opposite her visitor. "I'm sorry, I know magpies have the reputation of being hoarders. I was a biology major, and I like birds, so I read about them. They're wicked smart."

"Oh, then you would know. I just heard about them. I grew up here, and there aren't any magpies in Pennsylvania."

"You grew up in Union Hill?"

Her visitor squirmed, uneasy. "Yeah."

"Cool," Kate said. What was up with Annie? She and Yvonne should start a support group for worriers. AA, Angels of Anxiety. "I didn't know magpies as a kid, either, in southern Arizona. But my family took a couple of road trips north, to the mountains, and I got to see them there. They make huge nests, hard to miss." Kate was happy to talk about the handsome birds. Maybe she was off the hook of helping Annie make up her mind about keeping the necklace.

No such luck. "What do you think? Should I—?"

Kate hid her hesitation with a sip from the La Brea Tar Pits mug. She was startled both that Annie coveted what looked like an inexpensive bunch of glass beads and that she wanted Kate's advice.

"Gee, Annie, I don't know. You could put it in the campground's lost-and-found box. I bet nobody claims it," Kate said. Logic wasn't the point; she only wanted to ease Annie's tension, wherever it came from. "Then when you're leaving, you could ask Yvonne or Duval for it back."

Annie blinked. "I wouldn't want to ask Duval for anything. He's the kind of guy who pushes you around. A short fuse, you know?"

Kate didn't know. Duval had never been difficult with her. "He's probably stressed out, with his new job. He'd rather be camping. Like us." She tried another smile.

Annie didn't smile back. "I'm in my van because my husband's divorcing me," she said. "Duval looks a little like him, so maybe that's why I don't like him."

Projecting, Kate's friend Marjorie would say. "I'm sorry."

"My husband isn't bald, though."

"Good." Kate squelched a smile. Annie was concerned with her about-to-be-ex husband's image in the mind of someone who was nearly a stranger? Then she was still emotionally entangled with him. And in pain. Not much Kate could do for her on that score.

"It doesn't matter about Duval, anyway, because I'm leaving pretty soon."

"I'm sorry to hear that." Honestly, Kate didn't care what Annie did with the pile of cheap glass. "Then you could say Finders Keepers and it's yours. Why don't you try it on?"

Annie's fingers were so quick with the clasp Kate was sure this wasn't the first time they'd fastened it.

"You look great. Here's a mirror. What do you think?" Kate opened the bathroom door.

Annie slid out of the dinette to admire her reflection in the medicine cabinet mirror. "Awesome," she breathed.

"It picks up the green in your eyes."

"Kate, thank you. You're awesome. Thanks for the coffee."

After Annie left, Kate felt sorry for her but was glad she'd stopped in. Maybe talking had helped her feel less alone. Okay, Annie had said *awesome* twice, essentially equating Kate to one of the ugliest pieces of costume jewelry she'd ever seen. But she didn't mind.

\* \* \*

"It's great you're willing to sit for me," Kate said that afternoon. She'd moved her boat off the picnic table, and Yvonne was lying on it, propped on one elbow, with a magazine open beside her.

"Sit? I can roll over and play dead, too," Yvonne said. "I'm full of tricks."

Kate shivered a little. Maybe she was superstitious, but she never said something was so good it was "to die for" or she felt so good she thought she'd "died and gone to heaven." After her recent experiences, death was nothing she wanted to joke about.

She hadn't drawn the human figure, or a face, in a long time, and the challenge was invigorating. She opted for charcoal and set up her easel, which hadn't seen much use recently because she'd been working on smaller pieces on the road. But for the fair she could produce larger ones. If something was too big to take with her and nobody bought it, she'd donate it to the library. Edna could sell it or exhibit it. Not that Kate would still be a local artist by then, but maybe Edna liked her work enough to take it anyway. If she hated the piece she could always give it to Goodwill.

Clouds gathered as she roughed out Yvonne's shoulder, hip, and legs, and Kate enjoyed the way diffused light softened the sharp lines sunlight had laid down. The air was warm enough that her model was wearing shorts and a scoop-necked top, the first time Kate had seen her wearing anything but a below-the-knee skirt.

"One of those big gray barges in the sky has got to drip sooner or later," Yvonne said, looking up. "We have just got to have some rain." Her hair was swept behind one ear, and the ear was giving Kate a little trouble.

Savvy came around the corner with her heavy pack.

"Hi, sweetie," Yvonne said. "Where's Carson?"

"He stayed after. Computer club." The girl dropped her pack at the back door and joined them, looking over Kate's arm.

"Wow, Mum, she's good." She looked closer. "Except your ear is kind of funny-looking."

"Honey—" Yvonne said.

"It's okay," Kate said. "She's right." She turned to Savvy. "I'm going to fix this ear. See?" She used the kneaded eraser, and then the charcoal pencil.

It looked better. She still wasn't satisfied, but Savvy was impressed. "You got your ear back," she said to her mother. "Can you hear better now?"

Kate laughed, then had a flash of what it was to be a child, to mix the real and the imaginary, even if you could tell the difference. She remembered being a cowboy when she was Savvy's age, riding a horse made of nothing but air, galloping along trails on sand or caliche, sometimes with friends who rode similar invisible mounts.

She missed that state of mind. But now she had art, which was another way to make the imaginary real.

She looked at Yvonne on the picnic table, who'd gone back to reading her magazine.

Or another way to make the real imaginary. Like being a kid again. But better.

# SIX

Savvy wanted to sit for Kate, too, so the next afternoon they went out together, the girl knocking on Kate's camper door after school and handing up her heavy backpack. She looked excited, in a good mood for a change, so Kate didn't remark on the weight of the backpack, fearing it would be an unpleasant reminder of homework yet to be done.

A ton of homework? In third grade? Savvy was a serious cookie, no doubt about it.

Or maybe she was having trouble getting her work done.

Yvonne had given her approval on the condition that her daughter stay with Kate. "Don't go running off," she'd said.

"I won't," the girl had promised.

"How about we go find a tree for you to climb?" Kate asked. A girl in a tree would make an interesting subject, and it might keep Savvy from getting bored. They walked along the path toward the river, Kate carrying her easel.

"Okay," Savvy said. She was wearing a turquoise turtleneck and jeans. "Gosh, Mum sure made a big deal about me having to stay close to you. I think she's afraid of the woods now. She didn't used to be."

"Oh, I bet she isn't." Kate made her voice casual. "Mothers have to be cautious, you know. It's their job."

"Maybe she's afraid of the hermit, but I'm not."

Kate didn't say anything to that. Yvonne was probably thinking less about the Loyalhanna Hermit and more about Savvy getting lost in the woods the way she had, twice, on the way home from school. "Find a nice tree," she said.

Savvy gave a little skip. "I know just the one. My favorite. I used to come out here a lot when I was young."

Kate kept her laugh to herself. Savvy might not understand why it amused an adult to hear a nine-year-old say "when I was young."

Her amusement faded when Savvy added, "But now I get stupid headaches all the time after school." A few steps later the girl stopped and spread her arms wide. "Ta-da!"

Kate could see why the maple was a favorite. Its lower branches practically begged a person to climb aboard, and it offered plenty of thick, inviting limbs farther up as well. It was a splendid tree, not far from the river. It was blazing red; sugar maples turn early.

She took a good look around, scanning the understory. The tree's only drawback was its proximity to the place where someone had startled Kate while she was drawing a few days earlier. She didn't mention the incident to Savvy, who ran to the maple like the old friend it was. The girl jumped to catch a branch, swung her ankles up and locked them around it. Her brown hair hung like a flag. In fact Savvy or Carson could easily, and innocently, be the person who'd been spying on her. Children are curious, after all.

Kate tried out a knee-high, flat-topped rock as a place to sit and work, but it was too close to the tree—almost under the branch she wanted Savvy to pose on.

"I like that rock." The girl's voice came from among the red leaves. A talking tree. "I sit there sometimes and watch the river."

"It's a nice one," Kate said, opening her easel. "I'll sit there to draw sometime. But not today." See? she told herself. Yvonne's kids loved the woods, as she had loved the desert and mountains she'd grown up with. The two  must come down here almost every day. Why had she let herself get frightened by the sound of footsteps?

Savvy came back down and straddled a branch as big around as her waist. "Where do you want me to sit?"

"That branch is perfect," Kate said. "If you want to climb for fun while I get ready, go ahead, then come back down to where you are now, okay?"

"Sure." She disappeared into the crimson cloud, and a minute later Kate glimpsed her head and turquoise shoulders nearly at the top. Savvy planted her feet against the trunk and held on with one hand over her head, her small body angled outward from the trunk like an extra branch. She waved with her free hand.

Kate had a twinge of fear as she waved back. She wanted to say "Be careful" but suppressed the urge. She'd lived with Marjorie for a few months, but her son was only four, his sister an infant. Getting to know Yvonne was giving her an inside look at what it was like to be the parent of an older, active child, and she was beginning to understand her new friend's worries.

On the other hand, she remembered climbing trees and jumping from rock to rock along the edges of high places and being annoyed by adults who told her to be careful. Most children who play outdoors are sure-footed, have good balance, and take it all completely for granted.

She taped drawing paper to the easel and got out her set of pencils. When she looked up, Savvy was back down on the big branch, with two leaves caught in her hair.

"You're a star," Kate said, and Savvy giggled.

Kate was surprised at Savvy's patience. Lots of kids her age would be too restless to model; ten minutes was a long time to a nine-year-old, wasn't it? A series of rough sketches was called for, rather than one finished portrait—partly because Kate didn't want to ask the girl to stay in one place for an hour the way Yvonne had, and partly because she wanted to try out different poses to see what worked. She asked Savvy to sit on several of the lower branches. In some sketches, when Kate finished them, the girl would be recognizable; in others her face didn't show completely and she could be any girl—any child, really—having fun. In one sketch Kate stood on the big rock and drew a close-up of Savvy's eyes surrounded by leaves. The girl's laughter percolated through the foliage.

Her hands busy, Kate tried to imagine what it was like to be nine. A lot of changes were looming over Savvy Chouinard. Over any girl her age. Adjusting to public school was just the beginning.

Back at her easel, Kate asked, "What does Carson's computer club do? Is he learning to program?" Maybe she could get Savvy talking about after-school activities and encourage her to join a group. The leading edge of puberty was not a good time to withdraw socially, as Yvonne was afraid her daughter was doing.

Savvy didn't answer, so Kate asked again.

"I don't know."

"Do they have enough computers at school so everybody in the club gets to use one?"

"I guess so. But he kind of—"

Kate was involved in adding shadows to flat contours to make the figure three-dimensional, and when she'd done the face she realized there had been a long pause in the conversation. Hard to work and talk at the same time. She replayed Savvy's last comment in her head.

"What, honey? He kind of what?"

"Oh, I don't know," the girl said again. "They're not always, you know, inside with the computers. Sometimes they go out."

Strange. A computer club that met outdoors? Maybe the club went on field trips to local businesses. Savvy sounded reluctant, so Kate let it go.

"What do you like to do? Are there any clubs you'd want to join?"

"I mostly like to read, and I like gym class. Watch this." She hung from the branch by her knees, her smile upside-down.

"Very cool, Savvy," Kate said. "I'm going to sketch you like that."

"But there's no gymnastics club or anything," the upside-down face said. "There's basketball, but I don't like basketball. Those girls are mean and stick to themselves."

Kate flipped her sketchpad to a new page. "I hope you can find something to do after school," she said. "It's a good way to make friends."

Was Savvy listening? Kate looked up.

The girl had somehow torqued herself around and lay on top of the branch. "Carson's even better at this," she said. "He climbs trees faster than me, even. But I wish I had a sister instead. I don't like him."

"You don't? Why not?"

"He, like, totally ignores me. We used to be buddies, but now I could be made out of air. Even when I try extra hard to say something nice to him. And he's mean to the cats."

Kate felt out of her depth: this was parenting territory. "Talk to Yv—talk to your mother, Savvy. Maybe she can help you and your brother get along better." Or maybe Yvonne could get Carson to stop being mean to his sister. And to cats.

Half an hour later, while Kate packed up her supplies, Savvy went to the top of the tree again. Kate didn't look up, so she wouldn't have to watch any more one-handed waving.

Then her head snapped up. A noise had startled her, a kind of a rasping scrape. It was Savvy's shoe slipping against tree bark, and it was just what she'd heard the night she couldn't sleep and was drinking tea at the picnic table.

Someone was climbing trees at the campground? She'd have to think about that.

\* \* \*

It was late as they walked the short trail toward Roll and Rest. The clouds had cleared, and low light came through the trees in bars. A gust of wind kicked up and the bars filled with swirling dust. No doubt about it, southwestern Pennsylvania needed rain.

"I like to sew," Savvy said. She was skipping every couple of steps, as if she were playing a game. "Want to come see what I made?"

"Sure," Kate said. "That would be fun. But we have to stop at my camper on the way, and get your pack, and I'll drop off my easel." She was glad Savvy was sounding so cheerful. Fresh air and a friendly tree could do a person a lot of good.

The girl's next comment surprised her. "I hope Daddy isn't home yet. He can be a grouch sometimes. When he gets home? Last night he swatted Shadow out of his chair with a magazine, and I couldn't find her for ages."

Oh, too bad. Yvonne must be right: Duval was working too hard. "He's probably tired after work, honey."

"Yeah, yeah." She skipped three times in a row. "At least he's in a good mood sometimes. Not like Carson."

Savvy's room was on the second floor of the old house, with a great view of the river, which widened farther north, flowing past a couple of small islands. A four-poster bed with a green canopy was positioned so someone in it could look out the double windows. Sitting up and reading, Savvy would have the river as a companion, and she could go to sleep looking at the distant hills or the stars. Across from the windows was a brick fireplace, its looks spoiled by a protruding gas heater, but the room was big enough to accommodate it and a bureau, desk and sewing machine as well as the bed.

Big room. "Was this originally the master bedroom?" Kate asked.

Yvonne had come up the stairs after them. "I think so," she said. "But it's kind of cold and drafty because it's at the northwest corner of the house. Duval and I were up here until last year, when we decided the kids were old enough that we could switch with them and take the downstairs bedroom. It's easier for us when an RV comes in late, and besides, the stairs are kind of steep." She laughed that deep laugh of hers. "And they keep getting steeper."

"I made the canopy," Savvy said, bouncing on the bed and looking up. "With the curtains open I can sail down the river. When I pull them closed it's like a tent, and I can pretend I'm camping. With cookies and a book." On closer inspection the canopy fabric was not solid green but a print of overlapping leaves.

"This is awesome," Kate said. "The canopy, I mean. Although camping with cookies and a book doesn't sound too shabby, either."

Shadow came into the room and jumped up on the bed with Savvy, who pulled the cat into her lap.

"She chose the fabric and made everything without any help from me." Yvonne sounded proud.

"I like the print," Kate said. "It's always summer when you go to sleep. That should keep you warm."

Savvy giggled.

"She made the window curtains, too," her mother said.

All the curtains had ruffles along the sides and bottom edges; valances across the top provided opportunities for more ruffles. Savvy was a Victorian at heart.

"Curtains are easy," the girl said. "The corners on the canopy were hard. They're not right angles, 'cuz the side bars are arched." She flounced herself back on the bed, and Shadow abandoned her for a pillow. "I made this duvet cover, too. And a cover for the sewing machine."

"It all looks perfect, Savvy." Kate was impressed. She could sew a button back on a shirt, but the only other clothing repair she did involved iron-on patches when she got a rip in a pair of jeans. And she had to borrow the iron.

Outside the window, a pair of crows swooped past, cawing. Kate laughed. "This little room is like a crow's nest. You know what I mean by that?" She didn't want Savvy taking it literally— a crow's nest was not a pretty sight, at least not to human eyes.

"Yeah, like at the top of a ship's mast."

"Right. You can see all the way to the next town. Well, almost."

"I see a lot. I can see when ducks fly under a full moon," Savvy said. "And geese. When Shadow sleeps with me and geese honk they wake her up. She watches them and snaps her teeth. Don't you, Shadow?" She wriggled to the pillow and stroked the cat's shiny fur. "I saw a deer swim out to that island once. Sometimes there are boats, little ones. The river flows north, you know."

Kate hadn't thought about it, but yes: Loyalhanna Creek joined the Kiskiminetas River, also northbound, which joined the Allegheny northeast of Pittsburgh.

"That surprises some people," Yvonne said. "Some children take maps too literally. If you hang a map on a wall, the rivers must all go south because gravity pulls them toward the floor, right?"

"Lots of rivers flow north," Savvy said. "Like in Germany." The good student, showing off. "The Rhine and the, um, the Spree. And the other one."

"What's the name of other one?" her mother asked.

Uh-oh. Quiz time. Savvy's mother had been her teacher, after all, until a month ago.

The girl hesitated. Three seconds, four. Five. "The Elbe."

Yvonne looked relieved. "Good girl."

Savvy looked relieved, too. She slipped off the bed and went to the window. Three more crows joined the pair at the top of an oak tree. The dark birds rearranged themselves, flaring and settling back down, cawing raucously at each other.

"You're the lookout for the house, up here in your crow's nest," Kate said, and smiled at Yvonne.

"I can tell there's a drought because there's so much dirt showing at the sides of the river," Savvy said. "It's like the kind of ribbon with loops along the edges, and the loops are getting bigger." She started hopping from one foot to the other. "I can see when clouds are headed this way. It's called a front. Sometimes I do a rain dance, like this."

"You've got the best room in the house," Kate said.

"Carson likes his room because it's not right over Mum and Daddy's." Savvy stopped dancing. "He thumps sometimes."

Kate looked at Yvonne, who raised her eyebrows.

"His room is always messy," Savvy said. "He's a boy."

"Hmm," Yvonne said, and went across the hall to a closed door. "It's Wednesday, so he's not home yet because of computer club." She opened the door, and Kate looked over her shoulder.

The room was smaller than Savvy's, with a bunk bed, bureau and small desk. The only window was darkened by the trunk of a good-sized tree. Savvy was right—the place was a mess. The floor was an airfield of model planes, some of them with broken wings. A rock collection and scattered clothes took up the rest of the floor space—it was unclear how the boy got to his bed. The window screen lay on the floor. The rocks were close enough to the closet that its door probably couldn't be opened. But the kid who lived here didn't need a closet, since he used the floor for storage.

Yvonne sighed and closed the door. "He's never been neat, but it really looks like it's getting worse. He doesn't listen to me. I'll have to talk to his father about it."

She said "his father" instead of "Duval" because Savvy was right there. Kate turned in time to see a pleased expression cross Savvy's face, and tried to remember if she'd enjoyed getting her siblings in trouble when she was nine.

* * *

Kate tossed her sketchbook and pencils into her pack and headed out. A few more drawings for the Fall Crafts Fair wouldn't hurt. The night had been cool, dropping into the high forties, but the temperature had climbed rapidly while she had coffee with Yvonne. Indian summer, people would call it. The Millers were out as they often were, soaking up sun.

Richard folded his newspaper as Kate passed their site and looked at his watch. "Hey, honey, we'd better get cracking."

"Oh, gosh, you're right," Donna said.

Her watch looked big for her wrist: ah, it matched Richard's. Togetherness. Kate smiled.

The older woman got to her feet and headed for the gray Hyundai. "We're taking the dinghy in to get worked on," she said to Kate, using the RVing term for a towed car. "The brakes are bad. We bought it used, and I think we got taken. We've spent so much money in the last—"

"Let's not talk about it," Richard said sharply. "C'mon, Juneau." He opened the Winnebago's door. "Inside. Go on, girl. Good dog."

"I hope it goes well," Kate said. After a few steps she turned back. "Do you two need a ride back here after you drop the car off? I could follow you there. It'd just take me a minute to stow things and unplug."

Donna put her head out the Hyundai's passenger-side window. "That's so thoughtful of you," she said. "Someone from the shop's going to drive us back. Part of the expensive service." She dropped her voice to a whisper for the word "expensive" and winked at Kate as the Hyundai started to roll.

What a sweetie Donna was.

* * *

Kate worked her way north all day, stopping often to sketch, enjoying the bright foliage and crisp air. Sometimes she followed the trail next to the river, sometimes she cut to the trail halfway between the water and Watkins Spur, the road the campground was on. Watkins gained elevation as it went north, following a ridge.

She ate lunch, then drifted like a wind-blown leaf. Wordless, her mind absorbed by shapes and shadows, she became part of the forest. Animal and human, she balanced at the seam of the world: above the hidden network of roots, below the network of branches dressed in brilliant foliage.

Trees talked underground, exchanging chemical messages and nutrients. Trees talked above her, too, rustling in the least breeze, their bright headdresses shedding handfuls of leaves. The leaves became memos about the cold season to come. She sat on a windfall tree and watched the airborne leaves high above the river, small and bright like snow.

She worked, and walked. Time didn't pass; it vanished.

Then, flipping open her pad, she found herself squinting at the sketch. Daylight was draining from the sky. She roused herself. Time to stash her supplies in her pack and hike more quickly; she didn't want to be in the woods after dark.

Moving fast didn't mean she stopped observing. A blue candy bar wrapper and, later, a blue-and-silver beer can caught her eye, both shiny. She picked them up and put them in the plastic bag she kept in her pack for litter.

I must be Australian, Kate thought, remembering her conversation with Annie. I'm a bower-bird and I like bright things, blue things. Bling!

A bit of bright orange caught her eye. Her next bit of bling. A tiny mushroom? She'd read about orange mushrooms called brick caps in the guide to Pennsylvania plants and animals she'd gotten at the library. No, too bright for brick caps. She picked up the object and looked at it as she walked.

A bullet. Had to be, although it was smaller than any she was familiar with. Most of it was gray metal: she'd never have noticed it if it hadn't been for the tip, encased in bright orange plastic.

Odd. She put it in the litter bag.

A hundred feet farther on, she saw another man-made item: a cell phone. Too bad it wasn't blue to please her inner bower-bird. Pink, it was larger than the one she'd already taken to the police. What was going on? Were people getting strangely careless with their cells?

Maybe the phones weren't lost. She'd heard of burners, used during crimes and discarded afterwards. They couldn't be traced if the buyers used cash for the original purchase as well as for the pay-as-you-go minutes that didn't require service contracts.

Even though she'd provided her name and phone number, the police hadn't called her with any information. Maybe they wouldn't do so even if they'd discovered something by following up on those scary texts. She was just the person who'd stumbled upon the phone in the woods, after all. Not directly involved.

Wait, surely they'd have alerted her if there were any dangerous people or activities connected to the phone. Union

Hill wasn't Manhattan, after all—they'd have time to follow up. The fact they hadn't contacted her probably meant she'd misunderstood the messages because she'd had no context for them. Maybe they were from kids fooling around, playing one of those games in which people take on roles and act out stories.

Out of curiosity, she'd try what Yvonne had suggested—figure out what the pink phone's number was, then try to find its owner. The Roll and Rest had Wi-Fi, and she might as well get some use out of it beyond checking her email and the weather.

Almost to the beach, she saw an animal in the middle of the trail. She walked more quietly for a few steps, but her excitement faded as she realized it must be dead. She skirted the body—a squirrel lying on its side, with a gaping wound behind its shoulder. Odd to see it in such an exposed place, since sick or injured animals often hide. Perhaps this one had been grabbed by a hawk that somehow hadn't been able to hold onto it. Or an early owl.

Back at the camper, she made a quick hummus-and-onion sandwich and got to work on her tablet. She searched on how to find a phone's number, and in less than a minute she had it: click on the Settings icon and then on Status.

Heck, that was easy.

Finding the owner was harder. The first two phone number look-up websites she tried told her the owner's information was unpublished; a third site wanted her to pay for the owner's address along with his age, education, employment history, criminal record, and a list of relatives. Discouraged, she gave it one more go.

Bingo. The fourth site yielded not only an address but a name. Walter Tremblay, 521 Watkins Spur. That made sense. A neighbor, more or less. A fellow hiker?

She typed the address into GoogleMaps, which flagged the last house on Watkins Spur. The road dead-ended about three miles north of Roll and Rest. Maybe she'd go to the house. It was always fun to have a destination for a hike or a bike ride, and Walter Tremblay would probably be happy to get his phone back.

Or his wife or daughter would. Funny how gender-linked a color could be.

Kate yawned, brushed her teeth, took a book up to her bunk. She couldn't think of a single man she knew who would let himself be seen using a pink phone.

# SEVEN

Yvonne had told Kate she could store her bicycle in the shed, and she had to admit it was handy not to have to get the Trek down off the overhead bunk whenever she wanted to ride. Walking to the shed with her trunk bag and helmet, she saw Carson dodge behind the big hydrangea bush between his parents' house and the shed.

Too late. He might have succeeded in hiding if he'd gotten behind the hydrangea before she came along, but she'd caught him in the act. Motion was a give-away, as every rabbit knew.

Or maybe he wouldn't have succeeded in any case. Those blue and green running shoes were practically fluorescent, and bushes don't wear sneakers.

"Hi, Carson!" she called out. He was probably avoiding her because she'd literally collared him over his treatment of Rusty, then outed him to his mother about shooting rubber bands at Shadow. But she wanted to get along with the kid, especially since she was becoming friends with his mother. She'd have to make it clear bygones were bygones. "It's okay, Carson. I don't bite. At least not most of the time."

He stepped from behind the bush. Was he unconcerned at being discovered, or just trying to look that way? The bruise on the side of his face had faded. One hand held something behind his back.

Curious, she kept her voice light. "Whatcha up to? What've you got there?"

"None of your business," he said. "I'm not doing nothing." He ran toward the house, switching the object to his other hand as he passed to block her view of it.

He didn't do a good enough job. She got a look: a roll of gray tape. Just ordinary duct tape. Why would he try to hide it?

What a completely weird kid. Both he and Savvy were going nuts in different ways. Maybe the transition to public school was going to be harder than Yvonne had realized.

A thought-beat later, Kate scolded herself for being judgmental. Annie had called Carson weird, but Marjorie frowned on words like that. He was immature, but that made sense. He was only twelve.

The shed was a rat's nest of tools and supplies. Metal shelving ran along each side and supported a wide board at the back that might once have functioned as a workbench. Shelves and board were heaped with hammers and wrenches, drills and saws, toolboxes of various sizes with their lids open. Under the board, two tires on wheels, and a battery. John must work on cars, too.

Yvonne had told her the shed was John's territory, and Kate agreed with her it was a miracle he could find anything. She was sure he didn't work in here—there was barely room to store her bike. She unlocked it from the metal leg of the bench and rolled it outside.

Ugh. Kate hated messes. She was happy to shut the door on this one, grateful it wasn't her responsibility.

She rode to Union Hill, into the downtown area with library, police station and a block of shops and restaurants, then took random turns through an old residential neighborhood. Five miles later she hit a stretch of newer, larger houses set farther back on their lots. Cars flashed past, tires hissing on the blacktop, and she put some oomph into her spin.

She felt light as a leaf. It felt good to fly.

Some miles farther on she saw the lions, one on each side of a driveway. Massive stone animals atop four-foot blocks. They looked so out of place Kate laughed out loud. Weren't there lions outside the New York public library in Manhattan? Maybe they'd decided to go out West and got lost on the way.

You can't bear down on the pedals when you're laughing. She checked her mirror and made a U-turn across the road, still chuckling. The gizmo on her handlebars said she'd gone ten miles, which meant she'd have twenty when she got back to Roll and Rest. Not a lot of miles, but she wouldn't stop there.

By the time she turned onto Watkins, she could smell the river, or feel it—the weight of moisture in the air. She passed the campground and the two or three neighboring houses on the left, hidden in the woods above the road.

After a couple of miles the pavement got bad and the road narrowed. Kate had to concentrate on avoiding potholes, which became more numerous and deeper. Not much maintenance going on out here—this end of Watkins Spur had apparently been abandoned. Its edges were overgrown with bushes and the ground was stony; she hadn't seen a house in twenty minutes. A truck or SUV had left tire tracks in a couple of dips, which must have been wet in spring but were dry now. Aggressive tread marks were preserved in hardened mud.

An oversized metal mailbox by the side of the road, its post tilted and weathered, told her she was almost to the house. The numbers were mostly worn off, but there were three digits, and the second one was a two. This must be it, especially since it was the only place for at least half a mile.

The box's door hung down, and the opening was filled with a mass of twigs. A bird's nest from last spring. Whoever lived at this address must get their mail at the post office.

If anybody lived here. Maybe Walter Tremblay had moved on. The address she'd gotten from the Internet could be outdated.

The house, a single-story Cape Cod style, was sound enough—the paint didn't look too bad and the roof, at least the front half Kate could see, was intact. But the yard hadn't been tended to in a long time, with its sad lawn and overgrown bushes. The grass had gotten high enough to fall over and mat, so the next time it got mowed the growth underneath would be a sun-starved yellow. If it ever got mowed.

She laid her bike down at the side of the road. There were no vehicles in the driveway. The single-car garage, connected to the house with a breezeway, was closed. Still, the dirt driveway showed tire tracks, fairly recent, the same knobby tread she'd seen on the road.

She found a flagstone walkway, almost lost in overgrown grass, and followed it to the front door. Lifted the knocker, green with corrosion, and rapped a few times.

Waited.

No sound reached her but the wind. It skittered a few leaves down the road and tossed the maples' orange manes. This place must be even more forlorn at night, Kate thought. No streetlights. No neighbors.

Was that a noise from inside?

She rapped twice more, good and hard, and the door opened a crack. Then wider, but not by much. Light fell on a face cross-hatched with age, its expression suspicious.

"What are you selling?" an old voice quavered. A woman.

"I'm not selling anything," Kate said. "I'm returning something."

"I don't want to buy nothing."

Kate spoke louder. "Is Walter here? I have his—I have something for Walter.

"I don't want a walker."

"WALTER," Kate shouted. "WALTER TREMBLAY." The woman must be deaf as the wooden door her fingers curled around.

The eyes narrowed, the face fearful now. "Walter? What do you know about Walter?"

"I have something that belongs to him," Kate said, keeping her volume turned up.

The old woman looked her up and down. "You'll need to come back. Late afternoon. Wednesdays. That's when he comes." She shut the door.

Oh, for Pete's sake. Trying to do a good deed shouldn't be this complicated.

She'd taken a few steps toward the road when she heard the door open again. "You're kind of old, you know," the woman said.

"What?" She'd heard, but had no idea what the woman meant.

"Old!" the woman shouted. The door slammed.

Kate laughed. The woman's voice was so hostile Kate felt like yelling "Look who's talking!" in retaliation. But the comment was so off the wall she was pretty sure the whole conversation had been a series of misunderstandings on both sides.

She hoped the information about Walter's schedule was reliable, at least. Leaving the pink phone with the woman didn't seem like a good idea: she was impossible to communicate with. Or bonkers. Or both.

Kate trudged through the grass to her bike. She'd come back when Walter was home. The vehicle that had left tracks would be here. There'd be somebody sane to talk to. Or maybe she'd just take the phone to the police and forget about good deeds.

But if she'd lost a phone, would she think of going to the cops to see if they had it? She didn't think so.

Pedaling back along Watkins Spur, she felt sorry for the deaf old woman, isolated in a dark house at the end of a bad road. At least the tire tracks said she had a relative or friend with a truck who made the trip out and probably brought her groceries.

Kate filled herself with fresh air and birdsong on her way home, grateful for her freedom.

* * *

Sunday morning. Kate felt lazy, got up late. Read a book for a while, something she usually did at night. She wasn't a church-goer, but she made Sundays special by getting in touch with friends by phone. This time she made herself call her mother first, which was usually not fun.

"How are you doing, Ma?"

"Still breathing."

It was her typical answer, but sometimes Kate wanted to shout "How about a little gratitude?" Of course she never did. She understood, after joining with her sister and brother to pull her mother through a bad period at an alcohol rehabilitation center, that depression was something her mother couldn't change any more than she could change her eye color or the shape of her ears. The doctors explained mood was controlled by levels of neurotransmitters in the brain. Kate wasn't immune to periods of depression herself, but she'd never had anything close to the crash-and-burn scenario she'd seen her mother go through.

Kate called about once a month out of duty, hoping to prevent another major episode. Occasionally her mother sounded as if she'd had a few drinks. Kate had done some reading that suggested a relapse was inevitable, so every call to her mother began in suspense. They'd ended, so far, in relief.

This time her mother sounded fine. She complained Tucson was "heating up like hell," with temperatures in the nineties. "It's October, dammit," she groused. "And it doesn't cool down at night as much as it used to."

Kate didn't mention climate change because she didn't want to get into an argument. She asked if either of her siblings had phoned recently, and was happy to hear her sister had. She didn't expect her brother to call; he saved himself for emergencies.

Let there not be an emergency.

Then she called Marjorie, an anchor of calm and good sense and the friend she'd called most often since taking to the road in her camper. Partly from her own curiosity and partly because Marjorie would be interested, Kate asked if it was normal for a twelve-year-old boy to be cruel to pet cats. "I've gotten friendly with the couple who run this campground, and their son shoots rubber bands at the indoor cat and throws stones at the outdoor one."

"That doesn't sound good. A pre-schooler might hurt a cat innocently, but twelve is far too old for a child not to know animals feel pain." The pause that followed wasn't common with Marjorie. "Is the family dysfunctional in other ways?"

"The nine-year-old girl is going through some kind of emotional upset. Her mother plans to have her checked out medically because she's suddenly having memory problems. Both kids were home-schooled until this year."

"And the parents?"

"I don't know the father very well—he has a day job—but the mother is a a lovely person. Her worse fault is she worries a lot, mostly about her kids. She really cares, and she's responsible and attentive."

"I ask about the family because there's a well-known association between animal abuse and domestic violence," Marjorie said. "A child sometimes acts out what's been done to him, substituting the pet as victim. The cat or dog might be the only family member less powerful than he is."

"That's horrible," Kate said. "I can't imagine any violence going on with the Chouinards." But a mental image of Carson's face the first time she'd seen him up close made her stomach lurch. "Wait, the boy did have a bruise on his face, after school one day last week."

Marjorie sighed. "That doesn't sound good."

"He said he fell."

"Victims always have a story ready. Abusers threaten them so they won't tell anyone, and anyway they don't think they deserve help. The husband would be careful. The wife might not know what he's doing, might buy the boy's excuses. Might want to buy them."

Kate felt sick. "The daughter said her father's grouchy after work. He's got two jobs, insurance at the office and campground business at home. He does the books, runs the website. In a way, he's never away from work."

"Sounds like he's busy, and probably stressed. Grouchiness is understandable, if it's handled right. Does the girl seem afraid of him?"

"No."

"That's good. But I have to tell you, if there's a problem it's usually the husband, though there are occasional cases of abusive women."

Yvonne hitting Carson? Not a chance. "What if there isn't any abuse?" Kate asked. "The school told the mother the boy's developmentally delayed. What if it's more than a delay, and he's not going to go any further? What if he's mean to animals simply because of who he is, who he'll always be?

"You're talking genetics. Rare, but when it happens it's the devil to deal with. Because children like that—CU, it's called, callous and unemotional—they don't care about feelings, in animals or other people. The worst of them enjoy inflicting pain."

"He can't be hurting his sister," Kate said. "Yvonne would notice. She's an involved, stay-at-home mother."

"Okay, but mistreatment of animals is a red flag. All is not well in that family. I'd keep an eye on the father."

"I just can't feature Duval hitting his children."

"Abusers aren't monsters. They're troubled people who can't handle their emotions."

"You amaze me, Marjorie. I know a few people well, my family and friends. I think I understand them. You understand and empathize with everyone. You understand people you don't know, will never even meet."

Marjorie laughed. "That's an unusual description of a psychologist's perspective. Not that I'm a psychologist."

"You will be," Kate said.

Her friend's voice sobered. "Please, if you see any evidence of abuse, report it. You might be able to do it anonymously, but even if you have to give your name the state's required to protect your identity. That's a federal law."

"Oh, man. It's a long way to go from chasing a cat to child abuse."

"Just keep your eyes open," Marjorie said. "I'm sorry this had to land in your lap. I was hoping you'd get some down time after the nasty experience in the Adirondacks."

* * *

Kate went for a lazy hike, without her sketchbook. Took a few pictures, went home for lunch. Napped. Woke. The novel she'd started was so good she picked it up again. *Piano Tide.*

She'd chosen it for its interesting title and Alaskan setting, and it delivered big-time. When she finished reading it she was startled to find herself in Pennsylvania again, with daylight ebbing from the sky.

A series of stretches brought her back into her body. She opened a cupboard, feeling lazy about dinner, too. Old Mother Hubbard of nursery rhyme fame popped into her head as she looked at her meager supplies. She needed to get herself to a grocery store soon, but in the meantime Ramen noodles would have to do. She put the crinkly package on the counter and slid into a dinette seat to pull down the blind on her big window. It was almost dark, the pathway lights already on.

As she reached for the cord, Richard came out of the Winnebago. Kate was surprised to see him stagger. Was he drunk? She watched him head for the Chouinards' house, weaving and stumbling.

Then she saw Juneau. The dog was following Richard and collapsing every few steps, then struggling to her feet.

What on earth? Dogs don't get drunk.

Kate left her camper door open and ran across the gravel. Richard had reached the office door and was knocking feebly on it. Kate gave the door a good couple of bangs, then turned to Richard. He was breathing deeply, shuddering. "Donna—" He fell to his knees. "Get her out—"

Kate thumped the door once more and heard it open behind her as she ran to the Winnebago, passing Juneau. The dog was on her side; her eye followed Kate.

The class C's door was open and she climbed on board. Donna was slumped on the sofa and looked asleep. Kate got her arms under the heavy shoulders and dragged her to the steps, then pulled her down them, using a knee to keep Donna's head from hitting the edges. She thought briefly of the friend in Maine she'd found dead at the bottom of a flight of stairs, but pushed the memory away.

Once she had Donna out of the RV she reached for her phone to call 911, but it wasn't in her back pocket; she must have left it in her camper. Damn. Yvonne or Duval would call, though— probably already had, and from the house, which was better anyway: landlines gave the 911 system more accurate locations than cells.

In the dim glow from the pathway lights, Donna's face looked flushed. Kate put two fingers at the side of the neck, feeling for the groove between tendons and trachea where the jugular vein sits. Gosh, Donna's neck was thick. And it had been a long time since Kate had worked as an emergency medical technician.

She pressed harder. Was that a faint beat? She was relieved to hear a siren approaching.

Kate felt for a pulse at the wrist. It was sometimes easier. Damn, she'd really lost her knack.

But the siren noise had drained away, the crunch of gravel replacing it as the ambulance backed toward the Winnebago. Duval walked beside it, then held up his hand. The truck stopped sharply and the rear doors popped open.

"Okay, miss, we'll take over now."

Kate scrambled out of the way of the team. A man and a woman set a gurney beside Donna, its legs folded, and lifted her onto it, slipping a plastic mask over her face for oxygen. They lifted the loaded gurney and slotted into the ambulance, the mechanical thump and click coming to Kate with incongruous sweetness, that of a once-familiar sound not heard in years. Red lights flashing, the vehicle shot down the driveway and made a fast right toward Union Hill.

Kate closed the Winnebago's door and turned toward the house. Duval had waited; he met Kate and put a hand on her shoulder.

"She'll be okay," he said.

Richard was sitting in one of the patio chairs, Juneau pressed against his legs. He was staring at the ground, his hand on the dog's head. They were both shaking. Yvonne came out of the house and put a quilt around the man's shoulders.

"Juneau saved us," Richard said. His voice was weak. "I was reading before bed, and almost fell asleep over the book, and then Juneau was barking and poking me with her nose. I got up, I had such a terrible headache, and Donna was asleep on the couch, and she wouldn't wake up, and that's when—" Either he ran out of breath or he was overcome by his feelings.

"No more talking," Kate said. "Save your strength. You and Donna need to get checked out at the hospital, and we'll find out what happened." Her guess was carbon monoxide poisoning. The Winnebago had been plenty warm when she'd gone aboard to get Donna, so the couple had been running the RV's furnace.

"We'll take care of Juneau," Yvonne said.

"Thank you," Richard managed. "I really feel sick." He folded his arms on his knees and put his head down. Juneau licked his ear but he didn't seem to notice.

"Do you think maybe you and Donna ate some spoiled food?" Duval asked, but Yvonne shook her head at him and murmured "Not now, honey."

The second siren of the night sliced through the air, and Duval went to the corner of the house to wave it in. Richard did his best to sit up; he seemed stronger than when Kate had first seen him lurching out of the Winnebago. She was more worried about Donna.

Yvonne knelt beside Juneau and hugged her. "You're such a good girl," she said.

The ambulance's back-up beeper sounded along the driveway and stopped next to Duval. An EMT jumped out of the back and looked at the group. "Which one of you is my patient?" he asked, his eyes already on Richard.

\* \* \*

After a subdued "Good night" to Yvonne and Duval, Kate went back to the Millers' RV and turned the thermostat to OFF. If the furnace was running badly enough to produce carbon monoxide, it might have other problems, and there was no sense risking a fire.

Restless, Kate walked around the campground. Annie's van was gone, and John's was overshadowed by one of those forty-foot trailers that probably had a washer and dryer and three televisions on board. The shaded windows were bright with lights, and canned laughter from a movie or TV show washed into the night in sporadic waves. Perhaps the people on board hadn't heard the sirens and didn't know about the real-life drama at their doorstep. Two smaller campers were dark and quiet, but outside the third a couple sat at their picnic table smoking.

"Say, do you know what was up with those ambulances?" Because of the walkway lights Kate hadn't brought a flashlight, so the woman speaking was a shadow, her face lit briefly by the orange glow of a cigarette.

"I think it was carbon monoxide poisoning," Kate said. "Make sure your alarm is working, okay?"

"Oh, of course," the woman said. "But thanks for the reminder." She said something else, but Kate hadn't stopped walking and didn't catch the words.

Worried about Donna, she didn't feel like talking. Such a warm person, so funny and kind. Kate took deep breaths of night air. The moon was low in the trees, gibbous, its light choked by a tangle of branches.

She went home to her camper, ate plain noodles for dinner and lay awake, worried and wondering. She thought of the great-horned owl she'd heard the last time she hadn't been able to sleep.

And the other sound. Who had been lurking in the campground that night? Could he have anything to do with tonight's events?

She reached past her fear for a rational explanation. The Winnebago's furnace malfunctioned. Its alarm failed. Period.

Still, she slid deeper into the sleeping bag, covering her ears with its hood. She didn't want to hear an owl.

# EIGHT

Morning brought coffee, and coffee brought greater perspective. She didn't think Donna and Richard's severe symptoms were from moldy cauliflower or a piece of chicken gone bad, as Duval had suggested the night before. Donna was an experienced cook and kept a clean kitchen. It was probably carbon monoxide, which would be easy to check.

What other candidates were there? Maybe botulism? Kate's days as an EMT were too far in the past for her to be sure the pathogen could strike with the speed she'd seen in the Millers. Richard's ragged breathing might have had an emotional rather than physical cause. But what about an airborne agent? Something respiratory? With all the dust in the air from the drought, was there a Pennsylvania equivalent of the hanta virus of the Southwest?

She'd gotten up early, and it was still too soon to join Yvonne for coffee, so Kate had time to check out the Millers' RV.

Taking a deep breath and holding it, she went up the Winnebago's steps. The thermostat was set at 80, and the propane furnace was opposite the couch where she'd found Donna. Kate took a quick look at the counter, opened the fridge. Everything looked clean enough. She got herself out of there in under a minute without breathing a molecule of on-board air. Just in case.

The next step was to check the vent on the outside of the rig. If it was blocked at all, incomplete combustion in the furnace could have produced carbon monoxide, CO. Scary stuff. You couldn't smell it, and it could kill in minutes.

The heater vent looked just like the one on her camper—a metal plate with a circular opening, the grid across the opening in the shape of a Y. The vents must be standard. This one looked clear, the airflow unimpeded by any debris.

The only thing not exactly like her camper's vent was a difference in texture in a rectangle around this one. Maybe the RV had been painted and the vent, along with all the other areas not to be painted, had been covered with masking tape. But that wasn't important—the main thing was to check if the vent was clear farther in than she could see.

She looked around, found a stick and poked it past the Y. It moved freely, encountering no obstruction. Carbon monoxide wasn't the problem, then, unless the flame was adjusted badly on the furnace itself.

Not something she felt confident assessing on her own. Maybe John could. It was too early to ask him, though.

"Whatcha up to?" Carson's voice made her spin around; she hadn't heard him coming. His tone of voice was hostile, sarcastic; she wondered if his question was conscious or unconscious imitation, since she'd used the same colloquial contraction when he'd tried to hide his roll of duct tape the day before.

His face was blank. Then he wrinkled his nose to push up his glasses.

Footsteps. Yvonne, running from the house, her face wet. Kate knew from the look on her face it was bad news.

"Oh, God, I can't believe it. Donna's *dead.*" Yvonne engulfed her in a hug, rocking back and forth, crying. Kate felt tears wet her ear, her neck.

Then Yvonne stood back, hands on Kate's shoulders, gulping. Kate met her eyes, feeling embarrassed she wasn't crying herself. She felt sad, yes—she'd liked Donna a lot, especially considering how short a time she'd known her. But she often didn't cry in situations that drew floods from others. She didn't understand it, but it was how she'd always been.

Yvonne had known Donna for years, of course. "I called the hospital to see how they were doing," she said. "It never occurred to me—" Her voice caught.

It had occurred to Kate. She realized she'd spent much of her sleepless night trying not to think about her inability to find Donna's pulse. Apparently it wasn't her lack of skill that was to blame. Donna hadn't been in the best of health, with her weight and lack of exercise. But hell, she hadn't looked that old. Sixty, maybe?

She hadn't made it off the Winnebago alive. Probably the hospital staff didn't tell Richard the truth until the morning, giving him a night of rest to recover from his own poisoning. That might be his last good night's sleep for some time.

Kate followed Yvonne's glance to the side. Carson was playing with a yoyo, throwing it sideways so it hung in the air, quivering, then returned to his hand.

"Carson—" But Yvonne apparently didn't know what to say to her son, who seemed oblivious to the drama and pain around him. Face neutral, eyes on the toy, he didn't look up at his name.

The back door opened and Duval strode toward them, Juneau trotting at his heels. Kate was relieved the dog was moving well and looked alert. That boded well for Richard's recovery.

Duval put his hand on Yvonne's shoulder, and she turned into his chest. They held each other. Kate knelt to Juneau and petted her, and the dog gave her a tentative lick on the chin. Kate remembered how much Juneau had barked at Carson, and she looked around for the boy. He was nowhere in sight.

More footsteps on the gravel. John joined the group, and the Chouinards separated, Yvonne to turn her back to John and wipe at tears with a sleeve.

"We're going to have a look at the Winnebago," Duval said. "John and me. Donna died of carbon monoxide poisoning, and Richard's blood levels of the gas were sky high. He's lucky to be alive. So's Juneau." He looked down at the dog, who wagged her tail at the sound of her name.

Kate decided to keep her heater vent inspection to herself. Maybe the two men would see something she'd missed.

John ducked around the front of the rig, to the driver's side; Kate figured he was checking the vent. When he came back he nodded at Duval and the two men climbed on board.

"Be careful, honey," Yvonne said, her voice a little quavery.

"The heater's off," Duval called back.

The big window above Kate slid open—he was playing it safe.

Yvonne sat on the bottom step, shaking her head. "Such a shock." Juneau sat in front of her and she fondled her dog's folded ears. "I know, honey," she said to the animal, "you're wondering where your people are."

Funny, Yvonne had called both Duval and Juneau "honey." Sometimes Kate called her bike "honey." Almost at the top of a hill, she'd say "Let's go, honey, go go go!" Was she talking to her bike or herself?

Honey. Just a word, but it helped people get through their days with affection.

Kate hadn't spent much time with Duval, but she was one hundred percent sure Juneau was a honey. She sat beside Yvonne and gave the dog's shoulders a rub. "You're such a good dog, Juneau. You saved Richard's life."

"I wonder how she knew." Yvonne said. "Carbon monoxide is odorless, isn't it?"

"Yes, it is. I bet she picked up on Donna's condition, not the gas itself. She knew something was wrong with her, and she alerted Richard."

"That must be it."

"Coming through," Duval said. The women stood up.

John shut the door and shrugged. "We turned the heater on and I got down there and looked at the flame. It's as blue as can be, no yellow at all. So it's burning clean. Shouldn't be any CO gas coming out of the thing." He scratched his beard, and a crumb fell out. "I dunno what happened."

"What about a CO detector?" Kate asked. "It's required by law, isn't it? It should have gone off. Those things are loud—they shriek."

Duval shook his head. "It isn't working. It has a green light that should be on all the time, and it's out. They bought the RV from a private seller they found on-line—Richard was telling me about it when they first got here, about what a good deal they got."

"That's illegal, isn't it?" Yvonne asked. "The CO detector not working?"

"Yes. A dealer would be careful about something safety-related like that. But a private seller, I don't know. And how would you prove it hadn't failed after the sale?"

"Some people figure out how to defeat alarms," John said, "because they can go off when nothing's wrong. Not something I'd recommend, though."

"Pretty expensive, that good deal of his." Duval's face was hard. "He should have had it checked out by a dealership. Or by somebody like John here. Somebody who knows what they're doing."

"What does he—oh, he's retired. But what did he do for a living?" Kate asked.

"Taught high school English," Yvonne said.

Her husband shrugged. "What can you expect from an English teacher? Not mechanically inclined."

Judgmental guy, Duval.

\* \* \*

Kate found it difficult to concentrate on drawing that day. Her art had become the most important thing in her life, and often it was intensely satisfying. But not every day was a complete high anymore, the way it had been in August. Sometimes life got in the way.

Sometimes death got in the way.

Her mentor in Maine had warned her about staying on track, guarding the momentum of her work-life. She'd lost art after college, slowly, through the daily attrition of her jobs as an EMT and newspaper reporter that claimed most of her time and energy. Realizing that had led her to take a year off to travel in her truck camper, feasting her eyes on beautiful places and filling her notebook with a harvest of images.

Some days she was filled with joy. Other days she just had to show up for work. In front of her sketchpad.

When she got back to her camper after a few hours of hiking and drawing, a police car was parked beside the Winnebago, and two officers were inspecting the furnace vent. One of them glanced Kate's way, nodded to her.

She hoped they found something. It was disturbing not to understand the reason behind Donna's death.

\* \* \*

It was a dream, and then it wasn't. She willed herself out of sleep, as if swimming from the dark water at the bottom of a pond.

The phone. Damn, she must have forgotten to bring it up to bed the way she usually did. She slid out of the bunk and stared. Not her phone but the pink one she'd found in the woods. Lit up, on the table, ringing and buzzing against the hard surface.

Half-awake, she snatched the thing up. "Hello?"

No answer. She wished she'd just let it ring.

No voice. Not even breathing. But something. A connection, she was sure. The caller hadn't hung up.

She waited, didn't say Hello again.

"Kate?" A male voice.

"Who is this?"

A laugh. A click. Dead air.

She turned the phone off. Went back to bed, trying not to miss out on more sleep by being angry. Or scared.

But she was both. Who was he? *How did he know her name?*

\* \* \*

John still hadn't gotten the parts for her generator, so Kate went to the office to pay for a second week at the campground. While she was signing the receipt, Richard called, released by the hospital and hoping Yvonne could give him a ride to the repair shop to pick up his Hyundai. Yvonne asked Kate to go along to drive the dinghy back to Roll and Rest instead of letting Richard do so.

"I don't trust him behind the wheel," Yvonne said. "He could hardly finish a sentence, kept breaking down." She hung a CLOSED sign under the smiling cats on the door.

"It'll take him a long time to get over this," Kate said as she got into Yvonne's old Dodge.

"If he ever does. I can't imagine—" She didn't finish the sentence.

"Right."

They rode in the semi-silence of the rattly green car down Watkins Spur and then right, toward town.

"Years from now, when he thinks he's dealt with Donna's death, it'll ambush him like it just happened. For a few minutes or a few hours, he'll be a wreck again." Kate said. "At least that's how it works for a lot of people." She was thinking of herself and her father, who'd gone missing when she was eleven. Sometimes she still dreamed of him. Rarely now, she had a bout of grief, or anger.

Yvonne didn't say anything, but dabbed at her eyes with a tissue.

It wasn't the right time for Kate to tell her about the early-morning caller.

They found Richard slumped in a wheelchair just inside the hospital doors. He looked up, his face pale, when Yvonne said his name. A young man in blue scrubs, perhaps a volunteer, tossed a newspaper aside and jumped to his feet, saying the hospital required him to take Richard to the car. No walking.

Newspaper. Kate went into the small gift shop off the lobby and bought a copy of the *Union Hill Star-Herald*. A weekly paper, and thin.

Richard's wobbly transfer from wheelchair to passenger seat was being accomplished as she ran to the Dodge. She got in the back seat.

"Thank you, ladies," Richard said in a low voice.

That was all he said.

At the auto repair shop all three of them went inside. Word must have spread. Two ambulance calls in one night in a town this size was major news. The woman behind the counter kept looking at Richard sympathetically.

While his credit card was being processed, Kate snagged the keys to the Hyundai.

"See you back at the ranch." Something her father used to say, meaning "See you back home." Yvonne nodded, but Richard looked so puzzled Kate almost stopped to explain.

She drove the Hyundai to Roll and Rest and parked it next to their—his—Winnebago. Found herself smiling over Richard's bewildered look. Imagined him, after she'd left, asking Yvonne, "What ranch?"

Kate laughed out loud and immediately felt guilty. Donna had just died, Richard was a train wreck of grief. Nothing to laugh about.

Then she was crying in her subdued way, arm across the steering wheel, head down. Donna was dead. What a ghastly fact.

She wiped her eyes with her sleeve and got out of the Hyundai, leaving the keys in the ignition. Maybe laughing and crying weren't the opposites she'd always taken them to be. Maybe laughter came from a hidden part of her mind that had seen death strike nearby and was celebrating the fact she was alive. In this dangerous, crazy world, she was still walking around. Maybe her mother's mantra, "still breathing," was actually a form of gratitude, the best the woman could muster.

Or maybe the laughter was a response to the absurd joke life played on everyone. It let you carry on for years, decades, loving people and pursuing goals and learning things you thought were important. It let you get good and hooked on the habit of being alive.

Then, sometimes with no warning, the party was over.

\* \* \*

She'd bought the newspaper quickly, on impulse, not realizing it had come out the previous Thursday. Nothing in this issue, then, about two Sunday night ambulance calls to Roll and Rest. Kate glanced through the six pages: a very local paper, perhaps a one-person operation. Township commissioners' meeting, high school football schedule, school lunch menu, Rotary meetings in nearby Latrobe. The last two pages were solid advertisements.

One story caught her eye: "Elementary School Parent-Teacher Conferences Big Success." Yvonne hadn't mentioned talking to any teachers; maybe she hadn't known about the program.

\* \* \*

Marjorie was sympathetic. "What a terrible accident, Kate. I'm so sorry." She moved quickly, though, to being alarmed for her friend. She hadn't known Donna, of course. "Is your heater okay? Have you had it checked recently?"

"I look at it now and then to make sure the flame's good and blue."

"Is that enough? Doesn't it need, I don't know, to be tuned up, like a car? By a professional?"

"I do have a working carbon monoxide alarm, but I suppose I could ask John to check out the furnace. He's the handyman here, and Yvonne says he knows what he's doing. He's supposed to fix my generator one of these days."

"Hmmm. 'One of these days' doesn't sound promising. Maybe you need a different professional." Behind her voice a baby's wail crested into a shriek. "Talk to you later, sorry."

\* \* \*

Kate wrote a note to give to the police with the second lost phone, describing the call she'd gotten at three in the morning as the work of a "malicious predator" and giving Walter Tremblay's address on Watkins Spur. That should get some attention. She'd fill out the lost-and-found information, as she had for the blue cell, but the form was too small for all the details.

Maybe the police would be able to determine the number of the last incoming call on the pink phone. Her note closed with a plea to be informed of any results. "The caller knew my first name," she'd written. "So I'm involved somehow. Please let me know what you find out."

But as she rode her bike to the police station with the pink phone in her pocket, she decided to insist on a face-to-face talk with someone in uniform. She needed more than a nod from the guy at the front desk. This wasn't about lost property any more. It was personal.

She got ten minutes with a woman officer who was sympathetic and wrote up an incident report.

"Strange that the caller knew your name—you're just passing through, after all." She gave Kate a searching look. "Sure you don't know anybody local?"

"Just the people who run the campground. Yvonne and Duval Chouinard, their handyman John—I don't know his last name—and a few of the other RVers."

"The Chouinards? Oh, they're fine," the officer said. "I'll see what we can do with this phone, but keep your eyes open."

* * *

Getting ready for the fair ramped up the pressure to finish drawings, and Kate was glad to have something to do besides think about Donna and heartbroken Richard. Most days she went for a walk in the woods and drew roughs in her sketchbook, either before or after coffee with Yvonne, and sometimes both.

Maybe she'd sell a few things at the fair. It would be great to earn what she'd need to pay John when he fixed the generator. If he ever did. He'd told her a few days ago that the wrong parts had been delivered and he'd had to send them back. She'd had a flicker of doubt. Should she believe him? It could be an excuse. But what did he have to gain from delaying the job?

Maybe she wasn't thinking straight. She was shaken by Donna's senseless and inexplicable death, which had come out of the blue.

Blue. That made her think of the first phone she'd taken to the police, which made her think of the pink phone. She wished the cops would come up with some answers. The three-in-the-morning phone call still gave her the creeps. The guy knew her *name*.

The mood during coffee with Yvonne had turned darker, mourning added on top of her worries about Savvy and Duval. The two women didn't talk much about Donna, but Kate knew the cheerful woman's death wasn't far from her friend's thoughts. It wasn't far from her own.

A few days after the terrible news, Yvonne finished the magenta shawl and cast on stitches for a thick men's pullover. The yarn's graphite color might have had something to do with her state of mind.

"I made an appointment with our family doctor for Savvy," she said, her fingers moving quick and sure, tugging the yarn and flipping it over the needles. "She didn't want me to, but I'm afraid something's really wrong with her. Morning headaches, dropping grades. And she's crabby all the time." The cup in her hand shook, and she put it down. "I'm afraid it's a brain tumor."

"Yikes, Yvonne, don't go there. Not without better information. It's probably something far less dramatic. A temporary hormone imbalance, something like that. She's on the verge of puberty."

"Yesterday she yelled at me. She's never done that before." Yvonne's chin quivered. "She used to be such a good kid."

"She's still a good kid." Kate was surprised at how sure she was.

Shadow popped into Yvonne's lap and did her falling-over trick. Perfect timing. The poor woman could use a kitty-fix right about now. Sure enough, she cuddled the cat like a baby.

With the chaos of recent events, Kate hadn't had a chance to tell Yvonne about the pink phone, the name and address the Internet had turned up, and the phone call she'd gotten at three a.m. So she filled her friend in and described her encounter with the old woman at the house on Watkins Spur.

"I didn't know anyone was living out there," Yvonne said. "The last I heard, the veteran who owned the place abandoned it, and then it went to a sheriff's auction because of unpaid taxes. It took a while to sell, and the county didn't spend the money to maintain the road. Which only made it harder to sell."

"Whoever bought it must have a high-clearance vehicle," Kate said. "I saw tracks—someone's getting through. I doubt it's the old woman who's doing any driving. She must have a relative who checks up on her, helps her out."

"I don't know anything about her. But we can ask Edna."

"The old bat was entertaining," Kate said. "She's either deaf or doesn't really want to talk, so the conversation was more or less a series of non sequiturs."

Yvonne was somehow knitting even though Shadow was still ensconced in her lap. "That call sounds scary, Kate. The phone was lost in the woods, so how could the owner have known your name? Anybody could have found it."

"I don't have a clue. Maybe he's been watching me? Following me?"

"Possible, I suppose. But how? It's not easy to walk around quietly with all the leaves on the ground."

Kate drank her coffee and watched her friend knit. Neither of them said anything for a few minutes: a comfortable silence. It felt so safe here.

"That house used to be a cute little place," Yvonne said eventually, "but it must be falling apart by now."

"It doesn't look too bad," Kate said. "The yard's been neglected, but the house looks okay."

"The guy who used to lived there, he was an Army buddy of John's. They were pretty tight when they first got out, but I don't know what John's friend did after he lost the house, if he stuck around here or left the area." Yvonne and Shadow touched noses. They were exchanging smiles, Kate was sure. Cats always look like they're smiling because of the curve of their mouths under the whisker-pouches.

Yvonne's smile was the brief, human version.

Kate decided not to talk any more about the disturbing message she'd gotten on the pink phone. Yvonne had enough to worry about, and she was doing a good job of it. Savvy had a brain tumor and Duval was going to give himself a heart attack from working too hard.

She tried a joke. "Maybe the Loyalhanna Hermit lives in the house. Maybe our hermit is an old woman."

"Who told you about the hermit?" Yvonne asked. "I don't believe there is one. Some opportunistic hiker down on his luck probably got tempted to steal. Only someone who's having a hard time would take small things from yards near the conservation land—a jar of peanut butter off a picnic table, a pair of jeans, a fork. Nothing big, and never from inside a house. I figure if somebody needs a loaf of bread that bad, they're welcome to it."

With her rattletrap car and overworked husband, Yvonne didn't have a lot to spare, but she had a generous heart. Kate was surprised her friend didn't see the hermit as an opportunity to worry. Maybe with Savvy in such bad shape, her mother's worry inbox was full.

* * *

95

After ten days at Roll and Rest without any time on the river, Kate came up with a new plan. She'd carry her boat down to the water when she went out to draw. The obstacle to paddling had been that she got wrapped up in her art and forgot about the rest of her life. Doing artwork engaged her in a deep way that could use up all her energy. With the boat in front of her as a reminder, she'd stop drawing sooner and get some upper-body exercise, along with a different view of the Loyalhanna. And why not take her art supplies with her, and draw on the water?

The path to the beach was wide enough for easy walking with her lightweight kayak, a gunwale hull hooked over one shoulder, her bag of gear and art supplies over the other, her PFD and paddle in hand.

The boat was a boat, but her art was a lifeboat. When she put Donna's death and Yvonne's worries out of her mind and concentrated on the scenes before her, she felt a surge of pleasure that came at her straight out of earth and forest, air and light, and out of the water flowing past her. She understood her sanity came to her as a gift of the planet, which was why she had to be outdoors as much as possible.

And maybe that was the gift of her art, to others—a reflection of the pleasure. It was nothing like what she felt, looking at a tree or a heron and drawing it, but people looking at her work might feel something similar. One step removed, though, so a weaker effect. As if they stood on the street hearing a symphony orchestra through the open windows of a concert hall.

Kate put the kayak on the ground near the maple tree where she'd sketched Savvy. After that session she'd finished three drawings of the girl, which she'd try to sell together. If nobody bought them, she'd give them to Yvonne. Meanwhile, the knee-high rock had become one of her favorite places to work. She dropped her PFD beside the boat and laid her paddle inside the hull. The paddle was a splendid one, a gift from a woman in the

Adirondacks who'd been grateful to Kate for discovering the truth about her son's death. Like most double-bladed paddles it came apart in the middle for ease of stowing, but she'd fitted the two halves together, ready to go.

A breeze nosed against her as she settled on the rock, so she taped the sheet of Bristol paper to her lapboard. For a change of pace she'd brought India ink this time, with a set of brushes and assorted pens. She wanted to draw some of the plants that grew in the clearing between the maple and the river, especially the Queen Anne's lace on its tall, brown stalks. The heads, ribbed cups made of stems each ending in a star of a seed, looked like rusty candelabra. She'd showed some photos of them on her phone to Yvonne, who'd called them Bird's Nests, which was certainly a more accurate name for the plant in the fall than anybody's lace.

After that, she might draw the boat; she loved its shape. Or she might paddle it first. She'd see.

She put the jar of ink on the ground and rotated it a bit, pushing down, so it wouldn't be easy to tip over. Then she took off the cap and dipped her brush in. The breeze sharpened, so she set the cap on top of the jar, loose. That should keep the wind from dropping dust or bits of leaf into her ink.

The big maple rustled—happily, she thought. She sank into her working trance. The maple rustled as if it were talking to her, remarking on the sweet weather, its freedom, Kate's freedom—

\* \* \*

A gurgling sound. Water flowing.

She had a headache.

If only she could go back to sleep. But it was so bright. She tried to turn on her side, felt the bed tilt under her.

What?

Disoriented, she sat up. The sky was blinding. At a distance, trees moved past.

She was in her kayak. She looked around—beside her, behind her. No paddle. Her jeans were soaked, her head hurt.

What the hell? She didn't remember launching. The last thing she remembered—

It didn't matter. She was headed downstream, toward the dam. She had to get off the river. Fast.

# NINE

Head throbbing, she looked at one shore and then the other. The one on the left looked closer. She used her hands to paddle, which worked better in this boat than in most kayaks, because it was narrow. The hull rocked side to side as she reached and stroked. She was comfortable with the degree of heel, but tried to minimize it: a flatter boat tracks straighter.

She cupped her hands and worked as hard and fast as she could, but hands don't make good paddles. The blades are too small, for starters, and they leak. She was jealous of ducks, with their big fan-shaped feet, and beavers, with webbing on their hind feet that made them great swimmers.

A white noise like radio static came to her. It was the lowhead dam, or rather the roar of the water slamming back into the river at the outfall. It must be close. The current was getting stronger, sweeping her along; it was pushing the bow to the right, so to keep the boat aimed at the left bank she paddled harder on the right.

Both her hands were numb with cold.

If she went over the dam she would either be thrown against rocks or drawn into the plunge pool, the hydraulic cycle at the base of any column of water, natural waterfall or spill below a dam. It would pull her down, let her rise and then snatch her back from the surface for round after round. She'd heard those vertical eddies called "drowning machines."

The river ahead had a line across it, like a horizon: the top of the dam, a gray line that could be, for her, a literal deadline.

The kayak rocked vigorously as she paddled. Her arms and shoulders ached. Her head was a little clearer.

She saw a strainer coming up, a hazard she would ordinarily work hard to avoid. But the situation was far from ordinary. Fight fire with fire, she said to herself. Fight water hazard with water hazard.

A strainer was an obstacle that worked like a filter, letting water pass through but stopping large objects like canoes or kayaks. This one was a fallen tree with its branches partially submerged. If she got tangled up in the woody net, it could capsize the boat or knock her out of it. The bow could run under a branch and the boat be forced underwater by the incessant current. Her along with it. If her shirt got snagged, underwater—

Dangerous. But an opportunity, since it extended out from the shore she doubted she could reach in time.

She didn't point the bow at the fallen tree, because of the current sweeping her along. She aimed upstream of it, making her strokes as fast and hard as she could. The boat rocked wildly as she thrashed closer to the bank, to the deadly strainer.

Almost! But she was going past it—

She grabbed at a dangling branch. It snapped and the boat spun, turning into the mass of branches, shuddering, running up on something that lifted it high in the water, pinned it.

For a second Kate thought the boat was wedged onto an underwater branch solidly enough that it would hold. But no, the water was relentless. It nudged the stern away from the bank, turning the boat at an angle to the current. Then the hull went fully sideways and the water hit it broadside, foaming an ugly yellow. The boat was sliding away from the tree, caught by the rush of the Loyalhanna.

She lunged for the closest branch. It wasn't very big—if it couldn't hold her weight, she'd be lost—

It held, at least long enough for her to go hand over hand along it toward a sturdier branch. Holding on pulled her half out of the boat. Relieved of some of her weight, the boat floated free and the current tugged it along until her feet were at the stern. She tried to guide it back under her, hoping to trap it in the strainer's tangle, but the effort was beyond her strength. She had to let the boat go. She held on with both both hands as the kayak spun away.

Under her full weight, the branches sagged. She was waist-deep in the river, arms tiring fast as the current dragged at her.

She felt with her right foot for something to stand on, some part of the tree she could use to lift herself higher. Found a foothold, stepped on it, looked for a higher handhold, found it. Bark bit into her soles; the current must have sucked away her sneakers.

Now the water roiled around her legs just above the knees. She was lucky the tree was still strong, hadn't been in the water long enough to rot.

She peered toward the shore, so tantalizingly close. Some of the tree's roots were still attached, keeping it alive.

Keeping her alive.

She worked her way higher. It was like climbing a tree, only sideways. She thought of Savvy and her maple tree gymnastics. If only Kate had the energy of a nine-year-old.

Ah. High enough to sit on a branch, which was a blessed relief. Her arms tingled and ached; she shook them out, one at a time, the way she might after a set of pull-ups at a gym. She was facing downstream, and the river rushed at her calves, nudged her feet forward, as if the Loyalhanna were telling her to walk, trying to trick her into making a mistake.

After a moment's rest, Kate evaluated her situation. She was tired and cold. She had to find her way through an obstacle course of branches and get to dry land, then get someplace warm and sheltered. She was thirsty, probably dehydrated, and her head throbbed.

She needed help. But first she needed to get ashore before hypothermia robbed her of her strength.

What the hell had happened? She searched her memory, got the tip of her brush going into the bottle of ink on the ground. And then nothing. Why was she in her boat, on the river?

Sooner or later she'd remember. First she had to get out of this predicament.

Easing her way along the branches, she always chose the larger one. If she were climbing up, each fork would have been a good place to stand. But she was climbing down, or would be if the tree were upright. In this direction, forks were obstacles to get around.

By the time she got to the main trunk, she was shivering. She clenched her jaw to keep her teeth from chattering. She craved rest, wanted to lie down on the trunk. But it was getting late, and she needed daylight to get out of the woods. If she tried to rest here it would be dangerously easy to roll or slip into the water. It would be the end of her.

Drowning would be as easy as falling off a log.

She didn't trust her balance in this shaky body, so she straddled the log and worked her way toward the bank by putting her weight on her hands and sliding a few inches at a time. Her legs were back in the water—the trunk was only a foot above the roiling surface. Her feet were numb. Each time she pushed herself forward on the trunk she felt it bounce. But she trusted it to hold. It had some give because the end in the river was resting on the thinnest branches, the crown of the tree distributing its weight among the tips of those many small branches that acted like springs.

She reached the wall of torn-up roots, but she was still over rushing water, since the tree had been growing at the very edge of the bank. It must have gotten undercut on the river side, and when the wind pushed from the landward side its fate was sealed.

Exhausted as she was, she'd have to climb the wall of earth and roots.

She dug a couple of recesses in the wall to use as footholds. Then she reached up, felt around for a surface root and used it to pull herself upward. Once she'd started she couldn't stop, since each foothold threatened to crumble, each handhold threatened to break loose.

At the top she got a leg over the crumbling edge of the root mass. She took a short breather, muscles aching in gratitude. But her perch felt precarious and uncomfortable. She found a foothold, and brought her other leg over.

With all her weight on it, the root she'd been standing on broke, and she fell into the black muck in the pit the roots had left when they wrenched free.

She was technically on dry land. But it wasn't completely dry. The mud suggested how recently the tree had fallen; the moisture in the pit hadn't had time to evaporate into the drought-stricken air.

Relief flooded her. She looked down at herself: her shirt and jeans and bare feet were black with mud. She could feel mud clotted in her hair.

She laughed aloud. What a mess.

Her joy at being safely ashore, or the laughter, or both, renewed her energy. After climbing out of the river's clutches, how hard could bushwhacking her way through the woods be?

It was brutal. The ground was uneven, like a half-drained swamp. Roots and rocks and fallen trees, puddles large and small—they all blocked her way, the wood slimy and the rocks covered with treacherous, slippery moss. She had to be careful where she put her feet, because she couldn't risk spraining an ankle—she could die of hypothermia if she didn't get out of the forest before dark.

How to find the road? She'd listen for the sound of vehicles, and aim for Watkins Spur, which ran more or less parallel to the river before turning toward town. She hoped she wasn't past the turn-off, but rivers almost always had roads running alongside. Rivers were the original roads, after all, before wheels got invented.

If she turned her back to the Loyalhanna and kept her course as straight as possible, she'd come to a road. If not a road, a trail that would take her to a road.

She bet her life on it.

\* \* \*

"Kate, I don't understand what happened to you," Yvonne said.

"Same here," Duval chimed in, the musical Quebecois accent strong in his voice. "You said you woke up floating down the river, in your boat without a paddle? It sounds like some kind of joke, about being up a creek."

"I'm not sure what happened myself," Kate said slowly. Her voice didn't seem to be working right.

She'd had a long hot shower at the house—her camper's bathroom had a shower in it, but it was small and not up to the needs of a woman encrusted from head to foot in dried mud. Duval, coming home from town, had seen her walking beside the road and had stopped to pick her up even before he recognized her. Yvonne, after a first gasp at the sight of her, offered a shower and a T-shirt and pants from her own closet. The clothes were a little big but they smelled deliciously clean.

"There's a lot missing from my, my memory. I don't remember—" What did you call it when you put a boat in the water? "Launching. Or even being close to launching. The last thing I remember was dipping a brush in the bottle of—" What? "I hadn't even touched it to the paper."

"Strange," Duval said. He stroked his bald head. "Have you had any bouts of amnesia in the past?"

"No. At least I can't remember any." After a beat, she laughed. Yvonne caught the irony and smiled.

"Hey, when I was hanging onto the strainer by a couple of twigs, was I grasping at—" Kate forgot what she'd started to say. Now Yvonne was frowning at her. "Seriously, I've never lost a piece of a day before. Never had any kind of blackout. I think what happened—"

Her pause wasn't meant to be dramatic. She had to hunt around in her head for the words. Plain, simple words.

Yvonne and Duval were waiting.

"I think somebody tried to kill me. Or scare me to death."

The couple stared at her.

"You're serious?" Duval asked.

Kate nodded. "I've got this lump on my head. I don't know how the heck somebody could sneak up on me where I was sitting, in the clearing above the beach. But somebody must have. And threw me in the boat and pushed it out into the current."

Yvonne and Duval looked at each other. Then at Kate.

"That's attempted murder," Duval said.

"It was a hell of a close call," his wife said. Kate had never heard Yvonne swear before but considered the "hell" to have been enlisted in support of a good cause: her own life.

"It was a lucky thing I came to," Kate said. "If the boat and I had gone over the dam I might not be sitting here."

"A clever plan," Duval said. "If you'd gone over the dam you'd have hit rock after rock. Nobody would have been able to tell one of the blows hit you before you went over."

"I hadn't thought of that," Yvonne said, looking sick.

Kate had. She'd been thinking about it as she showered.

The shampoo had smelled heavenly, the suds were beautiful as they slid over her arms and down her torso and legs, turning first tan and then white as the dirt washed away. As hard as she tried she could not get her memory to fill in the gap, to open the black box in her mind full of the sights and sounds that would tell her how she'd gotten into the boat.

Damn, it was a good boat. Irreplaceable, given the state of her bank account. And it was in all likelihood smashed to bits.

Then she'd felt the lump. Winced as she probed. It was big, the size of a quarter. Sore, and throbbing after she touched it. Her fingers came away bloody. She washed her hair gently.

In a way, finding the lump made the incident more understandable. Something had hit her. Now she knew why she'd lost consciousness.

In other ways, the information only made things more inexplicable. Because of the strange events of the past ten days, she'd been alert. She couldn't believe the hermit or anyone else had been able to sneak up behind her to whack her on the head. Leaves would have rustled if an assailant had approached.

Yvonne and Duval were looking at her. Had one of them said something?

"The woods are so dry," she said. "I would have heard footsteps. I'm sure of it."

"Kate," Yvonne said. "Your voice sounds funny." She looked at Duval. "What do you think?"

"Yes," he said.

"I'm just tired," Kate said. "I think a good night's sleep will take care of it."

"I don't think so," Duval said. He pulled the keys to his pick-up from his pocket. "You need to get checked out at the hospital. I'll take you. Come on."

Kate started to object, but maybe he was right. Someone suffering a blow to the head and being unconscious for a few seconds or a minute was one thing. She'd been out like a light for much longer. How long? She had no way of knowing. But long enough to almost get badly injured or killed. She might have a concussion, so maybe Duval was right that she shouldn't go to sleep.

When she got up from her chair in response to his urging, she felt dizzy. He took her arm, and Yvonne opened the door for them.

She felt weak and shaky. But her condition could be due to exposure and fatigue, not a concussion. As Duval helped her into the front seat of his truck, she was still debating with herself whether it was a good idea to go to the hospital or not. It would be expensive.

Duval started the engine and backed down the driveway. "You're going to be fine, Kate."

He meant well, but she remembered him saying Donna would be fine after the ambulance had taken her away a few nights ago.

She must be thinking slowly. They were halfway to town before she decided he was right, she should get checked out by a doctor, especially since she didn't know what had hit her or how hard. Yes, it would cost something, and she'd lost her medical insurance when she'd gotten laid off almost a year ago, but taking care of her brain was worth it.

It was a good thing she'd turned down the aspirin Yvonne had offered. She'd been thinking of her stomach, but if she had a bad enough concussion to cause a brain bleed, aspirin would have made it worse.

The next thing she knew Duval was shaking her. He'd parked outside the emergency room and opened the truck's passenger door.

"Kate, wake up." He looked worried. "I've got a wheelchair."

\* \* \*

Yvonne came to the hospital to pick Kate up the next day around noon. She'd been awakened once an hour overnight, a routine lasting until six in the morning, and then she'd fallen asleep until ten, when the doctor okayed her to go home.

She still didn't feel great, but the lump on her head didn't hurt as much, and she was able to talk without fumbling for words.

"Take it easy for a week," the doctor said. "If your symptoms of dizziness or fatigue get worse, come back." He was younger than she was, and looked as if he hadn't gotten much sleep himself. Maybe this town wasn't as quiet as it seemed.

"Will I recover my memory of what happened?" Kate asked.

"It could go either way. Sometimes people remember, sometimes they don't." Had he worn his white coat for whatever cat-naps he'd managed to get? It was rumpled. He needed a shave.

She'd bet he had a number in his mind, the percentage of head-injured patients who were able to open the frustrating black box containing a piece of their memory. "Which way do the odds point?"

"Most people don't, unfortunately," he said. "Convenient for criminals."

The hospital staff must have passed her story on to the police, because a tall guy in a blue jacket and ball cap with UNION HILL PD on it came to her room right after the doctor left.

"So what's up?" he said, slouching in the bedside chair. "Somebody klonked you on the head?"

"That's what I think, but I can't remember."

"Got any enemies? Any ex-boyfriends around here? You're from Massachusetts, right?" He must have read her admission record.

"Right. Traveling in my camper, taking a little vacation." He wasn't taking notes, and he glanced around the room as she spoke. "I'm staying at Roll and Rest, and I've gotten to know the Chouinard family there. That's it for local contacts. No boyfriends."

His eyes came back to hers. "You been drinking at all when this happened?"

"No." She held his gaze. She didn't want to be dismissed as a drunk vagrant who'd nearly killed herself by boating alone and dropping her paddle.

"Okay," he said. "Any idea who would want to whack you?"

"No." She wasn't going to suggest the Loyalhanna Hermit, and have him think she bought into the locals' wild stories. "But I found a couple of cell phones in the woods and turned them in at the station."

"That so?" He couldn't have looked less interested. What was she forgetting to tell him?

Oh. "Some creepy texts came in on them, and a guy called me at three in the morning and knew my name. It scared me." She told him about the two phones and the reasons she believed they belonged to criminals.

He still didn't seem concerned. "Okay," he said again, and stood up. "So if you think of anybody who might have it in for you, give us a call, all right? And take care of yourself." He tucked a card under the plastic water carafe on the bedside table and sauntered out.

Kate wasn't reassured by the visit. Somebody tried to kill her, and all he could tell her was to take care of herself?

# TEN

She was home, in her camper, with no idea who wanted to hurt her. Or kill her.

Should she leave, make her way farther south?

That wouldn't be much of a solution, since she didn't know who her enemy was. He could just as easily drive her off the road, or find her at a boondocking campsite, the kind she had planned on using most of the time on this trip. No, now was not the time to find a lonely spot in a National Forest to take advantage of the free camping.

And she was still waiting for John to work on her generator. The second set of parts hadn't come in yet, he'd said when she'd seen him a few days ago carrying some tools to the shed. Disappointed, she'd started back toward her camper. Then thought of something she'd been meaning to ask him, and backtracked.

"Say, John, do you know a guy who lived out at the end of Watkins Spur? Yvonne mentioned you and he were in the Army together."

She'd startled him. He dropped a wrench, picked it up. "Yeah, I had a friend who lived out there for a while. He's moved on, though."

"You know where he went?"

"Back to Wisconsin, maybe? He had some family up there, a sister, I think, and his parents." He brushed the wrench off with dirty hands. "He wasn't in real good shape."

Was there more? No, John was squinting at her. That was all the information she was going to get. "Okay," she'd said. "Thanks."

So the man who used to own the house wasn't still living in the conservation area—if she believed John. He could be protecting an old friend. Had he not heard her coming back, or was it her question that made him drop the wrench?

No, she wouldn't leave. Her generator was still broken, and Roll and Rest was a safe harbor with people who'd become friends. She'd rather be here than alone or at another campsite. Besides, she wanted to stay for the Fall Crafts Fair in a few days and still needed more drawings for it. Edna had passed the word to Yvonne that Kate's drawings at the library had attracted attention. People were asking to buy them, so Kate had suggested prices. Then Yvonne told her Edna had put higher prices on them. Kate let them stand because Edna was probably a better judge of the local market.

Kate was delighted when two of them sold. Which was great, but now she needed to produce new work for the fair.

She'd sold only one piece before this, to the artists' retreat in Maine where she'd gone the previous summer. It was exciting to be paid for doing something she enjoyed so much. Yvonne said Edna was telling people there was a gypsy artist passing through town, which made Kate laugh.

* * *

After her exhausting experience on the river, she gave herself an easy day, long sessions of reading in bed broken up by short walks around the campground. Yvonne had rescued the sketchbook, ink and other supplies from the beach the day before and left them on the camper table. Two of the brushes were broken and the little bottle was empty, but the drawings Kate had worked so hard on were undamaged. She stared at the brushes, hoping to unlock the blank space in her memory, but nothing came to her.

Yvonne, that sweetie, brought her an apple muffin in the morning and a ramekin of apple strudel in the afternoon, letting herself in with the spare key Kate had given her. "Big apple harvest this year," she said. "Hope you don't mind."

"Mind?" Kate asked. "Home-baked yummies delivered to my bedside? Are you nuts?"

Yvonne laughed. "Bedside? I'm not climbing up there, so you'll have to settle for the foot of your bed." She laid a copy of the *Union Hill Star-Herald* next to the strudel. "Here's the paper you asked for. We get the Pittsburgh paper on Sunday so I don't usually read this one. It's all ads, anyway. Except this time there's an article about you, and one about Donna. Don't mail a copy to your mother."

"Right," Kate said, and then she remembered. "Say, did you go to the school to talk with Savvy's teacher, and Carson's?"

Almost to the door, Yvonne quickly took the three steps back toward Kate's perch in her bunk. Full maternal alert. "No. Should I have?"

"I meant to tell you. Last week's *Star-Herald* had an article about what a great success the week of parent-teacher conferences was."

"That's the first I've heard of it." Yvonne's brow bunched, eyebrows angled. "Thanks, I'll check it out."

After her friend left, Kate read about her own close call on the river—on an inside page, between a story about a Boy Scout litter clean-up campaign and another one about graffiti damage to a pair of stone lions on Rte. 119. She wasn't named, described only as a Massachusetts tourist who had narrowly escaped injury on the Loyalhanna after her canoe capsized. According to the reporter, she'd avoided going over the dam by swimming ashore and hiking back to the Roll and Rest campground.

Where had the *Star-Herald* gotten its information? The hospital? The police? The source hadn't done her any favors. She sounded like an idiot. The story hadn't even gotten the boat right. And the paper had missed the opportunity to run a much more dramatic story about attempted murder. Isn't drama what boosted circulation? Why hadn't a reporter knocked on her door? It would have been easy to find her at this small campground.

The story about Donna was even more bland, and barely two column-inches. Ohio woman, accidental death, cause unknown, authorities looking into the matter.

Kate stared at the two stories. The *Star-Herald* must be more interested in its readers feeling safe than in complete or accurate coverage. She was glad the *Danvers Daily News*, where she'd worked as a reporter for three years, had put the truth first. She'd still be there if a merger hadn't resulted in half the staff being laid off.

For a moment she was at her desk in the Danvers newsroom, one of a flock of desks, her fingers pattering over the keyboard, voices rising and falling around her, telephones ringing, the police scanner blatting from its shelf in the corner. Her first day on the job she was sure she could never write in such a noisy place, but within a week she'd tuned it all out. What noise?

She swallowed, felt a lump in her throat. She missed that place, that life.

No, not all of that life. She didn't miss her boyfriend Mike. His betrayal had erased her feelings for him completely, which surprised her. She'd felt hurt at first—she remembered thinking of Mike with pain as recently as last summer. But since then the wound had closed, and she hadn't noticed until now. Startled by her own freedom.

She took another walk around the campground. Two RVs had arrived, each around forty feet long, each with a back end that hinged open to become a ramp for the vehicles inside, probably ATVs but possibly small Jeeps or those tiny SmartCars. Kate walked past the big rigs happy she didn't have to deal with their maintenance issues. Or pay for the diesel fuel their tanks swallowed.

At the edge of the Chouinard property, in the corner near John's van, a squirrel lay under the bushes. No, only part of a squirrel. The fluffy tail and the body, its belly open as if it had been ripped apart by a dog. The head was ten feet farther on, the white throat black with old blood. The second dead squirrel in a week. The predators around here were as bad at hanging onto their dinners as the human were about hanging onto their phones.

She ambled back to her camper, thinking about the *Star-Herald.* It certainly felt odd to be on the other side of a newspaper story, even as an unnamed tourist.

The watered-down version of the attack on her, which didn't even make it clear it *was* an attack, wouldn't generate public pressure to catch the person who'd tried to kill her. Maybe the police hadn't told the whole story because they wanted her assailant to think they didn't suspect a crime. A false sense of security might make him more likely to make a mistake that would get him caught.

Or maybe the cop who'd visited her hospital room hadn't paid attention to a word she'd said.

* * *

That night she called Marjorie and told her about waking up in the boat and almost going over the dam. Kate made it sound funny, but Marjorie wasn't fooled.

"It sounds terrifying, Kate. How awful. The last time we talked it sounded like you were settled at a nice campground, getting some artwork done, making friends with the Canadian family. The only difficulty was the boy who was mean to cats. Now it sounds like you're in a war zone."

"Maybe not outright war. But hostile territory. Except I don't know who the enemy is."

"How's your head now?" Marjorie asked. "Are the concussion symptoms gone?"

"Yes, my balance is fine and I'm not groping for words anymore," Kate said.

"And emotionally? Are you frightened?"

"I suppose I should be. Okay, I am. But I'm pissed off, too. The cop who talked to me before I left the hospital didn't seem terribly interested in following up. Of course, I couldn't give him any details about what happened. No sighting of the perp, no local contacts to consider as suspects. Nada."

"The memory lapse must be frustrating."

"You bet it is. I want to be free to enjoy the outdoors without looking over my shoulder all the time. I need to do my work. Having to be watchful when I want to concentrate on a brush stroke or getting some shading just right—it makes me angry."

"Would it be wise to leave? You've told me you don't usually connect the water and sewer hook-ups, you just plug into what you call shore power. So to leave, all you'd have to do is unplug and put the cord away somewhere, right? Easy as moving a toaster oven. Except your toaster oven has wheels."

Kate laughed. "Right, that's how easy it is to leave. But since I don't know why I'm a target, I don't know if leaving would solve the problem. It might just isolate me."

"Is there any chance you launched the boat yourself, then had some kind of blackout and didn't remember doing it?"

"I don't think so. I wasn't wearing my PFD, which I always wear, and—"

"Sorry, Kate, what's a PFD?"

"Oh, you'd probably call it a life vest. PFD stands for personal flotation device. I always put mine on. A lot of paddlers just have theirs loose in their boat, because that's what most states require, and some people say PFDs are uncomfortable to wear. But it's nearly impossible to get the things on after you're in the water. And by then you have other problems."

"You wouldn't have gone paddling without it?"

"Never. I know I'm already violating a major safety recommendation, the one against paddling alone. So even though I sometimes feel a little silly—say it's a hot, calm day on a lake—I always wear the thing. And of course how could I go out without a paddle? I laid it inside the hull when I got to the beach, but it wasn't in the boat when I woke up on the river."

"Yes, that's pretty convincing," Marjorie said.

"And if I just went and launched the boat myself, why do I have a lump on my head?"

There was a pause. Marjorie was so rational, Kate could almost hear her thinking.

"Where's the lump? Back of your head?"

"Right on top. Almost center."

"Like something fell on you. From above."

Kate had been imagining someone behind her. She'd been sitting, so if someone had struck her the blow would hit her on top of her head. But something falling on her would also fit the lump's location.

"I hadn't thought of that, Marjorie. I'm going to go back to where it happened and see if being hit from above makes sense."

"If you have to go larking about in the woods with a sketchbook, why don't you ask someone to go with you? Your friend who runs the campground, maybe?"

"I could. But she has a life. A family to take care of." Kate hated the idea of having a baby-sitter.

"Stop and think, Kate. What's more important, doing your art or staying alive?"

Kate hesitated. "You know, they're almost the same thing."

* * *

For a few day she didn't go into the conservation area alone. Yvonne had the same idea as Marjorie, and volunteered to go along. She carried a folding lawn chair and sat working on her knitting; Kate drew her friend a couple of times. But as much as she liked Yvonne, the situation wasn't comfortable. Kate couldn't talk much because it broke her concentration. And she felt like a burden. An invalid. A child.

Savvy came with her once, under Yvonne's strict orders not to go out of Kate's sight. Kate had grown fond of the girl, but she sometimes chattered. She also disobeyed her mother and wandered away, down to the riverbank to skip stones or into the woods to look for good climbing trees. Kate felt a jolt of panic each time she realized she couldn't see Savvy, so she had to tell Yvonne the arrangement wasn't working out.

Then Yvonne asked her to text every hour when she worked alone, which was slightly less distracting than having a minder physically present. But even this system was disruptive to Kate's preferred work style, which was simply to get lost in the series of tiny choices that art required.

So she set an alarm on her cell phone for every ten minutes. When it went off she stood and turned in a circle, examining her surroundings. Occasionally she discovered Rusty had followed her. The big cat pestered her for attention for a while and then prowled off to find other feline amusements.

She returned to the rock she'd been sitting on when attacked. As Marjorie had suspected, it was close enough to the maple that someone could have dropped an object on her head from one of its branches, which would explain why she hadn't heard footsteps from an approaching assailant. She wouldn't sit there again.

After half a day working at her dinette and she simply had to go outdoors to draw. The camper had one large window, three smaller ones, and a skylight, but even so the light inside wasn't great, and the tiny space felt confining after a few hours. At that point staying inside would be courting depression.

Her days became a balancing act: art versus safety. The ten-minute periods were too disruptive, and she settled instead for texting Yvonne at irregular intervals, between sketches.

\* \* \*

One morning, only a few days before the fair, she woke early and packed up. Texting Yvonne as she walked, she went north on the lower, leafy path, not the higher one through pines. The river flashed in the sun through the red and gold trees. She set up at a bend in the trail and drew it. The trail gave depth to her drawing, inviting the viewer into the dappled space bordered with ferns and sumac bushes. The sumacs' composite leaves always made her think of the French painter Henri Rousseau: the spacing of the leaflets made each of them stand out separately the way his naïve renderings of trees did.

After a few hours there and another text to Yvonne, Kate noticed a cave at the top of a rocky outcrop. Her next subject? She left her easel beside the trail and shouldered the daypack with her sketchbook. As she picked her way through boulders, up a rough, little-used path, she smelled smoke.

No, that didn't make sense. Despite how dry the woods were, she'd heard no reports of wildfires. Surely Yvonne would have warned her.

When she reached the top of the trail, the odor did make sense.

On a flat ledge behind two big rocks, a trickle of smoke rose from a campfire. Its star-pattern style suggested that someone had spent some time here, pushing logs into the coals in the center. This was not a quick, heat-water-for-coffee kind of fire a fisherman or a hiker might build. And the site was a good choice for camping: the rocks would block any wind that came from the direction of the river, sheltering the fire and anyone tending it. Perhaps someone had stayed here overnight.

What had looked like a cave turned out to be only a shallow recess. It was low, and extended into the rock face far enough to protect someone only from rain only that was falling straight down. Not that rain had been much of a factor recently.

As far as wildfire danger, this campfire was probably safe, although it should have been put completely out. Always true, but especially now because the woods were so dry. Kate wouldn't have left it smoking. It was built on rock, though, surrounded by rock. Whoever laid the fire here knew what he was doing.

Just an ordinary campfire. But when she thought of the stalker or the hermit or whoever it was who'd knocked her out and pushed her into the dam-bound current, the cozy fire frightened her. Anyone hiding behind these rocks would be able to see a good stretch of trail. A trail Kate had walked many times in the past two weeks.

She held her hand over the ashes at the center of the star. Heat rose to her palm. The fire-builder hadn't been gone long. And because the fire wasn't out, perhaps he meant to come back soon.

Kate looked carefully, slowly, along the rock field below her, then down to the stretch of woods between the river and the rocks. No motion caught her eye. No bit of color other than the reds and yellows of the foliage, the ordinary shadows and tangles of a forest.

It was a glorious spot to work. The campfire, the view over the trees to the river. But tension blew through Kate like a cold wind. She couldn't work here. Not without a dog. Or a gun. Or both.

.

# ELEVEN

Westmoreland county's Fall Crafts Fair was set up on the high school football field in the nearby town of Latrobe. Kate was surprised at the size of the event: rows of booths and tables stretched from one goal-post to the other, with dozens of people unloading pick-up trucks and small trailers. Some vendors had put up tents, which looked gloomy inside but would have saved the day if the weather had turned out to be rainy.

Edna's site was in the open, which was fine with Kate. Outdoors was always better than in, especially on a day like this. The foliage was near peak, the woods around the field lit like torches flaring orange and yellow.

Yvonne had driven Duval's pick-up because of all the bulky things they needed to bring. Edna's site was inexpensive because it was in a row along one edge of the field, too close to the bleachers to drive to. So Kate and Yvonne carried the folding table, and Edna slung a bulging trash bag over her shoulder. An odd bundle of wooden rods was bungie-corded to the table.

"My quilts travel incognito, in black plastic," the librarian said, struggling to keep up with her taller friends. "Please don't let anyone throw a greasy napkin or an unwanted cup of coffee into this bag."

"I have trouble with the concept of unwanted coffee," Kate said.

Almost to the site, Edna stopped. "Wait, please. I need a break." When the others paused, she switched the bag to her opposite shoulder and wiped a palm across her damp forehead. "Indian summer," she said as she started up. "Oops, Native American summer."

"That's an Eastern thing," Kate said as they reached their place in the row, between a beekeeper selling organic honey and a woman offering baskets made of rope. "From the Rockies west people say 'Indian.' Even the Indians."

"Oh, good, then I can call it what I called it as a kid, with a clear conscience." Edna unhooked the bundle of dowels from the table and began connecting them into what might be the frame for a small cabin. "It ought to be named for the Indians, since they were here first. And that's true all over the country."

After they set up the table, Kate and Yvonne went back to the truck and carried more quilts and sweaters and the portfolio of drawings to their site. Most of the people bustling around them were also vendors setting up, but a few eager fair-goers with empty hands were already scouting the scene.

Yvonne unpacked sweaters from duffel bags. The ones Kate liked best were abstract patterns in multiple colors, designs Yvonne had said she made up as she went along. The variety of styles was vast, from thin and sparkly shawls for parties to thick pullovers that could fend off Pennsylvanian snowstorms. She'd made all different sizes, including cute cardigans for kids, with buttons that looked like ladybugs or curled-up kittens. She folded the sweaters on the table, grouping them by size.

"Wow," Kate said. "You've done a ton of work. Beautiful. Is this what you've made in the past year, since the last fair?"

Yvonne laughed. "Oh, no, this is about a third of what I've made. I sell some by word of mouth and some on concession at the crafts store in Union Hill. I can knit a sweater in three days, depending on what's happening with Duval and the kids." She shrugged unhappily. "Now that he's working so much we can't go anywhere, and campground business has slowed down for the fall, I've come up with a bumper crop of sweaters."

Kate had hit a gardening center the day before and bought sturdy stakes and four flowerpots. She turned the pots upside down and jammed the stakes into the ground through the drainage holes. Then she tied string between the stakes, near the top, and used clothespins she'd borrowed from Yvonne to clip drawings to the string. She put up her favorites; she had extras to replace whatever she sold.

"Instant gallery," she said as she stood back to look at her work. A clothesline of art. "I hope the day stays as calm as it is now. A stiff breeze could put me out of business."

Finished with her own set-up, she looked at her friends' displays. Most of Edna's quilts were king or queen size, and they weren't like any quilts Kate had ever seen. They were more like paintings, but using cloth for the shapes and colors. The librarian had put up two stands that showed off one quilt each, hanging on high bars for full visibility to passers-by. Another rack had a series of bars that swiveled, so people could look at quilts as if they were turning the pages of a book

One of the solo racks showed a quilt with the traditional squares, only larger, each square containing a leaf. Some leaves were realistic, some were like no leaves in nature—a blue leaf with crimson veins, for instance—but all were vivid. The other solo quilt was a textile landscape, a sky with moon and stars, a forest running down to a cliff above a river. The longer Kate looked at it the more animals she saw: a moose among the evergreens, an otter in the river, a fox curled up in a sunny glade.

"These are magical," she said. "You went to a fantasy forest to get those leaves, didn't you? And the next time you went, you brought back the whole place."

"Thank you," Edna said, and blushed. Her light complexion didn't do anything to hide how pleased she was.

She browsed along the line of drawings, stopping often. "Kate, these are marvelous. You're the real thing."

Kate grinned. "We go well together. Mutual admiration society, all three of us." She looked at Yvonne expecting a smile back and got instead a startled expression.

Kate turned in the direction Yvonne was looking. A man who seemed oddly familiar, like someone she'd known a long time ago, was walking past with two girls a little younger than Savvy, one on each side. None of the three looked at Edna's table.

Yvonne was flustered. "That's Gaston," she said. "He lives in Pittsburgh now. What's he doing out here?" She was tracking him like a pointer dog. "I'm still mad at him for bailing out of Roll and Rest. And we haven't seen him since then. The kids miss him, especially Carson. For a while he asked me every day when Uncle Gassy was going to visit. Thank goodness he's stopped doing that."

"He must not have seen you," Kate said. She'd been helping Yvonne unpack her sweaters, and dropped the last pile onto the table. No wonder he'd looked familiar, with his brotherly resemblance to Duval. Why was he ignoring his sister-in-law? "Are those his daughters?"

"No, I don't know who they are. He and his wife don't have kids. They're separated now, anyway. The marriage broke down last summer, about the same time he took his money out of the campground."

"Yikes, so Gaston lost all his relatives at once," Kate said.

"Duval's still shaking his head over it," Yvonne said. "They used to be close. Family's the first priority for us, and we can't understand how his brother could just cut us off. Or why."

Kate wrote her prices on pieces of light blue cardstock Yvonne had given her, clipping a sign to each of her three clotheslines of drawings. Yvonne taped her price list to the front edge of the table, while Edna put hers on top and weighed it down with a ceramic pot. Its label read ASHES OF CHILDREN WHO MADE NOISE IN THE LIBRARY.

Curious, Kate lifted the lid. The pot was full of red-and-white peppermints in clear cellophane twists.

"I'll mind the store while you get the rest of the stuff," Edna said, and Yvonne and Kate walked back to the truck. The bed still held folded lawn chairs, a cooler full of cold drinks, a huge thermos of coffee, and enough ham-and-cheese on rye sandwiches to keep them fed, Kate was sure, for a week. Plus enough pickles and olives to last the week after that.

Yvonne took the lawn chairs while Kate carried the cooler with the cardboard box of sandwiches set on top of it.

"Looks like a good turnout," Yvonne said. "We certainly lucked out with the weather."

Kate pivoted, scanning the parking lot. Cars and trucks were streaming in, dust rising and hanging in the air over the gravel. Kate was thankful the air was so still.

"By the way, thanks for letting me know about parent-teacher week," Yvonne said, her voice hardening. "I talked to both teachers. The school sent notices home with all the students, and parents were supposed to sign and return them to get an appointment."

"Oh, no, you lost yours?"

"I never got any. Savvy doesn't remember any forms, so I talked to Carson. He shrugged and said he'd signed both of them and gave them back to the teachers."

She stopped talking while a couple of people passed them, a woman with a pleased expression hugging one of Edna's quilts to her chest followed by a man wearing a fisherman-style sweater that might have come from Yvonne's table. Kate smiled sideways at her friend, but Yvonne's mind was clearly still on Carson.

"He checked the box that said the parents weren't interested in a conference," she said. "So I told him he can't watch TV for a week, but he didn't act like he cared. I don't know what to do."

"What did the teachers say?"

"Just what I expected: Savvy's a space shot and Carson doesn't give a hoot. When he gets scolded for not paying attention, he just shrugs."

Kate didn't know what to say.

Nobody had passed them carrying any of her drawings, but there were quite a few people clustered at the trio's table, and more than a few of them were looking at her work. The sight cheered her up. People were looking, really looking, standing in front of a landscape or portrait long enough that she felt appreciated.

Edna looked a little flustered, making change out of the fanny pack she was wearing backwards, unzipped and gaping, bills going in and out. "I'm a money marsupial," she said as Kate put the cooler down behind the table. "And I'm busy. Glad you're back." She was folding the sold quilts and putting the largest of them into trash bags for her customers, and slipping sweaters into the plastic grocery bags Yvonne had brought.

With three of them behind the table, change was made, work was bagged, and the crowd thinned. Three of Kate's drawings had found new homes, and she was thrilled. She'd already made more than enough to cover the generator repair. She filled the empty places on the strings with work from her portfolio.

* * *

"Boom and bust," Edna said. They were eating sandwiches and drinking coffee even though it wasn't quite noon.

Kate was excited. "We all sold a bunch. And you seemed to know at least half your customers."

"Librarians get around."

"That sounds like a bumper sticker," Kate said.

"Edna knows everything that moves in Union Hill," Yvonne said. "On two feet or four."

"Don't forget wings," Edna said.

"Oh, right. She shares her house with a bunch of parrots. Those doggone birds are really smart."

"I haven't taught them to read yet."

"Just a matter of time," Yvonne said. "Say, Edna, do you know who's living at the place way out on Watkins Spur? Some deaf old woman?"

"I thought that house was empty," Edna said. "And falling down. What were you doing out there?"

"It was Kate who did the scouting."

"I went out there to return a lost cell phone, but the owner wasn't at home and the old woman was deaf as a door."

"Deaf as a donut," Yvonne said.

"Deaf as as a dandelion," Edna said. "A dozen dandelions." After she stopped laughing at her own dandelions, she said, "I've been meaning to ask you how Savvy's doing."

"Our family doctor couldn't find anything wrong with her, but she's not getting any better," Yvonne said. "I've made an appointment with a neurologist in Pittsburgh, but it's not until November."

"Here comes another crowd," Kate said. "People travel in packs, like wolves."

Before the crowd got to them a familiar-looking guy in a blue jacket, coming from the other direction, stopped at the table.

"We got ourselves a lone wolf," Edna said. "What's up, Brandon?"

"Wanted to let your friend know we recovered her boat."

"Oh, man, my kayak? Fantastic!" Kate recognized him from the hospital. He was the cop who had questioned her and told her to take care of herself.

"Hung up in a strainer right at the dam. Wasn't safe to try snag it from the water, so I had to send a guy in through the woods to get a line on it." He turned to Kate. "Nice one. Has a few fresh scratches, but no real damage."

"That boat scratches if you look at it hard," Kate said. She was grinning. She and that kayak had been a few places together. But of course it wasn't perfect. "It's supposed to be made of a composite of Kevlar and carbon fiber, which I guess isn't as tough as it sounds. Isn't Kevlar what bulletproof vests are made of? I hope SWAT teams wear something tougher than my kayak."

"The stuff they make that boat out of is so thin it couldn't stop a mosquito bite," Brandon said.

"That's what I thought." She smiled, and heard Edna and Yvonne laugh.

"If we'd found that boat and I hadn't already seen you at the hospital after that, ah, adventure of yours, we'd have been looking for a drowning victim a few miles down the river. That was a close call."

"Don't suppose you found the paddle," Kate said.

"Go for broke, girl," Edna said.

"You gotta be kidding. It's in Pittsburgh by now." He picked up one of Yvonne's sweaters, a gray pullover. "This looks warm as toast. How much is it?"

He left with the sweater, after telling Kate she could pick her boat up at the police station.

* * *

It was a busy day, and a profitable one. Yvonne sold the most, in terms of numbers of items—she'd brought three big duffel bags but needed only one for the sweaters left at the end of the day. Kate sold more than half of what she'd brought, which pleased her enormously. Her work was out there, part of people's lives.

Edna declared herself delighted with the four quilts she'd sold. She felt the same way as Kate, happy that the art she'd created would be used and appreciated often.

"Some people hang them on the wall like paintings," she said, "especially the landscapes. Other people use my quilts like any old quilts, putting them on beds and sleeping under them. Either way, they're looking at them every day. It tickles me."

"That's where we part company," Kate said. "I hope my buyers hang my drawings and don't try to sleep under them."

"Don't worry. Winter's coming, and your drawings aren't anywhere near warm enough."

It was late, the air tinted with dust stirred up by the tires of the cars and trucks that had left. Vehicles still parked on the flattened grass were burnished by the low sun. Tired from a day spent mostly on their feet, the three women were nibbling on their still-plentiful supplies. Edna ate two ham and cheese sandwiches and declared she could eat another two but had better not.

Kate took the ham out of one and ate it along with an apple from the bag she'd brought. She tossed the core into the trash as a girl came up to look at the drawings. She moved quickly along the string.

"I want that one," she said, pointing to a charcoal-pencil landscape that featured the boulder near the river, the one Kate was sitting on when she'd been attacked. She'd drawn that rock because it had become important to her, something of an emotional landmark, but she didn't mind selling. She could easily draw it again for herself.

It was odd the girl had barely looked at it before deciding. Maybe she'd come by earlier in the day. She did look a bit familiar.

Kate unpinned the drawing and took it to the table to wrap in acid-free tissue paper. The teenager pulled crumpled bills from her pocket and tossed them onto the table, not making eye contact. She kept turning, looking over one shoulder and then the other. Maybe the poor kid had some kind of attention deficit problem.

The drawing slid out of Kate's hands as her last customer of the day grabbed it and ran.

# TWELVE

Kate was behind the table, and the girl was fast. No chance of catching her. Shrugging, Kate turned toward her two friends. Edna had a sandwich halfway to her mouth—she must have decided on a third one. Yvonne set down her coffee and said, "Well. That was strange. And rude."

"You know what, Yvonne? I think we saw her earlier today. I think she was one of the girls with Gaston. He must have sent her. Did you see how she was looking over her shoulder the whole time?"

"I think you're right. But why not buy it himself? Why is he avoiding us?"

"Beats me." Kate picked up the money the girl had left. "Holy cats."

"What?" Yvonne and Edna, in unison.

"There was a ten on top," Kate said. "The bill underneath? It's a hundred."

Edna whistled. "She sure wasn't paying attention to what she was doing."

"Now why would a girl that age be running around with a hundred dollar bill in her pocket?" Yvonne asked.

"Because she couldn't get change," Edna said, and the two of them cracked up.

Kate didn't laugh. She was looking down the aisle between the rows of vendors, toward the parking lot. Was that the girl, still running?

"That's the best sale I made all day," Kate said. "And it's the only one I don't feel good about."

* * *

The next morning, after some of the excitement of the fair had worn off, Kate made a list of unusual events, large and small, since she'd arrived at Roll and Rest two weeks earlier.

1. electrical box vandalized
2. someone spying on me at the beach, then running
3. someone spying on me at the campground at night
4. two cell phones left in the woods
5. sinister messages on cell phones (text and call)
6. Donna dying from CO poisoning
7. someone hitting me, setting me adrift
8. campfire on ridge, still warm
9. girl paying for drawing with $100 bill

Numbers 2, 4 and 8 suggested someone was living in the woods, or spending a lot of time there, and not your average camper: two dropped phones suggested someone careless. That person could also have caused the blackout and spied on her the night she couldn't sleep, numbers 1 and 3. But there was no evidence to make those connections.

And of course the Loyalhanna Hermit, or whoever was living out there, hadn't necessarily been the one to drop the phones. It could have been a hiker. Or two different hikers.

Living in the woods wasn't a crime, and Kate actually sympathized with the independent spirit and outdoor skills of someone who was able to do it. Losing a cell phone? If that were a crime then millions of people had committed it, including herself.

The two most important items on the list, 6 and 7—Donna's death and the attempt on her own life—were very different from each other. Knocking Kate out and setting her adrift was a deliberate act, but Donna's death was accidental, the inanimate culprit a malfunctioning heater.

Or was it? Kate's mind circled around the Winnebago furnace problem again. How could it be operating normally after it poisoned Donna? That didn't make sense.

She made another list, this time of the people around her. The Chouinards: Yvonne, Duval, Savvy, Carson. Richard Miller. John, who still hadn't fixed her generator. The deaf woman in the old house. Walter Tremblay, even though she hadn't met him.

Who had been at the campground and left? Red-haired Annie. And the two men in their twenties with the pop-up camper, the bearish guy who'd asked about her boat and his friend, whose names she didn't think she'd ever heard. A dozen other RVs had come through, big class A buses the size of Greyhounds, but they only stayed one or two nights. People heading home after their summer on the road, or snow-birders migrating south. They hadn't been around long enough to be involved in the weeks-long list of incidents.

She crossed out Yvonne and Savvy, neither one of whom she could feature sneaking up on her and throwing her in the river. She hesitated at Duval's name. He was certainly strong enough. And Yvonne had mentioned he sometimes met with clients at their houses during the day, so he could have been free to follow her to the riverbank. But why would he want to harm her?

Marjorie had suggested keeping an eye on Duval as a possible abuser of Carson. The boy's face had been bruised when he'd come home from school on Kate's first full day at Roll and Rest, but she hadn't seen any later injuries. His father was gruff sometimes—both Annie and Savvy had said so. But he'd never snapped at Kate, and Yvonne hadn't complained about his behavior.

She was deeply loyal, though, so she might not say a word even if he did mistreat her.

Yvonne was an attentive mother, and she talked things over with Duval. Kate thought of his hand on her shoulder, briefly, after the ambulance took Donna away; his willingness to examine the Winnebago's furnace; his insistence that Kate go to the hospital with a possible concussion, and his driving her there. Come on, she told herself. Don't let this attack make you paranoid, unable to tell friend from foe. Duval wasn't perfect, but he wasn't a lurking murderer. She crossed off his name.

Carson? He was a sneaky boy, no question. Marjorie had called his behavior a red flag. Was he simply immature for his age or was something more deeply wrong with him?

If she looked at him as a candidate for the two serious indications of evil intent, though, the electrical box vandalism and the attack on her, she had to dismiss him. The Millers had been right, that morning after the blackout when a group of campers had been chatting—the boy wasn't tall enough or strong enough to cut the fat wires in the breaker box. She didn't like him, especially because of the way he mistreated Shadow and Rusty. But even if she imagined him carrying something to stand on and granted him the strength to cut the wires, that still didn't qualify him as a suspect in the assault on her. He could have dropped something on her out of the maple tree, but he never could have gotten her down to the water and into her boat.

She shuddered at the memory of waking up adrift in her boat and crossed Carson off the list, putting him in the best light she could: a kid trying to grow up, hitting some bumps in the road to adulthood. With good parents like Yvonne and Duval, he would straighten out eventually.

She'd been staring out the window, lost in thought, for what felt like hours. Her mind cleared and the day came to her—it had turned into a dark one, with thick, fast-moving clouds, their bellies full of water. Good.

She looked back at her lists. So far she had one suspect, the hermit. She didn't know if he even existed. A hiker or hikers could have dropped the phones she'd found, made a campfire, crashed away through the woods.

Focus, Kate.

The next name on her list was John.

Looking scary and needing a good hot shower weren't criminal offenses. Neither were muffin crumbs in his beard. And Yvonne and Duval trusted him. Still, you had to wonder about a guy in his thirties living in a camper, didn't you?

Kate had to laugh at herself. She was in her thirties and lived in a camper.

But she took showers, washed her clothes, went out most days. She made friends. She had an occupation, her artwork, and after the success of the fair she was beginning to think of herself as a freelance artist.

With his wiry build, John was easily strong enough to carry her to the river. And he could have damaged the breaker box knowing Yvonne would hire him to fix it.

She'd rarely seen him outside his van since the morning he'd repaired the box, and she'd never seen him drive off his site. He could have done so while she was out hiking and drawing, of course—he'd said he was helping his brother work on a house. His van was a high-top, so it had standing room, but the floor space was minimal. What did he do with himself in there all day? And how could he stay in such good shape, spending so much time in such a small unit? Even her truck camper, which was at the small end of the RV spectrum, was bigger than his van.

The old woman way out on Watkins Spur was strange but not dangerous. Walter Tremblay was an unknown quantity, but he seemed to have a regular schedule, implying a job of some sort— he was free to help the old woman only on Wednesdays. That made him part of the small community of Union Hill, less questionable than an unemployed person. Still, he was somebody to keep in mind.

Gaston. She'd almost forgotten Duval's brother.

She'd never met him, either, only seen him briefly at the fair, but he might well have some kind of an ax to grind with Roll and Rest. The abrupt, unexplained withdrawal from his brother suggested some old family wound that could have smoldered for decades even if Duval was unaware of it.

So the list of names had contracted to John, Walter, Gaston, and whoever might be living in the woods. Yvonne would be able to describe her brother-in-law's personality. She'd mentioned he lived in Pittsburgh, and that was only an hour away. Kate would ask more about him the next time she had coffee with Yvonne.

The hermit? She'd have to find out herself if he was real or a rumor.

\* \* \*

Before planning her campaign to find the hermit or discredit the myth of his existence, she drove her truck to the police station to pick up her kayak. It was behind the building, secured to a fencepost with a chain around the aft thwart.

The officer who took the padlock off it grinned. "We didn't lock it because we were worried about theft," he said. "We locked it so it wouldn't blow away if somebody sneezed."

"Yes, that's a problem with this boat," Kate smiled back. "You know how they make these Hornbecks, don't you?"

"No, how's that?"

She tried to look serious. "Origami."

He laughed. "You got me with that one. I guess you don't need help getting this to your truck."

"Thanks, I've got it," she said, lifting kayak happily to her shoulder. "It weighs about as much as a piece of cake."

\* \* \*

Roll and Rest had WiFi, and Kate used GoogleMaps to bring up the nearby stretch of Loyalhanna Creek on her tablet, looking for places in the conservation area where a hermit might set up a campsite for a long-term stay. But even in satellite mode, the topography didn't show up very well. The image was of the forest in full summer dress, its canopy as dense and green as heads of broccoli.

She went to the house and borrowed a topographic map from Yvonne. Heading back to the camper, Kate was disappointed that it wasn't raining; only a few stray drops ticked against the laminated map. She'd hoped for a downpour. The drought took her back to being a kid in Arizona, watching the sky, seeing dry rain evaporate before it reached the ground, thrilled by monsoon thunder.

The map helped to narrow her survey of good sites. The ridge where she'd found the still-warm ashes of a campfire would be an attractive place if someone were carrying plenty of water. But to camp for an extended period, choosing a place near the river would make more sense. Water is essential. You didn't have to grow up in the desert to know that. And carrying water was a pain in the neck. The stuff was heavy.

Unless there were small springs someone local might know about that didn't show up on the map, Kate figured the best places to look would be close to the Loyalhanna. The protected land stretched for twenty miles along the waterway; its width varied from half a mile to four miles, the broadest patches offering the best opportunities for undetected camping. Keystone, the adjoining state park off to the east, with its established RV sites, would be more populated, and patrolled by rangers. Not hermit territory.

She wouldn't try to see her whole target area in one day. Studying the map, she decided she'd make two day-trips, one upstream and one downstream. She was grateful her boat had been recovered, and her spare paddle would get her back on the water.

The first rule for any outdoor activity was not to go alone. Kate routinely paddled and hiked solo because she had to do it that way or not do it at all, a consequence of her nomadic lifestyle. She often had to disregard the second safety rule, too, which said to tell someone where you're going and when you'll be back. Usually there was nobody to tell. She carried a cell phone in a waterproof pouch, checked it frequently for coverage, and relied on common sense to keep herself safe.

But this time there was someone to tell. Yvonne would be happy to be her check-in contact, Kate was sure. Her trips would combine exploring, hermit hunting, and drawing. She'd be cautious—nobody was going to sneak up on her again. Being on the water, where she'd have 360 degrees of wide-open visibility, would be reassuring. She had the feeling that the person who'd attacked her was land-based, comfortable in the woods, able to move quietly.

If she found a hermit, she wasn't planning on any kind of confrontation. A conversation might be helpful, but only if it was voluntary on both sides; she wouldn't pursue him. She needed to know what was going on, and if she uncovered the existence of an evasive or unfriendly hermit that in itself would be useful information.

She'd seen a bumper sticker once that said "God is my co-pilot." She didn't have that kind of faith; she was counting on the police to be her back-up. But she had to give them facts.

Because of the autumn temperatures, she'd favor the west side of the river for her search since it would catch the morning sun and be more appealing to a camper. The first day she'd paddle south, upstream; then she'd tackle the longer paddle to the north that ended in the dammed-up Loyalhanna Lake. The area surrounding the lake was heavily used for recreation, so she didn't need to check its shores. Her prime target was just south of it, where the swath of conservation land was broadest.

* * *

Yvonne was at the secretary, running Kate's credit card for another week at Roll and Rest. "Gaston? He and Duval were close growing up," she said. Kate had made her question casual, not wanting to let on to her worry-prone friend that her brother-in-law was on Kate's list of suspects. "Duval loved his kid brother, even though he thought Gaston could have done a lot more with his life. He was always looking for a good time instead of focusing on school or a job." She'd put her hair up in a bun and looked regal.

"The two of them sound way different," Kate said. "Duval's hard-working and responsible."

"Thank goodness for that," Yvonne said. "They had a rough period in their twenties. The worst was when Gaston scared Duval really bad, speeding, drunk, getting chased by a police car and getting away from it. Duval swore he'd never ride with Gaston again."

"Gaston evaded the cops?" Kate asked. "That's not how the story usually ends."

"He drove through people's back yards." Yvonne's expression radiated the same disgust that colored her voice. "Took out

140

clotheslines and fence posts and a couple of bicycles. Lucky he didn't kill someone." She closed the secretary and settled at the table. Slid the receipt across.

Kate signed it. "Is he an alcoholic?"

"Duval says Gaston doesn't have an alcohol problem, he has an excitement problem. He likes action, doesn't care about the risks." She picked up her knitting. "Then he seemed to calm down. He got married, and we had some good years with him and his wife living nearby, stopping in here a lot. Gaston was a wonderful uncle to our kids, especially Carson. He looks up to him."

"But not anymore." Kate's cup was empty. She got up, fetched the pot, filled both cups. Nice to feel at home.

"Right, not since he pulled out of the business. Maybe he thought we'd be too annoyed with him to be nice. Maybe he was embarrassed." She shrugged. "I liked his wife. Duval and I were stunned when we got a note from her saying she was leaving Gaston and moving out of state. Didn't even say where she was going."

Kate glanced at the receipt and tucked it in her pocket. "I'm into my third week here? So much has happened, I feel like I've been here a couple of years."

"I know what you mean." Yvonne smiled at her. "You're an old friend now."

* * *

The next morning Kate paddled hard against the current, heading south. The topo map showed a couple of bridges crossing the river, one not far from Roll and Rest and the second just before Latrobe. The air was cold and quiet, the water dark. She made good time, slipping under the first bridge and digging in for a long straightaway. A breeze sprang up behind her, which helped her speed.

Eventually the Loyalhanna curved left, doubled around in the shape of a big backwards C, then straightened. The next bend was gentle, and even before she saw the cement span Kate knew she was near Latrobe because of the sound of traffic. Just before the bridge, buildings on both sides of the water came into view, and she U-turned and drifted, putting a blade edgewise into the water now and then to correct her course.

She'd gotten up early. Patches of mist still drifted over the river. A hermit wouldn't camp in plain sight of paddlers, but he might use the same route from his campsite to the river on a daily basis to get water. She looked along the banks for places that showed use: an opening in the bushes, a trampled area at the water's edge, the erosion of repeated footsteps.

She paddled to the first likely spot and stepped ashore. Her legs were in for a workout getting in and out of the boat so much; their usual, less demanding job was bracing her against the pegs while shoulder and back muscles did most of the work. The lost paddle was carbon fiber, the spare one plastic and much heavier, so she'd get some extra weight-bearing exercise up top, too. She'd sleep well that night.

Darn, the path marked a small launch site. Bushes had hidden the rough trailhead, with room for two or three vehicles. Not a likely place for a hermit camp, but an excellent place for breakfast. Kate dropped her pack next to a log and sat. Poured coffee into the cap of her thermos and inhaled the steam.

A great blue heron glided in, low, and settled near her kayak, apparently agreeing with her choice of breakfast spot. She studied the big bird, letting the anticipation of drawing it calm and excite her at the same time.

What a gift. She took a couple of photos with her phone, then got her sketchbook out of the pack. Let her eyes and pencil follow the sharp lines of beak and eyes, the soft lines of plumes along the back of the elegant neck.

She'd gotten most of what she wanted before the heron hefted itself into the air, croaking as it flew around the next bend with a few heavy wing-beats. She could finish the drawing from the image in her mind and the one on the phone—or from the bird itself. She'd probably see it again, since it had flown downstream.

Kate stood in the shallows and looked in both directions. Had something startled her feathered model? She didn't see any other boats, or anyone on shore. But her recent experience dictated caution.

All right, back in the boat. Not that there was any rush—she had all day. But she was only one curve away from a view of the Latrobe bridge.

She sat motionless and floated. Studied the banks, especially the left, ruddering now and then, a drifting hunter. Where the current was strong, she paddled backward to slow her progress downstream. Dark whirlpools spun off the blades. If she weren't busy looking for the Loyalhanna Hermit, she'd enjoy watching the whirlpools flatten slowly and disappear. Water was hypnotic, following its movement a form of meditation.

In and out of the boat. She lost count of how many times. Her thighs ached.

And the sketchbook was filling. The edges of pages she'd worked on were gray and slightly fuzzy from being handled by her graphite- and charcoal-smudged fingers. On the last page she drew a map of the shorelines with trails and landmarks, adding to it as she found them. Not many blank pages left.

When the sun blared down from its highest point and the shadows of trees sharpened and shrank, she took a lunch break ashore. Eating underway, she might miss something. Sitting on a rock, she ate a piece of sharp cheddar, an apple, and a smaller piece of dark chocolate: fat calories to fuel her paddle.

In and out of the boat.

At one stop a cluster of salmon-orange plants at the edge of the water caught her eye, and she sat on the bank and sketched them. Fine hairs caught the sunlight, giving the spiky leaves a fur-like quality. She rendered the bright water behind the plants as untouched paper with the sparest of pencil lines to show the angle of current. She liked using bare paper, negative space, as an active part of the drawing.

When the east bank looked familiar she knew it was the stretch she could see from the beach below Roll and Rest. Almost home to her camper. She paddled to the middle of the river and dug in, enjoying the short run back to the scrap of sand. She'd stopped at dozens of places and was reasonably sure she hadn't missed any favored sites for getting water. Hermits probably lived in Westmoreland County south of Roll and Rest, but as far as she could tell they were the kind who preferred houses to tents.

But she hadn't wasted her time. A null result is still a result. Besides, it had been a good day for mind and muscles and pencil.

The late sun cast a golden light, and the scrap of beach glowed. Kate carried her kayak up the short trail, slid it onto the picnic table and put the cable loops around bow and stern to lock it up. Carson was sitting in one of the patio chairs, watching her, a small rifle in his lap. He didn't say anything, so she broke the ice.

"Hey, Carson, how're you doing?"

He blinked at her. She'd seen lizards with more facial expression. What an unreadable boy. She'd try one more time. "Cool rifle you've got there."

As if he'd come out of a trance, he jumped up. Maybe he'd been dreaming; kids did. "Yeah, it's great. My Uncle Gassy gave it to me. It really shoots!" He held his hand out flat. "Here's my ammo."

Small pellets with orange plastic noses lay on his palm. Like the one she'd found when she was hiking, at least a mile north of the campground.

Carson got around.

They looked small enough not to do any real damage, but they would probably sting if they hit bare skin.

He jammed them into a pocket. "Wanna see? You pump it up like this—" He pulled a lever under the barrel in and out three times. "And then you put one of 'em here—" He stuffed a pellet into a chamber at the rear of the barrel, doing everything quickly, carelessly, then pointed the rifle down and yanked the trigger. Bad form.

The pellet bounced off Kate's knee. Carson ran a few steps to pounce on it. "I only have ten left," he said. "Don't want to lose any more."

"Hasn't Yvonne—hasn't your mother told you that you never, ever, point a gun at anyone?" Kate was perturbed. Yes, it was an air gun, and she'd barely felt the impact of the pellet through her tough paddling pants. But there was a principle at stake.

"It didn't hurt you. It just hit your leg," Carson said. "Don't be a baby."

"Listen." Two steps, and she caught him by the shoulders and held on even though he squirmed. "A leg is part of a person. You don't ever point a gun—any kind of a gun—at a person. Any part of a person. Do you understand?"

Motionless now, Carson glared at her. No answer. An alarming thought came to her.

"If I ever, ever, catch you shooting at Rusty or Shadow I will tell your parents, and then you will be in a lot of trouble." The thought that he might shoot at the cats made her furious. "Your mother took away TV when you chased Rusty last time, remember? You could lose TV again. You could lose dessert."

What could she use to motivate him? "Your mother could say you couldn't go to computer club."

He hadn't reacted until the last of her threats, and then his face changed. From wary to something more complicated. Kate was suddenly tired of trying to figure him out. She let him go and he walked quickly away, past the house, past the shed, moving his shoulders around as if to shake off the memory of her grip.

She was trembling with anger. Growing up in Arizona, she'd been taught to respect guns. Air guns weren't technically firearms but were often used to train new shooters, especially young ones. Safety practices applied. She didn't like any kind of a weapon in the hands of a boy like Carson, who hadn't shown himself to be responsible. She imagined him stalking one of the cats, how it would turn and face him the way Rusty had behind Annie's front tire. How even that underpowered pellet, at close range, if it were to hit an eye—

Her blood boiled. She'd have to tell Yvonne, although this would make a third time she'd complained about Carson. She felt like a rat, but some people needed to be ratted out.

She'd watch him when she could.

And it seemed as if he'd decided to watch her, too. The next afternoon, when she came back from a long walk, he was in the same rocker on the patio. She didn't say anything. He didn't have his rifle, and she hoped his mother had taken it away from him. Yvonne had looked so despondent at their morning coffee when Kate had described the incident that she wished she hadn't had to say anything.

"I'm sorry," Yvonne had said. "I don't know what to do with that boy. He's gotten worse, I swear, in the last few months. He finally stopped asking about Gaston, and I thought he was making friends at school and not thinking so much about his uncle." Her sigh was deep. "Gaston gave him that rifle, and a box of ammunition. Duval told him he can't have any more, after he uses that box up."

"He probably re-uses the pellets, if he can find them," Kate said. "They have a bright orange tip that makes them easy to spot."

"I'll get Duval to talk to him, too. You're right, he shouldn't be pointing that gun at anyone. Your story scares me."

# THIRTEEN

"Have fun," Yvonne called from the back door as Kate unlocked her kayak. "Call me if you can't make it back upstream, and I'll pick you and your boat up with Duval's truck, wherever you come out of the river." She'd found a large, clear plastic bag for Kate to put her biggest sketchbook in, the opening rolled and secured with masking tape. Kate didn't have any drybags that size. The larger drawings she'd done for the fair had excited her about the format—and they'd all sold.

The air was still chilly. The forecast claimed the high would go to the low sixties, but that was hours away. For the second day of her hermit hunt, Kate zipped up her paddling jacket and did a few jumping jacks before taking her boat to the beach. She'd worn high boots this time. Just cheap rubber ones, but they kept her feet dry. Too clunky to use with an ordinary kayak—the thick soles wouldn't fit in the tight space forward where the pegs were. Another reason to like this deckless Hornbeck.

First stop: she landed above the lowhead dam and carried her boat around it. After putting in far enough downstream that the water was calm, she held the gunwale and watched the outfall for a moment. Couldn't help having a momentary image of what might have happened if she'd regained consciousness too late to save herself from going over the dam. Shuddering, she pushed off gratefully downstream.

She'd brought her easel, a lightweight aluminum model, and set it up at four or five locations. One of them was mid-river, where the bottom was sandy and the water shallow. She laughed and took a picture of it with her phone. Not a selfie, just the easel looking misplaced and mysterious with its ankles in the water. It made her think of Magritte. If he were setting the scene, the easel would have a canvas on it. A painting of the river, perhaps. Or a cat in an upside-down bowler hat. Or a rainstorm of green apples. She liked the quirky imagination that informed his work.

In a deep stretch, a couple of fishermen were casting from the shore. She gave them plenty of room as she paddled past, and then pulled out on the opposite bank to draw them. She'd enjoy working that sketch up, adding detail. She liked the way the lines came off the tips of the rods, expanding the presence of the anglers across the waterscape.

Drawing was thinking. Composition was the deepest pleasure she knew.

\* \* \*

Landing, drawing, launching, paddling, landing. Being on or near the water made the time dream-like. Wavelets tickled the hull, a breeze pulled a yellow slant of leaves from a stretch of frilly river birches, an occasional birdcall bounced across the sky. She lifted her paddle to a group of other kayakers in a tandem and two solos. They nodded back as they passed her but nobody spoke.

A few hours later, soaked in solitude and the satisfaction her work brought, it occurred to her how easily she could become a hermit herself.

Trails ashore were hard to see because some trees had already lost their leaves, which blended forest with footpath. She found a few trails and added them to her map, but most paralleled the river and didn't look like they were used much.

Probably made by people wanting to fish who clambered down the ridge from Watkins Spur.

When the Loyalhanna broke into multiple channels she knew from the map she'd floated close to the lake, so she swept the boat around and headed back, upstream. Having to paddle harder kept her from sinking back into that daydreaming state. Just as well: she'd be more observant.

Entering a backwater, she looped a line around a tree branch and ate lunch in her boat, an apple and a mint-chocolate protein bar. Mid-bite, she was startled by a large bird landing on the trunk of a dead pine only twenty feet away, his scarlet cap underlined with black and white bars, his yellow eye huge. The biggest woodpecker, the pileated. Kate had seen a few, but never this close.

Moving slowly, she put the protein bar down in the boat, careful not to rustle its wrapper. Got out a small sketchbook, watched the creature. Two toes up, two toes down, his big feet clutched the tree below a patch where the bark had fallen off, and he whacked busily with his huge beak at the bare wood. He must be angling his head a little, side to side, the way Kate would chop with a hatchet, because a shower of pale wood chips sprayed below him and a rectangular hole appeared in seconds. Impossible to study his technique: the action was too fast.

A few carpenter ants scuttled away to hide under the bark at the edges of the bare patch. Those were the lucky ones. Woodpeckers have tongues so long they wrap around the inside of their skulls when not extended. She couldn't see his sticky tongue, but if he'd mainlined into a nest then thousands of ants would be boiling around in there, easy targets.

And Kate would bet he'd found a nest. This guy knew what he was doing.

She drew him, although she was so interested in his project she looked at him more than at her own work. How long would he stay? Others she'd seen flew in a minute or so.

He stayed a lot longer. The hole he made was huge, six inches tall and two inches wide. He must be slurping down ants big-time.

And then he cocked his yellow eye at her and launched.

"You made my day," she said to the flown bird. Head down, she was drawing the hairs that protected his nostrils from wood chips and didn't see where he'd gone.

The four words sounded loud. She smiled as she picked up the protein bar and finished it. Only thirty-two, and she was losing it. She'd always talked to birds and animals and even plants on occasion, and now she was talking to the air in places they'd just left.

And startling herself.

"I guess you've found the hermit," she said aloud, "and her name is Kate. She thinks you're a blabbermouth."

She ate her apple in silence.

Pulling her line back aboard, she got underway. The channel narrowed, the current was faster. She had to put her back into paddling. The banks were overhung with dense foliage; here and there a tree had fallen into the water, and she was careful not to get too close. She was grateful to the strainer that had saved her from being swept over the dam a week ago, but she kept her distance from these. Dangerous critters, strainers. And not the kind of critter she talked to.

She landed frequently, working her way along the west side of the river and adding the trails she found to the map at the back of her smaller sketchbook, now otherwise full. These trails weren't on the topographic map; local people, hikers or boaters or anglers, must have made them. Wildlife may have contributed, deer's hooves helping to keep the trails open. Coyotes, she knew, often follow a trail because it's easier traveling, just as it is for humans. Why bushwhack, on two feet or four, if a highway's available?

In a couple of places near the riverbank she found the charred wood of old campfires, some of them in clearings where a backpacker could have pitched a tent and spent the night. Or they could be the work of fisherman frying up their catch or heating water for coffee or tea after cold hours in their waders. She'd been imagining the hermit had a permanent campsite, but the number of possible tent sites reminded her that he could be as nomadic as she was, on a smaller scale. Maybe she'd find a temporary shelter like a tent. Or something hard to see and easily dismantled, like a lean-to made of evergreen branches propped against a ridgepole lashed between two trees.

Paddling out of the main current, she found a side channel, a narrow one past a small island she'd missed on her way downstream. She landed quickly and pulled the kayak out of the water. The bank was low, with well-worn areas and a group of boulders that looked as if they'd been moved there to serve as seats.

Several trails tempted her. Were these more fishing trails, or had she discovered the hermit's haunts? The island would screen him from most kayakers, who would stay farther out on the main part of the river.

One of the trails crossed a dirt road that angled upwards toward the ridge and the last stretch of Watkins Spur. Given the road access, maybe the boulders had been deliberately moved to the riverbank, by truck or an all-terrain vehicle. They were grouped like chairs in a hotel lobby. Forest furniture.

After adding the intersection to her map, Kate walked up the road for a few minutes, looking at the ground. The surface was dry and hard, which didn't show tracks well, but higher up the surface had been improved with gravel. The stones looked disturbed, with small heaps and valleys suggesting foot traffic.

The road looked like it ended in a wall of trees, but it was too wide and clear to just stop. It must make a hairpin turn. Kate looked uphill. She should be able to get a glimpse of the roadbed farther on, above her, as she approached the turn and the amount of foliage between her and the far side of the turn decreased. Yes, she could see the light gray band of gravel above her.

From the woods ahead, something glinted in the sunlight. She stopped.

In the trees beyond the point of the hairpin, something large and dark interrupted the leafy light. A cabin? She went closer, keeping to the edge of the road because her footsteps were quieter there. The soil was beaten down, packed. A lot of people had come this way, going down to the river.

Or one person, many times.

After a few steps, she looked again. The thing was hard to make out in the shadows. If it hadn't been for that spark of a reflection, she might well have missed it.

She got to the point of the hairpin and scanned slowly. She saw a line that didn't fit with the rest of the scene, a straight silver arrow cutting through the clutter of foliage.

An antenna. The telescoping metal kind that older cars have. Bling! The dark bulk was a vehicle, some kind of van, a dark color.

Whoever had parked it here had chosen the site because it was relatively flat, and near water. He must have cut down a few trees to make room, and taken the felled trees elsewhere so they wouldn't reveal what he'd done.

Or maybe the van was abandoned. In her years of hiking, Kate had sometimes come across vehicles left in rural places, although that happened more commonly out West. A truck isn't wanted anymore because it needs too many repairs, so its owner drives it into the desert and throws the keys into a wash.

Now that she was looking carefully, Kate could see that some branches had been arranged between the edge of the road and the van. She picked out various branches that just stopped, unconnected to larger branches or trunks. Their leaves were beech leaves, yellow and bronze. The trunks of nearby trees wore the ridged and scaly bark of red oaks; none showed the smooth gray bark of a beech. The cut branches had been brought from somewhere else.

Concealment, not abandonment.

Kate had seen enough. She didn't want to meet the hermit, or disturb him; she only wanted to know if he existed, if there was someone living out here in the woods on a long-term basis. And now she knew. The safest course was to retreat, and think things over with this new information.

She turned back. Caught sight of a figure by the water, and stopped.

Her view down to where she'd landed was clear. Someone was standing beside her kayak.

This was a good test of the hermit's attitude. If he was hostile, he'd push the boat into the river. She'd just gotten it back after a close call at the dam, and she'd hate to lose it. But she didn't want to risk getting into a fight with this guy. He could be dangerous.

The hermit sat on one of the big rocks, watching the river. Tugged the brim of his cap down.

Kate was surprised. Hermits are hermits because they hide. They aren't supposed to sit on rocks, waiting for boaters to reappear. But that was what this one was doing.

And he looked familiar. She couldn't see his face, but something about the way he held himself rang a bell. She'd go a little closer, see if she could figure it out. Somebody she'd seen at the fair? Or the campground? She started back down the road to the trail.

He'd gotten up and was leaning against a tree trunk, looking at the water. Head down, shoulders slumped: a despondent posture. A confrontation didn't seem likely, based on his body language.

Kate's foot crunched a leaf, and he turned toward her.

He was a she.

"Annie!"

# FOURTEEN

Her expression was one of relief. "Oh, Kate, I thought it was you. I recognized your boat." The smile was wobbly: Annie was still as stressed as she'd been when she asked Kate's advice about the green necklace a couple of weeks earlier. Probably because of the divorce she was going through, which would haunt her for years.

"Annie, wow, am I surprised. " Kate remembered Annie getting testy when the subject of the Loyalhanna Hermit came up with the Millers. No wonder: it looked like she *was* the hermit, living in her hidden van. She must have been taking a break when she stayed at Roll and Rest. "Hey, I have some sandwiches, and coffee. Is it too early for dinner?"

Annie gave a weak laugh. "It probably is, but I won't turn you down." She took her cap off, and her red hair fell down and glowed. Kate would have recognized her a lot sooner without the cap.

Pulling her pack out of the boat, she scrumbled through the gear inside for provisions. She spread a red kerchief on one of the rocks and set the food on it. Two Granny Smith apples gleaming next to the brown grainy texture of six half-sandwiches and the shiny wrappers of food bars: a good subject for a still life.

"So Annie, what are you doing out here? Have you been boondocking in your van up there since you left the campground?" She didn't want to sound nosy or judgmental. "I boondock a lot myself, but I had to stop at Roll and Rest when my generator broke."

"Oh, you saw the van." Annie hesitated. "Then I'll have to tell you about my brother Steve." She sat on a rock and took a bite of sandwich.

After two tours with the army in Afghanistan, she said, her brother hadn't adjusted well to civilian life. "I came down here from Wisconsin a bunch of times to visit Steve because I knew he was in trouble. He kept hearing gunfire, and he thought people were sneaking up on the house. He kept the curtains closed even in the daytime, and he couldn't sleep. I wanted him to get help, but he didn't think he needed it."

"That's trouble all right. What was his specialty in the army?"

"He was in the K-9 corps. His dog was a combat tracker," Annie said. "About three months ago he asked me not to visit anymore. I thought he'd figured out my husband didn't want me to be away so much. For a while Steve called me every couple of weeks, but then he stopped doing that."

"You must have been worried," Kate said.

"I had to find out what was going on. When I got here, he wasn't in the house on Watkins Spur, some old woman was. I didn't know where he'd gone. I checked the town records and found out he'd lost the house. He never paid the taxes on it, not a dime." She'd finished the first half sandwich and took another.

"Are you talking about the house way out on Watkins? The one just before it ends?"

"Yes, that's the one," Annie said. "We grew up there, playing in the field behind the house and in the woods here, all along the river. We had a golden retriever and in the summer we swam in the river, all three of us. My brother loved that dog."

She paused, looking out at the river. "My mother left the house to Steve because I was up in Wisconsin, married, all nice and secure, right?" She sounded sad. "She died before his second tour."

"I'm sorry."

Annie shook her head. Her mind wasn't on her mother. "When I found the old woman in the house instead of Steve, I was afraid he'd done himself in." She took a deep breath and let it out slowly. "I'd been hoping I could live with him for a while and look for a job around here—good for both of us—but I had to regroup. Roll and Rest wasn't too far from the house so I stayed there for a week while I figured out what to do."

Her face was calmer. Telling her story was doing her some small, temporary good. She started on an apple.

"The Millers talked about the Loyalhanna Hermit and I knew it must be him. I went looking, walked around in the woods calling his name."

He'd stepped from behind a tree, she said, looking a decade older. Bearded and gaunt, his clothes patched with duct tape, he told her civilization was sick and he was better off on his own in the woods.

Even after he started camping, he'd managed to get a couple of jobs, Annie said, the first with a veterinarian. But he felt too sad for the sick dogs. Then he worked for a photographer for a few months but had a fight with him. Without money he stopped going to town, and his ties to local people faded. But his paranoia didn't. He followed hikers and fishermen, unseen, tracking them until they left what he considered his territory.

No wonder Kate had felt she was being watched.

"How's he doing now? Where is he?" Kate hoped his sister had convinced him to get into a rehab program for veterans with PTSD.

"I don't know." Annie looked around. "Probably watching us."

Well, that made sense. Kate suppressed the urge to look around too. She probably wouldn't see him anyway, considering she'd been looking for him pretty much since she arrived at Roll and Rest, after the first morning's disrupted drawing session, without success.

"So for now I'm just hanging out with him," Annie said. "The two of us live in my van, and I cook him a decent meal once or twice a day. I brought a little money with me, and we don't pay rent, and eventually maybe I can talk Steve into getting some help. We can't live like this forever."

"What do you do for food?"

"He bow-hunts, mostly rabbits. He can't take a deer because we don't have any way to preserve the meat. The fridge in my van is tiny, and smoking would mean a big fire, which isn't going to happen because it would attract attention."

"Do you have a good heater?" Kate asked. "The nights are getting cold."

"Yeah, we're good and cozy, we both have warm sleeping bags. He slept on the ground, after all, until I showed up." She'd eaten the apple down to the core, which she held up. "Thanks for this," she said, and tossed it behind a bush.

"Now it's rabbit bait."

"Yeah." Annie shrugged. "I'll have to drive into town pretty soon, to get propane for the heater and the stove. He'll scout first, make sure nobody's around to see me leave. I can get some veggies, too, and gas. We need to run the engine to charge the battery. For the heater fan, not for lights. He doesn't like lights. We use a candle lantern after dark, and he's got the curtains taped at the edges and the bottom so light doesn't leak. You can't tell we're there."

"Not much of a night life, then," Kate said. "No big parties?"

She got a smile. "Not even small ones."

Kate was glad she always packed more food for her day-trips than she thought she'd eat. Along with the sandwiches and apples she had a large thermos of coffee, which she normally didn't finish until she got home, using the microwave to reheat what was left if it had cooled down in the mostly-empty thermos.

This trip she'd found a better place to put the food than her own stomach. At the rate it was disappearing, it was obvious the hermit's sister appreciated the gift. She'd eaten three of the sandwich halves and an apple, and was tearing the wrapper off a protein bar.

Kate put the thermos between her knees to unscrew the cap.

"Hi," Annie said, and Kate looked up.

A thin man with a ragged beard was standing next to Annie. Red-haired like his sister, he had the wiry build as John at Roll and Rest.

"Hello, Steve. I'm Kate." She nodded at the plastic cup dangling from his hand. "Want some coffee?"

"Sure," he said.

The real Loyalhanna Hermit.

Kate stood and filled his cup from the thermos. He drank it fast, and she gave him a refill. A fellow java junkie, she thought, but he handed the cup to Annie, who took a swallow and handed it back.

"Great stuff. Thanks." He sat on a third rock, relaxed but wary, like a crouched cat. Tore the wrapper off a protein bar with his teeth, his eyes on Kate.

She reclaimed her own rock and drank from the thermos cap. "Beautiful place you have here." She waved a hand toward the river, the woods, all of it, wanting him to know she didn't object to his living in the conservation area. The National Park Service might not agree with her—there was probably a limit to the number of consecutive days one was allowed to camp here—but she wasn't a park ranger, just her own outdoorsy self.

"Um. Yeah," he said. "It is." The bar was gone and he took two sandwich pieces.

"I've been hiking around, doing some paddling, and drawing pictures." That wouldn't be news to him. "Sold some at the Fall Crafts Fair." He must know the event, since he'd grown up in Union Hill.

His gray eyes were intelligent, his hair long and tangled. He actually looked cleaner than John; no muffin crumbs littered his beard. Duct tape patched the camo fatigues, and his shoes were taped so thoroughly she couldn't tell what kind they'd originally been.

"That's a good boat of yours," he said. "Weighs about as much as a rabbit."

Kate laughed. "Never heard it described like that, but you're right." He could know that from watching her carry it. Or had he checked it out more closely? While she was walking the trails looking for him, he could have been assessing her boat, lifting it, admiring it. He could easily have stolen it. Apparently he wasn't that type of guy.

Was he the type who would knock her out, put her in the kayak and push it into the current? She didn't know a thing about him, although he seemed more fearful than aggressive. Annie's dedication spoke well for him. But Gaston was Duval's brother and that didn't make Gaston a person you could trust.

Steve had certainly had the opportunity to attack her. He was good at moving around the woods quietly. He was quiet at the moment, but how volatile was he?

"Kate's at Roll and Rest," Annie said.

"Good place," he said. "I feel a little bad about it, though."

"Hush, Steve," his sister said.

"You had a power outage—"

"Steve, don't."

He kept on. "A power outage because I—"

"You'll get in trouble."

"I'm not planning on telling anyone," Kate said. She looked at Annie and then Steve. He must have been through hell, and she wasn't going to tell anyone anything about him. Not even Yvonne, because Yvonne would probably tell Duval and Kate didn't know him well enough to know what he might do.

"I cut the wires." He slipped a multi-tool out of his pocket, fiddled with it, turning it into pliers, a saw, a screwdriver. A knife.

"Why?" Kate asked. Her voice puzzled, not accusatory.

He was looking at the gadget in his hands, enjoying it, swiveling the different tools in and out. It was probably his most valuable possession, something he used every day. He snapped the knife blade in and out and ran his thumb across the edge.

At her question, his face went dark. "I told him I would only do that one thing. That was it. And I quit right after that."

Something told Kate not to ask who "he" was. Yet. She looked at Annie, who looked both scared and angry.

"I'm glad to hear that," Kate said. "I won't be telling anyone you did it, but Duval and Yvonne can't afford to pay for any more repairs."

"That's what I said," Annie said. "Once was one time too many, as far as I'm concerned." She looked at Kate. "He did it before I got here. The man he used to work for is evil. I told Steve to quit."

"I didn't work for him very long, after I found out. But now we don't have any money," Steve said. He put the multi-tool back in his pocket and stared at the ground.

"Steve can't work at a regular job," Annie said to Kate. "He can't be around people for very long. He wouldn't even come visit me at Roll and Rest, after I found him. That's why I moved out here."

"Too many people," he muttered.

"You're a devoted sister," Kate said.

"That sneaky kid, I didn't like him," Steve said.

"Carson?" Kate asked.

"The squinty little kid with glasses. At the campground."

"Yes, that's Carson, the campground owners' son."

"He saw me that night I did the box," Steve said. "I looked around, made sure nobody was out and about, then I turned off the main breaker and did the damage. Waited a couple of minutes afterward, making sure nobody had come along and seen me. Flattened myself against the wall of a shack, behind a bush."

Kate knew the bush he was talking about, the hydrangea between Yvonne's house and the shed.

"Little bast—little brat, I mean," Steve said, glancing at Annie apologetically. "He was pressed up against the shed wall, too, hiding in the same place I chose, right next to me. He must've been watching me the whole time. Kinda freaked me, I'll tell you." He wiped his forehead with his palm. "At first I pretended I didn't notice he was there. But after a bit, I looked right at him, and he shot off like a rabbit. I guess I scared him. He's lucky I didn't—"

"Steve," Annie said.

He stood up. Two quiet footsteps in the leaves, and he'd melted into the forest.

Moments later a pair of kayakers passed, using the narrow channel near the bank rather than the main course of the river. Steve must have heard the splash of a paddle, or a voice, and hadn't wanted to be seen.

Kate raised a hand in greeting to the paddlers, who nodded back. After they were out of sight she lifted her eyebrows at Annie. "Steve knew they were coming?"

She shrugged. "My brother's half-wild. He has hearing like a dog's."

\* \* \*

Kate paddled hard upriver toward the campground, paying less attention to the kingfishers and herons than she usually did.

Why hadn't Carson said anything about the man he saw vandalizing his parents' property? Why would he protect Steve? The kid was such an odd duck. Maybe he thought the crime was exciting. Maybe he was frightened Steve would get even with him if he told.

Her own curiosity was satisfied, but she wouldn't pass the information on. She understood why homeowners whose land abutted the conservation land would object to people camping on it long-term, but she didn't want to make trouble for Steve and Annie. For one thing, she knew they would be responsible to the land. They wouldn't litter, or pollute, or start a forest fire. They weren't careless people. And she believed Steve wouldn't do any more damage at the Roll and Rest.

In fact, even though Steve was the Loyalhanna Hermit, he wasn't necessarily the one who'd stolen the items that had gone missing from nearby houses, the flashlight or loaf of bread or whatever.

Kate would visit the two again; she'd said as much to Annie after Steve had left them. Annie was amazing. Not many sisters would do what she was doing. Steve had been through a lot, but maybe he could pull himself out of it with her help. The next time she talked to Annie she'd try to find out who had asked him to damage the breaker box. She hadn't wanted to rush things, but the creep should be called to account.

Kate hoped Steve wasn't the person who'd set her adrift. He was deeply troubled, and given his paranoia he could believe he had reasons to lash out. The way he played with the multi-tool, pulling out the knife blade and testing the edge against his thumb, might have made her uncomfortable if Annie hadn't been there. And what had he been about to say about Carson?

Steve and the boy both hiding against the shed wall was funny, now that she had a chance to think about it.

She'd take more food next time, land at the same place. She could do that a couple more times before she said goodbye to the Roll and Rest and to Pennsylvania. Yvonne and Savvy, and Annie—she'd miss them.

The thing about this traveling life, she was starting to see, was that you made friends and moved on. Maybe some of the friends were keepers, people you stayed in touch with even as the miles multiplied between you and them. They were special people. It took time to sort out who would be a keeper and who would drift out of touch, and it wasn't all up to Kate. Staying friends took effort on both ends.

Carson was more than sneaky. He hadn't stopped playing with his yo-yo when Yvonne had run from the house, crying because Donna had died. Was he one of those rare children Marjorie had described as CU, "callous and unemotional"? Kate imagined him at age sixteen or eighteen and felt prospectively sorry for Yvonne.

What would Savvy be like when she was twenty? Kate liked the girl and hoped the best for her. She'd have to get through this difficult period of headaches, forgetfulness and irritability, but Kate would bet that a loving daughter would greet Yvonne on the other side of those problems. Medical issues had to be ruled out, of course, but probably Savvy's brain and body were expressing the hormonal storm called puberty.

Stay tuned, Kate told herself.

She paddled to the middle of the river, the water catching the dim gold and orange light that seemed to come from the trees' bright canopies. She was tempted to stop and work longer, but she had an hour's paddle ahead of her. She'd be landing at the beach near the campground at dusk even if she didn't stop.

A figure at the edge of the river startled her. Two-legged, dark. Was it wading to intercept her? Just because she'd found one hermit didn't mean there wasn't another.

It whirled and fled, and Kate saw a white patch flash. A deer. The back half had blended into the shadows of the woods before it turned, and the forward part had caused Kate's heart to jump.

She put the energy into her paddling.

Close to Roll and Rest, she made out a big raccoon in the shadows at the water's edge, washing some tidbit. "I like your tail," Kate called, then realized how that comment could be taken, and laughed. "I hope you like my tail. Are you free tonight? Want to take in a movie?" Its eyes stared at her from the mask. "Wait. I don't go out with bandits. Are you the bad-ass who stole Duval's jeans?"

She landed on the scrap of sand and carried her boat up the trail. Nearly dark, with no moon. Kate thought of the raccoon again when she saw Carson on the patio. He was whittling a stick, and he stopped and stared just like her ring-tailed date had. She couldn't see his face in the gloom, but she bet it had that blank lizard look.

Come on, this was stupid. A feud with a twelve-year-old?

"Hey, Carson. Want me to draw you sometime?" It had occurred to her that he might be jealous—she'd had Savvy pose, but not her brother. Savvy had volunteered, of course, but he might not know that. "Want a drawing of yourself?"

He didn't respond. Okay, maybe he couldn't see her, but was he deaf?

The door opened and Yvonne came outside, looking around. "Carson?" she called, even though he was right in front of her. Kate remembered how, when she was a child playing in the back yard, her mother would call her in when she could still see perfectly well outside. To people in a house with the lights on, it's black out there. And when they step outside, their eyes don't adjust to the dark for several minutes.

"Yeah?"

"Oh, there you are. There's a friend on the phone for you," Yvonne said. "That girl."

Carson got up quickly and went inside, and so did Yvonne. She must not have seen Kate. The door closed, and like an afterthought the light beside it went on.

Kate locked her kayak to the picnic table. Carson had a girlfriend?

# FIFTEEN

The next afternoon Kate drove to Union Hill for groceries, adding some items for Annie and Steve, then down Watkins Spur past the campground. Because of her truck's high clearance, she was able to go far enough that she could park near the river access road that switchbacked past Annie's hidden van.

But drawing came first.

She prowled around the woods, then made herself comfortable on a fallen log near a clearing. River birches caught her eye first; she enjoyed their salmon-colored trunks and ruffled bark. After half an hour she was thrilled when a wild turkey emerged from the underbrush, followed by others. The rafter, or flock, numbered a baker's dozen. Wary at first, bobbing their heads and peering at her, they eventually relaxed and picked through the leafy litter.

Since the birds looked almost black in the shade, she drew the ones that came farthest into the sunny clearing to forage, their bronze and chestnut colors clarifying individual feathers and the way they fit together. She translated the variegated plumage into pencil strokes on paper.

Turkeys were tough old birds, even the young ones. They had to be—they didn't migrate.

The huge creatures scratched and pecked like oversized hens. A tom came within twenty feet of her, an old guy judging by his beard, that tuft of central chest feathers long enough in his case to brush the ground. He cocked his head at her, eyes bright against the bare, gray-blue skin, then went back to feeding.

An encounter with wild creatures put Kate into a paradoxical state of calm excitement. Mysterious, the lives that looked back at her from furred or feathered bodies. Mysterious too the communities of plants that surrounded them, supported them, wove them and her and all living things into the biosphere.

After the turkeys moved on, she worked for another hour and then climbed up to where she'd left her camper. Leaning her frame pack against the back bumper, she loaded it with the heavy groceries: two gallon jugs of water, four jars of peanut butter, two loaves of whole-wheat bread, and a bag of oranges. She placed the treat, a cherry pie, on top of the load and pulled the flap taut over it. Then she sat on the step below the pack and got the shoulder straps in place and the hip belt tight enough to take most of the weight.

An external frame pack was considered old-fashioned, but it was still the pick-up truck of the trail, and this one made trekking the provisions down to the switchback easy.

"Annie?" Kate called, not too loudly. "Steve?"

After a minute she tried again.

The camouflage job with the cut branches was effective; she found the van easily only because she already knew it was there. A lot of hikers would watch their footing closely enough on this grade that they'd miss the dark bulk in the shadows, and not that many fishermen would drive the gravel road because of the steepness and sharp turn.

She saw a faint path and followed it. Plainer a few feet in, it led to the back of the van. The silence said nobody was home.

The reclusive pair had made a table by placing a small board across two fallen trees, the surface disguised with painted swirls of green and brown. Should she leave the food there? The peanut butter was probably safe—the jars shouldn't have much odor since they were sealed—but the bread, oranges and pie were probably already stimulating the noses of hungry creatures she couldn't see. She didn't want Annie and Steve to come home to a mess of plastic bags and an aluminum pie plate all torn apart and littering their back yard. And calling attention to their campsite. She imagined the scene, adding a half-dozen raccoons sprawled around the edges of the disaster, rubbing their bellies and groaning with pleasure. Honestly, sometimes she had to admit a cartoonist lived in her head.

She knocked on the door and waited a bit, then tried the latch. Unlocked. She dropped the pack to the ground and slid everything inside without looking. She didn't want to intrude on her friends' privacy. Closed the door quietly, and turned. Steve stood like a tree among trees, straight and still. It was getting late, and with his slight build and dark clothes he could have been a shadow.

"Thanks," he said, eyes downcast. "Annie went for a walk. You know we can't pay—"

"I know," she said. "You're welcome to it, Steve."

She retraced her steps, scuffling the leaves as she came out to the road to disguise her tracks. When she looked back, Steve was gone.

Getting late. As she climbed up to to Watkins Spur, Kate's mind drifted toward dinner. She'd sauté Portobello mushrooms, drizzle spaghetti sauce and grate cheese over them and add a sprinkle of finely chopped onions and parsley.

Deep dusk by the time she reached the Spur. Her camper loomed, its white bulk turned gray by the failing light, and she jumped in surprise as a figure stepped from behind it.

"Hello?" It was a girl, with long dark hair. "Can you give me a ride home, please?" The voice was light and high, like birdsong.

Kate got out her flashlight and shone it at the girl's knees so she wouldn't blind her.

She was about Carson's height; Yvonne had said he was small for his age, so the girl might be younger than he was. Eleven, ten? Her hair hung almost to her waist. Above the leggings and suede boots, the frilliness of her blouse fought with the practicality of a down vest. The frills reminded Kate of Savvy's curtains.

"A ride home? Where do you live?" Kate asked. The house with the loony old woman wasn't far. Could this girl live there? No, that was walking distance, easy.

"In Union Hill. On the east side. Magnolia Street?" She looked hopeful, and sweet.

"Sure, I can give you a ride." The girl was shivering. "Are you cold?"

"Yeah, a little."

"I want you to put this on, all right?" Kate took off her leather jacket and held it out, low. The girl turned and slipped her arms into the sleeves. Her hands, of course, didn't come out at the cuffs.

Kate hit the button to open the truck. The lights flashed and the locks popped. A dog barked in the distance, and the girl whimpered and ran to the passenger door. She yanked on the handle, but it was too high for her.

"Hang on," Kate said. Another bark, another whimper. "Are you afraid of dogs?" She opened the door and the girl scrambled in without answering.

As she got behind the wheel, it crossed Kate's mind how trusting the youngster was. Maybe she should say something, tell the girl not to assume every adult was kind-hearted and safe to be around. But maybe it would alarm her unnecessarily. Kate wasn't a parent and wasn't sure what to say. When she got the girl home she'd walk her to the door and maybe talk with the mother a bit. The mother who must be wondering where her daughter was.

"I'm Kate," she said. "What's your name, honey?"

"Sharon." But she'd hesitated.

"Hey, Sharon, do you want to call your parents on my cell phone? They must be worried."

"Oh, no, they think I'm—"

The fit of coughing that interrupted her answer sounded fake. Okay, the girl was being evasive. All the more reason to have a word with a parent.

Kate gave it one more try. "How did you get so far from home, this late?"

"I was hiking, you know, with friends. I got lost."

Hiking in a frilly blouse and boots with heels? Not convincing, kiddo.

Kate drove to the edge of town and asked Sharon for directions, which took them to a residential neighborhood. Kate had biked through it. Older homes. Quiet. A breeze stirred the big maples, and the leaves clouding the streetlights cast the houses in orange light.

"The next corner," Sharon said.

"The corner house?" Kate pulled to the curb, and Sharon jumped out of the cab, leaving Kate's jacket on the seat.

The kid did everything fast. "Hang on a sec," Kate called out. She doused the headlights, put the truck in park, and turned off the engine. The passenger door was hanging open, which would normally annoy her, but the big truck door was too heavy for Sharon to close.

Kate slid from behind the wheel into the night and went around to the passenger side. "You can wear the jacket up to the door, honey," she said. But the girl wasn't there.

What the heck? Kate looked around but didn't see anyone. She took a few steps toward the front door of the corner house, but there was no girl on the porch and all the windows were dark.

"Sharon?" she called.

Uneasy, she walked to the intersection and looked down the quiet streets. Movement caught her eye, but it was just a cat beetling across the road. A dog barked twice, many houses away.

A dark night, the new moon having turned its back on her world.

She didn't know what to think. What was such a young girl doing so far from home, and so late? Sharon, if that was her name, had lied and had used Kate, that was obvious. Nothing she could do about it now.

The youngest in her family, she wasn't used to dealing with children. Maybe she was the one who'd been overly trusting, not the girl. She'd tell Yvonne about the night's adventure, get her opinion about whether she should report it.

Feeling sad and somehow lonely, she drove to Roll and Rest and skipped dinner in favor of calling Marjorie before it got too late, wanting to share the news about discovering the Loyalhanna Hermit and his sister. If there was time, she'd talk about Sharon, too.

Kate recapped her conversations with Annie and Steve for her friend.

"I must say, ever since you left Massachusetts you've been getting involved in the oddest situations."

"Yes," Kate said. "I don't know why. Moving around, I guess, always meeting new people."

"One place is all I can handle. And I'm happy where I am. My children are ninety percent fascinating and only ten percent exasperating." Marjorie laughed. "We'll see how it goes from here."

"And you have psych coursework on top of taking care of the kids and the house."

"Speaking of which, I've done some more reading about conduct disorder in children, thinking about that boy you're dealing with. You might ask his mother if he showed any guilt or remorse when she scolded him about hurting the cats. If he did, that's a good sign. If he didn't, he may be one of those rare people who doesn't have the capacity to care about the feelings of others."

"I don't have to ask. I was there. It was a day or two after I'd arrived, so I wasn't sure how Yvonne would take it, a customer dragging her son by the collar to her door. But she was great. She read him the riot act." Kate thought back. "He just looked at her. He didn't say anything."

"I wish he'd at least looked at the floor," Marjorie said. "I'm a little worried because he's doing bad things on his own, not hanging around with a bunch of other boys. Peer pressure can get a basically decent kid into trouble. But he's acting on his own inner impulses."

"Cats are bad enough, but he could be the same way about other people?"

"Exactly."

"I'm astonished he didn't tell his parents who cut the wires and caused the power outage the first night I stayed here," Kate said. "He isn't a very loyal member of his family. But even more than Carson, I'm worried about Steve."

"Who? Oh, the hermit?"

"Right. He's withdrawn, paranoid, his clothes and shoes patched with duct tape. He was living like a coyote, hunting rabbits and hiding, until Annie showed up."

"She sounds like a dedicated sister."

"Absolutely. But she's not that strong. It's a huge strain on her to try to pull Steve back from the brink of—I don't know what to call where he's headed, but it's not a good place."

There was a pause. "Psychosis is a possibility," Marjorie said. "I'm concerned about Annie. If he loses touch with reality, he might become violent. Might mistake her for one of the enemies he thinks surround him."

"That's an awful thought." It hadn't crossed Kate's mind that Annie could be in danger.

"I'd be willing to talk to either one of them, although it sounds like getting him on the phone with me is unlikely. But the sister? I could do my best to support her, and maybe tell her some things to watch out for. If he's getting worse, she might have to bail to save herself."

"Yikes," Kate said.

"The best thing for her to do would be talk to a local counselor or therapist. Do you think she would?"

A picture of Annie waiting beside the kayak came into Kate's mind: head down, shoulders slumped. "I doubt it. She looked awfully depressed."

"I figured. Inertia is such a problem with depression." Another pause. "Do you think she'd talk to a friend of a friend, namely me?"

"She might. I'll ask her," Kate said. "That's generous of you."

"Don't forget to keep your eye on that boy. And his father. There's trouble in that family, I'm convinced."

# SIXTEEN

The next morning over coffee, Kate described her encounter with Sharon. She put air quotes around the name.

"That's pretty strange," Yvonne said. "A kid that age, way out there? And the story she gave was fishy? Doesn't sound good."

Kate stirred her coffee, which didn't need stirring. "I wonder what she would have done if my camper hadn't been there. And what if the driver wasn't me? A guy could have showed up. With really bad luck, a not-so-nice guy."

Yvonne looked pained. "Let's not go there. Without you she would have had to walk back to town. Which isn't impossible, really. It's only about three miles. But after dark? In those boots you described?"

"I don't get it," Kate said. "Why did she run away from me, when I'd taken her home?"

"That's an easy one," Yvonne said. "I'm a mother, so I can guess what she was thinking. You knew where she'd been, and she didn't want you to tell her parents." She ripped the corners off two packets and poured sweetener into her cup. "I'm onto her. She was doing something bad."

Kate's mind was trying to cope with the sweet kid she'd met being such a trickster. "I said her mother must be worried about her and she said 'No, my mother thinks I'm at—' and then she didn't finish the sentence. She had a coughing fit, but she was faking it. She wasn't a good actor."

"Something's definitely up. When a girl that age lies to a parent, nothing good can come of it." Yvonne's face was grim.

"She wasn't that far from the house with the old woman," Kate said.

They looked at each other.

"Maybe there's something going on out there," Yvonne said finally. "Which is a creepy thought. Although the police should have been able to put a stop to it, since you gave them the address."

"Well, maybe it's time to talk to them again."

"Yes," Yvonne shivered. "I'm getting goose-bumps. Something going on with youngsters at an isolated house is the kind of thing you hear about on the news."

"Not something you expect to happen in a quiet country town like Union Hill," Kate said.

"Telling the police about the girl a good idea. I'll go with you. I know some of the guys at the station, and they know me. Let's go now."

It made sense. Kate would have more credibility if she showed up with a local citizen than she would by herself, a stranger passing through, a transient RVer with Massachusetts tags on her rig. The three conversations she'd already had with the police—two at the station and one at the hospital—had apparently accomplished nothing.

"I'd like that." Kate said, pushing back her chair.

\* \* \*

The police treated the report about Sharon seriously. A sandy-haired, freckled Sgt. Dewey joined her and Yvonne in a bare interview room and videotaped her story, which made Kate uncomfortable at first. He said it was routine.

"Look at me," he said. "Not at the camera. About what time did you park on Watkins Spur?" Even his hands had freckles.

"Let's see," Kate said. "I parked there around 2:00, and spent the rest of the afternoon drawing." She'd packed food to Annie's van and seen Steve, but didn't want to mention either of them. "It was almost dark when I headed back to my camper—"

"She's a really good artist," Yvonne put in.

The sergeant put up an index finger in Yvonne's direction without looking at her: Wait.

Kate smiled her thanks at Yvonne and then got back to business, describing the girl who'd startled her, waiting beside her camper.

"The child accosted you?"

"Accosted? She asked me for a ride to town, said she lived there."

"I just want to get this clarified." He glanced up at the camera on the ceiling. "You did not pursue her yourself, or entice her to go with you?"

"No, not at all. She must have seen my truck camper parked on the road, and waited there for the driver. Who turned out to be me."

He took her through the events, Kate throwing in every detail she could remember, the way he'd instructed her to at the beginning. "Nothing isn't important," he'd said. So she told him how Sharon was dressed and how likely it seemed she was lying, probably not even giving her real name. Then Kate jumped to her experiences with the two found phones, their disturbing messages, the house at the end of Watkins Spur, and a brief account of the attack that nearly put her over the dam. She tried not to sound impatient.

"It was over a week ago that I brought in the second phone and told a woman officer about the house. She wrote up a report. And I told the cop who visited my hospital room, too."

"Oh, it was you who brought in the phones? You've been busy," the sergeant said. "We went out to that house and checked around, but the only person we found was an elderly woman."

"There's a man, too. She told me he was around on Wednesdays after work."

"Oh?" He thought a moment. "Our guys went out on Tuesday, I think. The cruiser couldn't make it all the way down the road, so they had to hike in." A smile flickered across his lips, and Kate wondered if the officers who got the assignment had complained. Patrolling in a police car is significantly less strenuous than dealing with a rough road on foot.

"Try a Wednesday," Kate said, disappointed. She gave the Union Hill police credit for checking out the house, but she wasn't impressed that they hadn't reviewed the information she'd given when she'd brought in the pink phone. Or had she failed to mention what the old woman had said about Walter Tremblay's schedule?

"I'll tell the chief," Sgt. Dewey said. He paused, and when it was clear Kate was finished, he asked Yvonne if she had anything to add.

"Just that I'm worried for my children's sake," she said. "If there's some monster out there kidnapping girls and—"

"We really don't know enough to speculate," he said quickly. "We'll check out the house again, see if we can get our hands on a few more facts. Thank you both for coming in." He pushed a button on the remote and a red light on the camera went out. "Ms. Corliss, I'd like to show you some pictures of runaways."

"Please call me Kate. But isn't this girl the opposite of a runaway? I took her home, or at least I hope I did."

"I didn't make myself clear, Kate. These are recently returned runaways. It sounds like this girl's in trouble. Sometimes runaways have experiences that get them in trouble even after they're reunited with their families. And sometimes they take off again. I'd like to prevent that, if it applies to this girl."

He slid a folder across the table to her. "Here are some photos. Have a look through them, tell me if you see the girl you gave a ride to. Take your time."

A dozen pictures. They made her sad: most of them were candids, a few were posed school shots, but all the children, mostly girls, looked happy, caught by the camera on a swing or playing with a dog or behind a cake with eight or ten candles on it.

"Do more girls run away than boys?" Kate asked.

"About seventy-five percent of runaways are female," Sgt. Dewey said.

"Why?"

He shrugged. "No good studies to tell us why. Maybe they're more sensitive to family problems."

Kate looked back at the photos. None of them showed the girl she knew as Sharon. She shook her head and pushed the file away.

"Thanks, Kate. I'll let you know if we have any more questions," Sgt. Dewey said. "And thank you, too, Yvonne. If there's anything, ah, unpleasant going on, we'll find out."

As Yvonne and she left the station, Kate said, "He sure didn't make any promises. He'll tell the chief. That's it?"

Yvonne shook her head. "I know. And he said they'd find out if anything 'unpleasant' was going on. Whatever it is, it's a heck of a lot worse than that."

They were both quiet on the ride back to the campground. The old Dodge, of course, was not.

\* \* \*

"How's Steve?" Kate asked. "How are you?"

Because of her late start, she'd driven as far out Watkins Spur as she could go. Spent an hour wandering in the woods, taking pictures with her cell and sketching. Now she and Annie were sitting on the boulders near the riverbank. The place had indeed turned out to be where the brother and sister came to fill plastic jugs with water they sterilized with iodine pills.

"You know, I really think he's gotten better. When I first found him he was always sure the bad guys were behind the next tree." Annie was eating orange sections one by one, savoring them. "Now he's calmer. Most of the time. Unless he has solid evidence there's someone around."

As Kate had expected, Annie talked about her brother and not about herself. "That's great, Annie," Kate said. "You're helping him."

"I know I'm helping nutritionally. He was eating mostly rabbit when I got here. Half-roasted, because he was afraid campfires would give him away." She wrinkled her nose.

"Now you have the stove on the van."

"Right, and I make sure the meat's cooked through. I feel sorry for the rabbits, but he deals with them. What he gives me looks like the chicken pieces you buy at the store, minus the tray and plastic wrap."

"You said he uses a bow. Does he snare them sometimes, too?"

"No, just the bow. It's quiet and he can recover the arrows. Nothing for anybody to find, like an unsprung snare."

"Does he hunt squirrels?"

"Ugh, no," Annie said. "At least not since I've been here. And I buy onions and carrots. We eat regular stew."

So the dead squirrels she'd found weren't Steve's doing. "On his own he'd eat all meat, all the time? That's called a Paleo diet these days," Kate said with a smile. "It's very popular." The other name for the diet was Caveman, but she kept that to herself.

Annie didn't smile back. Kate herself wasn't deeply immersed in current events and culture, but Annie was even less so: no newspapers or magazines out here, no Internet. Did she even have a cell phone? She'd probably never heard of the Paleo diet.

"You're helping with more than nutrition. Now Steve has somebody to talk to, somebody who understands, somebody he trusts—that's a huge gift. Don't underestimate that," Kate said.

The green eyes filled, and Annie put her face in the crook of her arm and had a little cry.

Kate put a hand on her back, gave it a few rubs. "You're both going to get past this."

After wiping her eyes with a flannel sleeve, the hermit's sister put together a wavery smile.

Time to find out if Annie would accept the other gift Kate had brought along with the oranges. "I have an old friend named Marjorie," Kate said, "someone I went to college with. She isn't a psychologist, at least not yet, but I think she's very smart about emotions."

Annie had stopped eating and was watching her carefully.

"I talk to her about my problems a lot. She's a good listener, and has great ideas about what to do." Marjorie had been invaluable in helping Kate get to the bottom of two murder cases, but she didn't tell Annie that. "She's taking courses toward a Master's degree in psychology, which is what she was doing when she found out she was pregnant and decided she had to get married. Now she's divorced with two little kids."

Annie went back to her orange, but slowly. "That doesn't sound like an easy life."

"It's not, for sure," Kate said. "But maybe it's made her even wiser. Would you like to talk to her? You can use my cell phone. We'd have to drive someplace where there's better coverage than here, but you wouldn't have to move your van. We could go in my truck."

"But I'm not the one who needs help," Annie said. "Steve is." She looked around as she said it, probably worried that he was listening. He'd gotten more relaxed about Kate's visits, but he usually came late and appeared suddenly, like a ghost of the war that had damaged his mind.

"You're coping amazingly well," Kate said. "But it's a strain to take care of someone with PTSD." Was that the first time she'd used the acronym with Annie? "Especially out here, where you're isolated and can't take a break."

"I'm fine," Annie said. She tossed the orange peels into the plastic bag they were using for trash.

"You're one heck of a strong woman," Kate said. "But your nervous system has to be screaming for relief. Think of how many times you cry during a day. Do you have trouble sleeping? Do you feel like you're always on guard?"

Annie looked at the ground.

Kate spoke gently. "Marjorie was telling me it's very common even for professionals to get burned out. She called it 'caretaker fatigue' and 'secondary PTSD.' It might be especially difficult if Steve has told you some of the experiences that are troubling him."

Annie was frowning and biting a fingernail. "I don't know," she said finally.

"Think about it, and let me know if you decide to take Marjorie up on the offer. She'd be happy to talk with you, and she's a great resource. It might help you help Steve."

* * *

Before leaving Annie, Kate pressed most of the air out of three plastic grocery bags of trash and stuffed them into her daypack. Just for fun she followed a new trail she'd found. She'd been on it once before, but only as far as the wooden bridge that arched over a stream, or what little the drought had left of a stream. She'd stopped there to draw the bridge, but this time she crossed it, her steps loud on the boards, and kept going. Since it headed west from the Loyalhanna it would take her up to Watkins Spur.

Packing out the trash might be even more helpful to Annie and Steve than bringing them food. They had to keep bags of trash inside the van, because any food scraps or wrappers put outside would attract critters. They couldn't hang food and trash from tree branches, high enough to be out of the reach of bears and smaller nuisance animals like raccoons and mice. That's what people who tent-camped often did, but hanging bags would advertise the van's location. So they piled up trash in the passenger side footwell until Annie made a grocery run.

Annie said sometimes the bags got smelly and the odors kept her awake. She had plenty of things to lose sleep over, and lack of sleep could undermine her health. Kate hoped Annie would agree to talk to Marjorie, who often came up with ideas and strategies Kate hadn't thought of. Coursework meant Marjorie was familiar with the latest therapies, too. She'd said caretaker fatigue was manageable, and so was PTSD, with good counseling.

The trail had looked like it would take Kate southwest, but it faked her out with a hairpin turn and headed northwest. She kept climbing, expecting another turn, but it didn't come. Rats. She was going to top the ridge much farther north than she wanted. And it was getting late. She was glad she had a flashlight in her pocket.

Finally she got to Watkins, its broken pavement a welcome sight that pointed her home to her camper. She looked forward to getting her daypack off; the stink of the trash on her back wasn't a pleasant companion. She wouldn't take her pack inside the camper since she didn't want to find herself lying awake with the odor like Annie. She'd figure something out. Maybe use bungee cords to tie the pack to her bumper, then hustle it into a dumpster as soon as she got to Roll and Rest.

Five minutes later, she saw the house she thought she'd never go near again. The breezeway light was on, and a black SUV was parked in the driveway.

Quiet. The only sound was her own footsteps. Good.

Then she jumped as a flash of light exploded silently, illuminating the meadow behind the house.

One heck of a flash. Much brighter than a lamp being turned on and off, or the blue flicker of a television. Kate had heard satellites occasionally give off intense bursts of light as they reflect sunlight to the earth, but this one hadn't come from the sky. It had come from the back of the house.

Again: a brilliant instant that opened the field behind the house and touched the trees beyond with silver.

Kate wracked her brain for things that made bright flashes and no noise.

Curiosity killed the cat, she said to herself. But she was already walking closer to the house. She had to pass it to get to her truck.

# SEVENTEEN

The front windows were dark. She wasn't going to snoop, but she'd be alert as she walked by the place. Whatever the flashes were, they made her uneasy.

Eyes on the house, she almost stepped on the small lump at the bottom of the driveway. The breezeway light caught fur ruffling in the breeze. Another squirrel. At least it was in one piece.

She turned on her flashlight and shielded it from the house with her left hand. No, the squirrel wasn't in one piece. All four paws had been amputated, and the stumps were packed with dirt. The animal had been maimed and left to run away on its stumps. Not the work of a hawk or an owl or a coyote. Only human cruelty could have such a result.

A door opened. Kate snicked her flashlight off as a teenaged girl stepped into the breezeway.

Short dark hair. Not Sharon.

Crouching, Kate moved quickly past the driveway and into the pine woods beside the road. She didn't want to be seen walking along Watkins Spur this close to the house. Her instincts told her she didn't want the man who came here to know she was in the vicinity. She wondered if the police had come to check the place out again. Maybe not—she'd given her statement to Sgt. Dewey only yesterday.

Another girl followed the first. Taller, with long blonde hair.

The first one opened the back door of the vehicle and both of them got in. Neither said a word. Kate eased herself behind a tree.

After a moment, a bulkier figure. A man. Behind him, another shape, and Kate's nerves jangled.

A dog. A big German shepherd.

She couldn't outrun a dog. And if the animal came after her, evading it would be only the first of her problems. The man would be right behind it.

The dog was looking toward her. The breezeway light reached the trees, and Kate withdrew into the shadow of the biggest one, standing straight in its darkness.

She heard a growl. A bright finger of light probed the space around the tree for a few long seconds.

"There's nothing there, you stupid mutt," the man said.

Kate felt a light breeze on her cheek, blowing her scent toward the house along with the potent smell of the trash in her pack. The dog's nose must be on fire: he knew exactly where she was. But the space around her had gone dark again.

"Zeus! Goddammit!" A jingle of tags.

She risked a look. The man was holding the dog's collar with one hand and opening the front passenger door with the other.

"Goddam rabbits," he said as the dog leaped into the SUV. "You've always been a jerk about goddam rabbits." He slammed the door and must have caught the dog's tail, because it yelped. He opened it and shut it again, then started around the front of the vehicle. Kate retreated behind the pine.

The driver's door slammed, the engine started. As the headlights backed down the driveway, she edged around her guardian tree to stay within its moving shadow.

Maybe what the man was doing with the girls was perfectly innocent. But maybe it wasn't. She didn't like their silence—that wasn't normal for girls their age, was it? Didn't they usually chatter and laugh, boisterous as puppies?

The tortured squirrel made her sick. She'd find a way to report it. Some authority needed to look into whatever was going on at this house, and if the police had missed their opportunity maybe getting some other organization involved could help. She hoped somebody figured it out before something awful happened to the girls.

Kate walked down Watkins to her truck, realizing with a shiver that Walter Tremblay had driven his black SUV right past it. He'd know she'd been in the area. She hung her reeking pack on the outside mirror and tried to calm herself. She'd never park here again.

He knew her vehicle, but he didn't know she lived in it. Or where she stayed.

* * *

She still felt edgy as she drove into Roll and Rest and backed into her site. Dinner was going to be simple. She had a couple of frozen entrees for nights like this, when she wanted something fast and simple.

When she got out of the truck to plug the camper into shore power, Carson was climbing up the tree next to the house. He was really athletic, as Savvy had said. Quick as the monkeys Kate had seen on TV nature specials. If she hadn't known better, she'd say he had a prehensile tail.

She was about to call out to the boy when the back door opened and his mother came across the patio.

"Kate, is that you?" She must have seen the camper's headlights from the dining room window. Her voice was strained.

"Hey, Yvonne." Kate hoped she didn't sound as rattled as she felt. But it didn't matter, since her friend sounded worse.

"I don't know what to do. I don't know where Savvy is." She wrung her hands. "Duval isn't here; he had to work late."

"Did you call the school?" Kate plugged her electrical cord into the post and met her friend on the gravel path.

"Yes, when she was half an hour late. We were supposed to go shopping, clothes shopping. She wouldn't want to miss that. Something must have happened to her."

"What about the police?"

"I called them too. They'll look for her. But maybe she's been kidnapped. She could be a hundred miles from here by now."

Kate touched her friend's arm. "Yvonne, hold on. She's been getting forgetful recently. She probably forgot about the shopping trip."

*"Then where is she?"* Yvonne turned away and put her hands to her face. "I'm sorry, Kate, I didn't mean to yell at you. I'm just so worried. I need to drive around looking for her, but I keep crying so hard I can't see."

"Yvonne. She's forgotten. She's been forgetting lots of things, and the shopping trip is just one more. She's not in danger," Kate said, with as much certainty as she could muster. "Where does she usually go after school?"

"She usually comes straight home. She isn't in any clubs like Carson."

"Do you know the names of her friends? I bet that's where she is, with one of them."

"No—" The word was a wail. "I don't think she has any friends."

"Let's do what you said, drive around and look for her. She's forgotten, or spaced out, or she's with a friend. Whatever's happening, if she sees the car she'll recognize it." Savvy would know the car blindfolded—the old rattletrap was audible for at least a block.

"Yes, yes, let's go." Yvonne's voice was more under control now that she had something to do.

"I'll drive. That way you can look harder, and be ready to jump out and give her a big hug," Kate said.

That, apparently, was what Yvonne needed to hear. She hurried to the Dodge.

They cruised slowly around the school. It was dark, and empty as far as they could tell. One car, an old Ford sedan, was parked in a corner of the lot, but when their headlights hit it two startled faces appeared above the headrests.

Yvonne looked, shook her head. "I hope she's not hanging out with some boy in a car."

"She isn't. She's only nine, for Pete's sake." Kate was thinking of the girl's personality as much as her age: Savvy seemed way too serious for backseat romance.

Kate followed Yvonne's directions, taking lefts and rights until she was completely lost. A neighborhood of larger houses, followed by smaller houses. Then an intersection that looked familiar.

"Is this Magnolia?" Kate asked.

"Yes," Yvonne said. "How did you know?"

"This is where the girl who got the ride from me got out, night before last."

"Oh, right, I knew that, you told me. My mind isn't working right."

"You're too worried to think," Kate said. Then she saw Savvy. "But you can stop. There she is."

Across the street, the girl was walking slowly along the sidewalk. She stopped, staring at her mother's car.

Yvonne erupted from the Dodge and raced to her daughter, who was lost to Kate's view by an overwhelming maternal hug.

I must be psychic, Kate thought. This was the scene she'd envisioned to comfort Yvonne, and that's how things had played out.

They came back to the car together, and Yvonne put Savvy in the front seat.

"Are you okay?" Kate asked. When she heard Yvonne close the back door, she made a U-turn.

"I feel okay. I just get so confused," Savvy said. "I went home and took a nap. And then I remembered I was supposed to do something, meet somebody, so I walked over here and looked for my friend Daphne. I think that was who I was supposed to meet, but I couldn't remember which house was hers. Then I got lost. Then I couldn't decide whether to look for Daphne's house or mine." She was crying.

"I'm glad I got you scheduled with the specialist in Pittsburgh," Yvonne said. "I really want you checked out." She was leaning forward from the back seat, with her hand on Savvy's shoulder.

"Ugh, doctors," Savvy said. "The family doc didn't tell us anything. And we can't afford a fancier kind."

"We're going to afford it," Yvonne said grimly as Kate turned into the campground driveway. She stopped at the back of the house and Savvy got out.

"Kind of a compliment that she thought she was meeting Daphne instead of you," Kate said, turning the Dodge off and handing the keys over the seatback to Yvonne. "Not every kid gets her mother mixed up with her friends."

"Maybe you're right. But I wish she didn't get mixed up, period." Yvonne opened her door, kept her voice low. "She told me the car was familiar, but she didn't know whose it was."

Kate got out of the old car and stretched, arms high, letting her muscles squeeze themselves free of tension. "I'm glad you're taking her to the guy in Pittsburgh."

"I wish the appointment was sooner. I hope I can hang on that long."

"You can. You're a trooper, Yvonne."

\* \* \*

The screechy noise that awakened her seemed to be coming from everywhere. Kate slid out of her bunk, fighting her way up out of a deep sleep and a dream of paddling against a stiff current with a German shepherd in the bow of her boat, growling and snapping at her hands. Was it the smoke alarm? The carbon monoxide alarm?

She finally pinpointed the shriek: her phone, which she'd left on the table next to the book about Pennsylvania wildlife. It was an alert from the National Weather Service about high winds in the area, in Allegheny and Westmoreland counties. A forecast of winds at fifty miles an hour, gusting to seventy-five. She could already hear moaning in the trees between the campground and the river, and her camper rocked a little on the truck's shocks.

Best to put another line around the boat on the picnic table. The table itself was bolted to a cement pad, so it wasn't going anywhere. The kayak wouldn't be blown away—it was locked to the table—but the cable was stiff and couldn't be snugged down tight like a strap. If the wind got under the boat it could shudder it around, lifting and dropping it an inch or so. That would be enough to ding the wood trim along gunwales where they hit the table. Not to mention making enough noise to drive Kate nuts.

She shrugged her way into her leather jacket and went into the blustery dawn. One of the compartments on the side of the camper yielded the bag of webbing straps she needed. She glanced at her watch: five o'clock.

What the heck, she'd put two straps on the boat. She took the first one out and dropped the bag on the edge of the table. The strap was in a loop, the end through the buckle. They were all like that, to keep the whole mess of them from getting tangled up with each other in the bag.

She undid the buckle of the first strap and got it around the boat. The ends dropped under the table, so the next step was a knee on the bench and her shoulders under the table, snagging the two ends and threading the buckle.

Way too much work, way too early.

She left the strap loose, sat on the bench, and pulled it until the buckle came to her. Found the end and snugged the strap tight. One down, one to go.

She hadn't bothered to zip her jacket, and wind stripped the warmth from her barely awake body. Lights were coming on in Yvonne's house. She glanced at John's van: his light was on, too. An extra-early morning for everyone. The big Winnebago was dark; Richard was away in Ohio, staying with family and making funeral arrangements for Donna. What a hard time for him. He'd asked her to keep an eye on the RV, and she'd check it after the kayak was secure, make sure all his windows were closed and nothing had been left outside.

The wind was blowing debris now, twigs and leaves. Her eyes felt gritty, and she sneezed. In a minute she'd be back inside her camper, safe from the wind's fury. Coffee. She should have hit the button on the machine before she came out here, and the magic stuff would have been waiting for her when she was done with this chore. She picked up the second strap.

Something large erupted toward her. Jaws clamped onto her right forearm, and she felt the vibration of the dog's growl in her bones.

The animal was large, a dark German shepherd, and it was pulling hard, its front legs were braced on the bench. One of them slipped off, and the dog lurched. Fireballs of pain exploded along Kate's arm. Then it got its huge paw back on the bench and tugged.

It was winning. Kate felt her shoulder, her torso, tilting toward the animal. Her seated position on the bench kept her from getting a leg out as a brace to stop her from going over.

She pulled her right leg up, swiveled on the bench, and put her foot into the dog's chest. Now the two of them were locked in place. The dog wasn't winning anymore, but it wasn't losing either.

Shouting at a dog in attack mode was useless. She tried to wiggle her arm inside the leather sleeve to see if she could slide out of her jacket, but that made the dog bite harder. Damn, that hurt. What could she do, with her right arm trapped? She had to break his grip, or he would keep pulling until he had her off the bench. And then he would go for her throat.

"Yvonne! Help!" The wind grabbed her shout and shredded it.

The second strap was still in her left hand. She held it in her mouth and used her free hand to grab the bag of straps and hold it over the dog's eyes.

The animal was surprised. The grip on her arm loosened, but only briefly. It didn't need to see to bite. Kate's arm throbbed.

She took the bag off the eyes and poked it into the gap between the teeth. She had to interfere with the dog's breathing. She hated to put her fingers anywhere near those huge teeth, but she had to.

It took some time. The bag was flexible but the straps inside less so. She just kept poking, pressing the bag against the dog's jaw with her palm and using her fingers to shove material into the gap.

It wasn't a very wide gap, because her arm wasn't much of a mouthful for this monster.

Finally she was rewarded with some hoarseness in its breathing, a hesitancy in the rhythm. But the grip on her arm didn't change.

She lessened the pressure on the bag. It stayed in place, and she cupped her palm over the dog's nose and pressed.

The hoarse breathing faltered. Stopped.

The jaws came off her arm and the dog dropped its muzzle, working its tongue against the nylon bag in its mouth.

The bag dropped to the ground. The dog coughed. And then lunged.

Kate kicked with her right foot as hard as she could, hitting it in the chest.

Still it came on. With both hands free now, she jammed the loop of the second strap over the dog's head, around its neck. The jaws caught her right arm again, but their hold wasn't solid. Most of what the animal had in its mouth was bulky leather sleeve.

This was the dog she'd seen outside the house on Watkins Spur, wasn't it? What had the man called it? Some Greek god's name.

Ares, maybe? "Ares! No!"

The dog released its grip a fraction, but it was only to get a better one. Its jaws landed in the place on Kate's arm that was already bitten. Stars exploded in her brain.

"Hades! No!"

The dog growled harder. As she'd suspected, shouting at it wasn't helping.

With her right foot braced against the dog's chest, Kate pulled with all the strength in her left arm on the strap. It tightened. She saw it disappear into the animal's thick fur.

Inspiration struck. Zeus. "Zeus! No! Goddam rabbits!"

The dog let go.

It was still breathing, but having a lot of trouble. Gasping. That's what had made it let go, not that she'd remembered its name.

A piercing whistle cut through the wind, and the dog dropped its front paws from the bench and half-ran, half-staggered away, past the house and down the driveway, the strap dragging beside it.

The dog's dark shape merged with the silhouette of a man's figure beside an SUV at the side of the road.

Door slam. Engine roar. Squeal of wheels.

* * *

"I know the dog," Kate told Yvonne.

"Later." She was focused like a laser on the road. Leaves and twigs and small branches skittered across the pavement. "Got to get you to the hospital."

"I don't think my arm's broken," Kate said. "I can move my hand. But it hurts."

"I know the dog," she told the nurse in the emergency room.

Kate had a massive bruise, but she'd been right: the arm wasn't broken. Her jacket sleeve was torn in too many places to count. Thank heavens she'd been wearing leather. She wouldn't need rabies shots, but the nurse gave her a pill for the pain.

"We'll call animal control."

"And the police, please."

"I know the dog," she told Brandon.

She knew his name from their conversation at the Fall Crafts Fair. At the end of her first hospitalization he'd asked her a few questions, but this time he stayed more than a minute. Things were looking up.

Or maybe not. It probably wasn't a good thing to be on a first-name basis with cops investigating incidents she'd had a part in, however unwillingly.

He sat in the other chair in the exam room and ignored her statement about knowing the dog. "So do you consider yourself accident-prone?" He was smiling. "Why do I keep finding you in the hospital?"

"My visits here aren't because of accidents."

He was chuckling. "Somebody's dog gets loose, bites you—or tries to bite you, doesn't give you a single puncture—" He picked up her jacket, looked at the sleeve. "Looks like you got gummed, not bitten. Did the dog have a Medicare card?"

"If it weren't for that leather jacket, I'd be in a lot worse shape." Kate was annoyed. "This was a trained attack German shepherd, set on me by someone in a dark SUV parked on the street in front of Roll and Rest."

At last he was listening. "And you know that because?"

"Because I saw him." She kept herself from rolling her eyes. "The person standing near the SUV whistled, and that's when the dog left me. The driver must have been watching, saw that the attack wasn't going well. He drove off with the dog."

"So you beat up a geriatric German shepherd?"

"His name is Zeus, and he belongs to somebody named Walter Tremblay, who saw my truck camper parked near his house at the end of Watkins around dusk. He must have figured out where I was staying and got lucky when the wind warning brought me outside."

She was suddenly tired, maybe from the painkiller the nurse had given her. "Ask Sgt. Dewey about it. He knows how I found Tremblay's name." She didn't want to tell the whole story again—blue phone, pink phone, Sharon.

"You're just full of information," Brandon said. "Anything else?"

But all those sentences in a row had taken the last of her energy. She closed her eyes and let her head fall back against the headrest. The pain medication was knocking her out.

"You've got all kinds of rabbits to chase," she said. "Goddam rabbits."

Brandon probably thought she was nuts, but she was too tired to explain.

# EIGHTEEN

Yvonne drove her back to the campground, and Kate crawled up to her bunk. Sleep fell on her like snow, soft and all-embracing, and she didn't wake up until noon the next day.

Her arm throbbed no matter what position she tried. Unable to summon the energy to do anything, even read, she settled for rest instead of sleep. Turned on her little radio tuned to NPR and set the volume low. She wasn't really listening, but the quiet voices were soothing.

Mid-afternoon. Yvonne knocked on the camper door and then climbed in, bringing two carrot muffins and a plastic container of soup. Kate had been thinking vaguely about food, but when her friend handed one of the muffins on a paper plate up to her bunk, hunger sharpened and announced itself with a major stomach growl.

Yvonne heard it and laughed. "Sounds like I'm just in time." She put the soup in the fridge, told Kate to call if she needed anything, and left her to rest.

The muffin was a godsend. It made her thirsty, though, so she climbed down and drank a glass of water. Too much trouble to make coffee? Yikes. She wasn't herself. Back to bed.

Half-asleep, she was roused by John's signature slaps on the door. He must be ready to repair the generator, but he sure had lousy timing. "Just a sec," she yelled, and climbed down in a fog, pulled on jeans and unlocked the door. Yes! He had a package of parts under one arm and a metal toolbox under the other. She went into the bright daylight and unlocked the generator compartment.

Pleased, she went back to the bunk and the twilight of near-sleep, her lullaby John's off-key humming and the occasional clatter of tools.

She must have fallen into full sleep, or maybe the handyman didn't want to disturb her again; he might have heard from Yvonne about Kate's canine encounter, or he could tell from her first sluggish appearance that she was under the weather.

When she woke it was quiet. And dark. She got up and heated half of Yvonne's split pea soup in the microwave, then read at the dinette, browsing through the book on Pennsylvania plants. Wasn't sure she'd be able to sleep after so much inactivity, but went to bed anyway.

\* \* \*

She woke at five, surprised she'd slept through the night and wondering if waking at this hour was a subconscious response to the twenty-four hour "anniversary" of Zeus's attack.

Resting and reading the previous day had been necessary, but a second lazy, unstructured day had less appeal. Living in the camper's small space made cabin fever an ever-present possibility. She'd have to get outside. She couldn't paddle or bike, but she could walk.

After awkwardly brushing her teeth and making coffee with her left hand, she sat and drank, staring idly out her dinette window, letting her mind wake up.

Then she remembered the maimed squirrel, and shuddered. An online search brought up the site for an organization called People for the Ethical Treatment of Animals. Its mission statement focused on animals in laboratories and the food industry, but it included rodents and birds considered pests. Close enough. She clicked on the complaint form and filled it out, typing on the tablet keyboard with her left index finger. Slow going.

She finished her coffee and watched leaves swirl around the patio, some of them claiming seats. Then her view of the chairs was eclipsed by a big diesel van with West Virginia plates that rumbled in and stopped outside the office. Good, more business for Roll and Rest.

She picked up a pencil, gently, with her right hand. Started to write her name: a test.

Sparkles of pain shot from elbow to fingertips. Damn.

Her forearm was a solid bruise, its colors evolving from reddish toward spectacular shades of blue and purple. The swelling seemed to have gone down some, but her two arms were considerably different in size, the right thicker than the left. The injured arm felt hot.

The bad news: she wouldn't be drawing for a few days. Which made it even more imperative that she go out now. Down to the beach. She'd sit in the sun and choose subjects for drawings she could only work on in her head.

She rinsed her cup, half-filled it with water and took a bottle of Ibuprofen from the medicine cabinet. The dull orange tablet dropped into her palm with a sting of memory: she and her former boyfriend used to call the drug Vitamin I because they took it so often after vigorous weekends backpacking, biking or paddling. Without him, she didn't push herself nearly as hard; she couldn't remember the last time she'd needed this stuff. After her relationship with him had failed and she'd become a nomadic RVer, her pain had been emotional. Nothing she could take for that.

She yawned, which reminded her of poor Donna. How Richard had said she'd been yawning, and he'd suggested she go to bed, and she'd smiled at him.

Her last smile.

The lump in Kate's throat meant the pill would have to wait. She sat at the dinette and ran her thumb across her La Brea Tar Pits cup, feeling the raised lettering. She was in a gloomy state this morning, wasn't she, with her mind running to her old boyfriend and to Donna? Probably a reaction to being sidelined as an artist.

The big white van started up. It was a class B camper built on a crew cab chassis and sat high on its wheels, which meant either four-wheel drive or just a jacked-up suspension. Four-wheel would be a good choice around here, with plenty of rugged roads to explore. She'd never driven a 4x4 but it must be fun.

The van rumbled off toward the middle of the campground. Yvonne would be ready for coffee and conversation.

She and Yvonne had been through a lot together. They'd known each other less than a month, but events had brought them close. With her generator repaired, Kate could move on. She'd miss Yvonne and Savvy. And Donna, too, in a different way.

But she wouldn't miss the disturbing events that had been happening around Union Hill. And she wished she could be sure the trouble wouldn't follow her. If she went a couple hundred miles the first day, maybe she wouldn't have to worry about that.

Kate swallowed the orange tablet, then pushed her cup away, trying to let go of her sadness about Donna along with it. Memories were important as long as she didn't let them act like tar pits, pulling her down and trapping her.

Her knock under the sign with the cartoon cats was left-handed.

"Hey, Kate." Yvonne's long nose reminded Kate of a heron's bill this morning. "How're you feeling?"

"I can't complain. My arm should be broken."

"You can complain all you want," Yvonne said, closing the door behind her friend and heading for the kitchen. "That must have been terrifying, having a hundred-pound dog clamped to your arm. I wish I'd heard you shout."

"I could barely hear myself, the wind was so loud," Kate said. She took her usual chair. "You've got a new customer. Where're they from?"

"New England someplace. And not them, he. Pleasant guy, Sean something. You'll probably meet him yourself soon enough." Yvonne put two coffees on the table.

The name gave Kate a twinge of sadness. Sean had been the name of the FBI agent who had saved her life in Maine last summer, when she'd stumbled into the middle of a major drug bust. He was a sweet man, and if she hadn't been traveling something more might have happened between them. But she was always leaving, in this new lifestyle of hers.

"Oh, Kate, Duval got a promotion!" Yvonne said. "And a raise. You know, so many bad things have been going on, it's such a relief to have something to celebrate."

"Give him my congratulations," Kate said. "That's great. You guys need a break."

"It'll help pay for Savvy's treatment, whatever that turns out to be. I'm worried it might be really expensive."

"A little less worry never hurt anyone." Kate rubbed her arm, wished she hadn't, and took a sip of coffee. Using her left hand was beginning to feel normal.

Holding a cup was one thing. She couldn't draw with her left hand. Damn the dog.

No, it wasn't the dog's fault. He'd just been doing what he was trained to do. She hoped his mysterious owner Walter Tremblay would end up sorry he'd set Zeus on her. "I'm still trying to work out why Zeus's handler had him attack me," she said.

"Maybe the police will get us some answers."

Kate liked the use of "us" instead of "you."

Besides Duval's promotion, the other Chouinard family news was that Carson had a girlfriend. "His teachers have been telling me he's socially backward, so this is an excellent sign," Yvonne said. "Not that I'm exactly looking forward to his teenage years. But of course I want him to develop the way a boy should." She smiled. "He was on the phone with her for fifteen minutes. I haven't had a conversation that long with him in years."

"Hooray," Kate said. "He's about to complicate his life. In a good way."

"He's going to complicate my life, too," Yvonne laughed. "It's what being a mother's all about."

* * *

She was headed back to her camper when the door on the side of the newcomer's van opened and a tall man in a black jacket and jeans got out and came toward her. Dark hair, gold eyes—

She stopped, her heart skipping a beat.

"Kate?"

"Sean!" she said. "What—how?"

"Let me translate. What am I doing here and how did I find you. Is that about right?"

He gave her a hug, then caught the look of pain on her face.

"What's the matter?"

"Oh, nothing, I mean—" She was still flustered. "I got chewed on by an aging attack dog. A bruise from hell, but no real damage."

"Your life is just too exciting."

"And yours?"

"Let's go for a walk, and talk about our exciting lives," he said. "I bet you've found a few trails around here."

Before Kate led him to the conservation land along the river, she stopped at her camper to get another Ibuprofen. Rusty was sitting on the picnic table at her site, next to her kayak.

"Do you like cats? This orange number is the alpha cat in the neighborhood. Probably in the whole county. He's the Boss, the Man, the grand poobah. Rusty, meet Sean."

"I understand you're a bigwig," Sean said to Rusty.

"Wig? No, I'm betting that fur is real," Kate said, and climbed into her camper for vitamin I. When she came out, Sean was sitting astride the bench, stroking the striped back. Rusty was looking over his shoulder at Sean, blinking slowly in appreciation.

"I guess you do like cats."

"Heck, no. This is self-defense, to keep him from nuzzling me in the ear."

"I should have warned you. Watch your ears around Rusty."

As they walked down the path to the beach, Sean said, "I'm lucky to have caught up with you. The tracker battery's getting pretty low, but it transmits only when you drive, and you've been sitting here for three weeks."

"Tracker? You were tracking me? How—" Then she remembered. "Oh, you weasel! Last summer in Maine I saw you do something to my truck, and I didn't know you were FBI, so I didn't want to drive it after that—"

"So you rode the motorcycle I loaned you—"

"And it got shot to bits—"

"Right out from under you."

They smiled at each other, and Kate felt a warmth spread through her that had nothing to do with the sunshine that gilded the beach and the water beyond. They stood together, not talking for a few minutes, the only conversation the one between wavelets and wind.

Then Sean cleared his throat. "So look, I'm a little embarrassed I did it this way. I should have called, but then there was an ATF task force forming up for a job in Pittsburgh, and I was already on the road for another job, and—so I didn't have that card with me, the one you gave me, with your phone number."

He looked at her, worry on his face. "You don't think it was creepy of me, do you? To just show up? I mean, I could see on the mapping software that your camper wasn't moving, and I wondered what was going on, if you were okay or if you'd had a breakdown—"

"And being FBI and all, you didn't have the resources to look up my phone number, of course—"

"Yep, you're right, I could have done that." He laughed, his face flushing with embarrassment. "But that would be too easy. Much more fun to drop in on you. And there was this great RV in the confiscated vehicles pool at the ATF in Morgantown, so even if I didn't find you I got a nice trip. Don't you agree that was the way to go?"

"Oh, I do. I absolutely do." Whether it was the Ibuprofen or Sean's presence, the pain in her arm had subsided.

"Seriously," he said, "I had some vacation days, and I wasn't very far away. Coming here just seemed like the right thing to do." He gave her a sideways smile.

"Seriously, it's fine."

"I have to warn you, though, I never know how much time off I'll get. My work life isn't nine-to-five predictable. I'm hoping I can have four or five days here—I'm owed them—but I can never be sure."

"Too bad you missed all the fun. My dog-bite's history."

"Not a bite. Dog-jaw compression injury," Sean said. "Don't exaggerate."

She punched him lightly with her left fist, and they shared another smile.

He looked at the lake, his face tightening. "I hope the trouble here is finished. But I'm not sure it is."

"I know a lot, and I've given all the info to the cops." They should have picked up Walter by now, found out what he was doing with the girls. "And I'm on red alert, believe me." She took a couple of steps, and he followed, and they ambled north along the trail. "The last time I hung around with you, in Maine, too much happened."

"My life since then has been almost as exciting as yours, but of course I can't talk about it with unauthorized persons." He smiled apologetically at the official phrase. "So bring me up to speed. What's been going on here?"

Kate gave him the high points, or maybe the low points: Donna's accidental death, the attempt on her own life when she was set adrift, her encounter with Sharon, and the man with the dog who was doing something shady with girls at the house on Watkins Spur.

"You think he's molesting children?" Sean asked. "Or trafficking runaways?"

"Could be both of those. Or maybe taking pictures. Child porn," Kate said. She described the flashes of light she'd seen coming from the old house. A strobe flash was her best guess.

"So the local cops are onto this guy?" Sean stopped and turned to her. "I don't like this, Kate. Why are you being attacked?"

"Maybe Sharon's connected to the dog owner, and talked about my camper, described it. But for sure he saw it on the road to his house, which probably convinced him I was nosing around. And there's only one campground near Union Hill."

"But the other time, when you went adrift in your kayak, that was before you'd found out about the house, wasn't it?"

"That's right," Kate said. "Why would I have been on the pervert's radar then?" They'd started walking again, and she was looking for the dead squirrel she'd found. Not there. Some bigger critter must have gotten it, maybe a coyote.

"Hey, she said, "you're a veteran, aren't you? Want to meet a fellow vet? He's in tough shape. Maybe he'd take advice from you he wouldn't take from me."

She filled him in on the Loyalhanna Hermit as they walked. "He's obviously dealing with the aftermath of some huge trauma," she said. "But withdrawing from society the way he's doing is not a good strategy in the long run."

"That's right," Sean said. "People are social creatures, there's no way around it." He gave her a look, eyes like gold foil shot with copper. "Sounds as if he's got a very understanding sister."

That look, those eyes of his. She was thrilled, and a bit scared. She liked Sean a lot, maybe too much. But he seemed to be all business, trying to make sense of the spooky events of the past three weeks. Except for that first brief hug, he hadn't touched her.

Maybe he was more comfortable solving crimes than dealing with women. But he'd come a long way to see her—that must mean something.

"You'll probably meet the hermit's sister. I'm not sure he'll show himself, especially to a guy. And be warned: he might be listening to everything you say, even if you don't know he's there."

"So he's bugged the woods?" Crow's feet bracketed Sean's eyes when he smiled. "I deal with bugging devices all the time in my line of work."

"The only bugs out here are real bugs."

"Real bugs, real trees. My kind of place."

"I'm glad you're willing to talk to Annie. I think it'll cheer her up to meet someone who's been in the service and isn't a wreck afterwards."

"Well, I didn't go through whatever happened to her brother. I saw some light action, but nothing disturbing. I got into the intelligence end of things early."

They sat on the boulders near the water where Kate had first seen Annie. The day had warmed up; Kate pushed the sleeves of her fleece up.

"Holy cats!" Sean said, looking at her arm.

"Hey, get your own line," Kate said. "I'm the one who says 'Holy cats.'"

"Okay, Holy—wombats," Sean said. "That's one ferocious bruise. Your dog may have been old but he was dedicated."

"Not my dog."

"Have to confess, I don't even know what a wombat is," he said. "Do you?"

"An Australian groundhog. Eats plants. Cute, furry thing."

"She know her animals." Annie's voice came out of the bushes, and then she stepped into sight, smiling. She was learning her brother's tricks.

Kate pulled her sleeves back down. "Annie, this is Sean. Sean, Annie."

They nodded at each other.

Annie sat. "Any friend of Kate's," she said.

"This is a spontaneous visit," Kate said, "or I would have brought some supplies. My friend here dropped in from—" she glanced at him, caught his warning look—"outer space."

Annie smiled again. She was looking better. Maybe she'd decided to talk to Marjorie. "You don't look Martian."

"All men are from Mars," Sean said. "I'm glad I don't look it."

"His antennae are retractable," Kate said.

On her way out the door of her camper, Kate had tossed some apples in her pocket. She offered them around, and the three of them sat comfortably together for a while, eating the crisp MacIntoshes. She didn't think Steve would join them, not with a stranger along.

"Your brother is a brave man with a big problem," Sean said.

"He gets nervous around people, doesn't trust anyone."

"He trusts you."

"He does. And he lets me see him the way he really is. But he gets embarrassed when something triggers his fear in front of other people."

"What are his triggers?"

"Mostly loud noises. Flashes of light, too, but mostly noises. A car backfiring, Harley accelerating., door slamming. Like that. Out here he doesn't have to deal with those things."

"What about thunderstorms?"

"Yes, that's the only natural trigger. He crouches, and wants to get to cover." She lowered her voice. "He looks really scared."

"I bet he doesn't want to do that around people who don't know him and don't understand," Kate said. "That's why he couldn't keep a job, right?"

Annie nodded. "You got it."

"Yep, I can understand that," Sean said. "I was really jumpy when I got back too. But I'm sure I didn't see anything as bad as what your brother went through. Was he Marines?"

"Army. K-9 corps."

Sean glanced at Kate and raised an eyebrow. Probably thinking of the dog that had bitten her. No, compressed her.

"Please tell your brother I wish him well," Sean said, standing. "I hope he sees this time in the woods as a transition. Next step? Counseling can be a huge help—there are counselors who've been in his shoes, in his combat boots. And he might get in touch with some of the guys in his unit. The VA would help him do that, and the Internet would make it easy, wherever they are."

"Thank you," Annie said. "I'll tell him that."

Kate and Sean walked farther, to the little bridge. They stood at the rail and listened to the water for a while. It was just a trickle, running along a crease in the mud of its bed, but it brightened every pebble it touched. Water was magic—take any stone out and let it dry, and it would be dull as dirt.

They moved on, not speaking much, glancing at one another now and then. When they heard voices coming toward them, Sean stepped off the path and pulled Kate beside him. Two hikers came into view, one man in his fifties and the other much younger, both carrying fishing rods and tackle boxes. They passed, nodding their hellos.

Sean and Kate got back on the trail. A minute later, he said, "Describe the older man."

"What? Why?"

"It's a law enforcement technique, but it's not a bad idea for others, too," Sean said. "To train your mind to notice and remember things, especially vehicles or people. Later, you could find out they're important."

"Okay, let's see. White guy, maybe fifty, just starting to get some gray in his hair, about five-ten. Spends a lot of time outdoors, face tanned and creased. Weight pretty good, maybe 180 or so. Fit. Wouldn't want to get into a fight with him."

"Hey, not bad," Sean said. "You could apply to the FBI."

Kate laughed. "Not a chance. Enough trouble comes to me already. I don't want a job where I'm supposed to go looking for it."

\* \* \*

Where the trail met Watkins Spur, Kate suggested they turn back. "That house I told you about is down this road. Besides, the trail is prettier. And the river."

"Isn't it odd how a place looks different depending on which way you're going through it?" he asked. "I've always noticed that. You can't really retrace your steps."

"You see the other side of things?"

He gave her a smile and a nod.

Thin clouds had dimmed the sun and the air got chilly. They walked a little faster on the way down.

As their footsteps thumped on the wooden bridge, a downy woodpecker flicked from a birch trunk and flew deeper into the trees.

Farther on, near the rocks where they'd sat with Annie, Sean cocked his head. "Do you hear that?"

Kate listened, then shook her head.

He turned and went up the dirt road. Stopped and looked back at her, then scanned in a full circle until she caught up to him.

They moved again, at the same moment but separately. His head was up, his movement tense. He was headed straight for Annie's hidden van.

He stopped again, and she heard it too. An engine running. Had to be the van's.

That was odd. The two hermits wouldn't want to run the engine during the day, when any hiker or fisherman passing by might hear it and find the vehicle. If Annie started the engine, it would be to go to town for supplies. Being seen was okay—as long as the van was on the dirt road, she'd look like anybody else with four-wheel drive who was spending the day in the woods. What she wouldn't want people to notice was that at the end of the day she wasn't going home like everybody else.

She'd get out fast, and get in fast. She and Steve probably had a plan for her returns from a trip to town: she'd park on Watkins Spur while he made sure nobody was nearby, and when he gave her the all clear, she'd hustle the van into the space they'd made and he'd cover the entrance with branches.

The engine running was not in itself a big deal. What alarmed Kate was that it kept running while the van wasn't moving.

A few steps behind Sean, Kate saw him reach the point of the switchback. It took him only a moment to push aside the scrim of cut branches and move behind it, but before he disappeared he pulled a small handgun from an ankle holster.

She slipped in after him, saw what he'd seen seconds ago: Annie in the driver's seat, collapsed on the steering wheel. Motionless.

Kate rushed to the front of the van. Sean had stashed his gun and opened the driver's door. He reached across Annie to pop her seat belt free, then got his hands under her shoulders and pulled her out of the cab. Her head rolled loosely against his chest. Her eyes were closed.

He laid her on the ground, turned off the ignition, and knelt down. Kate knelt beside him as he put two fingers against Annie's neck.

"Godammit," he said softly. Then he scrambled to his feet and disappeared around the back of the van.

Annie's face was flushed, her eyes closed. Kate reached for the pale wrist, knowing it was too late. The hand was cold.

She looked at Annie's face, remembering how she'd smiled as she stepped out of the bushes just a few hours earlier. But Annie wasn't here any more.

At her throat, the green necklace sparkled. Dressed up to go to town? Kate remembered Annie's child-like excitement when she'd tried on that necklace. Awesome, she'd said.

This wasn't what was supposed to happen next.

Kate stood, eased her way around the van, and found Sean crouched inside the rear doors. He shook his head. "Nobody else in here." He scanned the woods around and above her. "I thought I heard somebody."

He came down the step and touched her elbow, moved past her, scanned the area again. Dropped to the ground and crawled partway under the vehicle.

Kneeling, Kate watched him take some pictures with his cell phone. She scrambled to her feet as he slithered out, stood, and went to the passenger side. He pulled the tail of his shirt out and used it to keep his fingers from touching the handle as he opened the door. He glanced at her. "Keep a lookout?"

She turned slowly, looking for movement. But the foliage was dense enough that she couldn't see very far, and that made her uneasy. What was Sean hoping to find in the van?

Then he was beside her, cell in hand. He looked at the screen. "Come on, I need more sky to get service. Let's go down by the rocks."

At the front of the van he swept the cut branches into his arms and threw them on the road, then moved toward the river. He looked around continuously, like a wild creature. At the circle of rocks, he caught her eye and pointed, sweeping his finger in an arc. She understood and faced away from him and the river, watching the woods for any movement.

He spoke quickly into the phone, in a low voice. And then his hand was on her shoulders, his voice in her ear.

"I'm sorry about your friend."

Tears ruined her vision. She wanted to turn, pull him against her. But she looked down, closed her eyes, breathed through the ache in her chest. After a few moments she said, "What happens now?"

"A coroner comes out from town. Tonight and tomorrow, local police examine the scene, looking for physical evidence."

He turned her by her shoulders. "Did Annie ever talk about suicide?"

"No, God, she was taking care of Steve. She had a mission. She wouldn't—"

"Okay, that's what I thought too. She was murdered, then."

It wasn't exactly a surprise; Kate had been thinking of Donna since she saw Annie slumped over the wheel. "How do you know?"

"The tailpipe's plugged, stuffed with rags. Exhaust system's got some leaks, up near the front." He was still vigilant, looking past her. "Maybe her brother wasn't as stable as she thought. Or as grateful as he should have been."

"Maybe it wasn't him. Could be someone we don't know. Those two hikers we passed?"

"Possible," he said. He didn't sound convinced. He'd know the statistics. Annie's brother was much more likely to have killed her than strangers. Most of the time there's a strongly felt reason for murder, and that kind of reason usually comes from a close relationship. Spouses, often. Other family members, too. Siblings.

"Let's wait," he said quietly. "We can get a ride back with the police. Let's just stay alert. We might see something useful."

They stood like two pointer dogs, he facing upstream, she facing downstream. Kate tried to keep from thinking, but it was impossible. Annie. Poor Annie.

Was it really Steve who had killed her? He seemed like the last person in the world to do it. He had so much to lose.

But who else?

And if he was innocent, where was he?

\* \* \*

The vehicles arrived together, a cruiser and a black Blazer with COUNTY CORONER in gold on the side, and parked

214

above them on Watkins Spur. Two policemen, one carrying a canvas satchel, walked down the road. Sean pointed to the van, easily visible with its door open and Annie's body on the ground behind the pile of branches.

The cop with the canvas bag got out a camera and took pictures from the road, then he and his partner moved around the vehicle slowly, looking at everything, the one guy taking pictures. They started with the passenger side, and when they got to Annie the camera snicked away rapid-fire. Lots of close-ups of the body and the ground around it.

The other cop came over to Kate, and Sean stepped away. She couldn't tell the officer much. She didn't know Annie's last name, or whether it was the same as Steve's, and she'd only seen Steve twice, the second time only briefly. She stammered a little, conflicted about exposing him. But she had to—he could be the killer. She described the other hikers they'd seen. Sean's asking her for details right after the two parties passed on the trail had fixed them in her mind. What a fluke. He couldn't have known how useful that would turn out to be.

The cop with the camera must have taken a hundred photos; now he was tying yellow tape to trees around the scene. The officer questioning Kate thanked her and moved on to Sean.

The Blazer eased down the road as far as the switchback, its back-up beeper piercing the quiet air. Two men got out, one of them opening the back doors and the other heading for Annie's body with what looked like a folded-up orange tarp. Kate turned her back.

The birches between her and the river were a gray and yellow blur. Kate wiped her eyes. Was Steve hiding and watching all this activity? He must be a wreck. The scene might bring back some dark memories. Kate worried that his sister's death might tip him over the edge, ripping away the stability Annie had helped him build. And she wasn't here anymore to tell him things would go a lot worse for him if he didn't come forward. He was the prime suspect, and if he tried to stay hidden he'd be vilified as the monster who killed his caring sister.

He'd be hunted. And sooner or later, he'd be found.

She felt Sean's hand on her shoulder and then it dropped away. They looked at the river for a few minutes. The Blazer's engine started.

"C'mon," he said.

Kate was startled: the cruiser was gone and Sean led her to the coroner's Blazer. He nodded at the driver and opened the back door. Getting in, Kate glimpsed a mummy-shaped orange package behind the seats. She didn't look any closer.

Sean got in next to her, shook his head as the Blazer lurched down Watkins Spur. "The exhaust system wasn't in great shape," he said. "And the engine, the part of it that sticks out from under the dashboard, between the front seats? Mechanics call it the doghouse. Not a great design. Anyway, the cover was cracked. It would have leaked exhaust." He looked out the window. "If that vehicle had been properly taken care of, Annie would still be with us."

"Which means a rag in the tailpipe wouldn't necessarily have been fatal?"

"That's true. But it doesn't mean whoever put it there shouldn't be prosecuted."

Going up the campground driveway, the Blazer was strangely quiet. Then Kate realized she was comparing its ride to the Chouinards' old Dodge.

Yvonne came onto the patio. Her worried look changed to relief when she saw them. "Oh, it's you two," she said, and laughed. "It's a little scary when a vehicle with CORONER on the side pulls into your driveway." Then she looked back and forth between them. "What's the matter?"

# NINETEEN

"It's Annie," Kate said.

"Annie Brady? Stayed here a few days in a rusty old class B van?" Apprehension clouded Yvonne's face.

"Yes," Kate said. "I'm sorry. She's dead."

And then both she and Sean stepped forward, because Yvonne looked like she was going to faint.

They got her through the door and into a dining room chair.

"Tell me," she said.

"Suicide or murder," Sean said. "The exhaust pipe had a rag in it. Either she put it there herself or someone else did. Maybe her brother. He wasn't around, at least not that we could see."

"Her brother's a vet with PTSD, back from Afghanistan, and she was out there trying to help him," Kate said. "He's been living in the conservation area for about a year, so he's the cause of the Loyalhanna Hermit stories." No reason not to tell Yvonne now, since Steve couldn't be protected any more.

Yvonne took a thick cardigan lying on the arm of her chair and put it on. She hugged herself but still looked cold. "Annie—" she said, her voice breaking. She tried again. "Annie didn't strike me as the type to do herself in. Of course she only stayed a week, so I didn't know her very well."

"That was Kate's impression, too," Sean said.

"A couple of hikers passed us, out on the trail, after we talked to her," Kate said. "So maybe they should be questioned. Another possibility is that creepy guy I told you about at the old house. It isn't too far from where Annie's van was hidden—it's above it, on the ridge. And we know he's at least ill-tempered, and possibly a criminal."

"That would be a random killing, if it's just based on proximity," Sean said. "I'd rather look for motive."

"Maybe Walter was afraid Steve or Annie would find out about whatever he's doing in his house with those kids."

Yvonne had been looking back and forth between her two visitors, dazed. Kate said, "Here we are chattering like magpies and I haven't had a chance to tell you," she said. "Sean and I know each other. We met last summer."

Sean was staring at the floor, thoughtful. "I'd like to see what the local police come up with," he said. "I'll see if they're willing to share information with me tomorrow."

"Would they?" Yvonne asked. "With an out-of-stater?"

Sean hesitated. "I'm in law enforcement."

"Oh, sorry, I didn't realize." She pulled her sweater closer, clearly still taking in the ugly news about Annie.

Kate would bet Sean didn't like revealing his official status. Most likely she wouldn't know what he did for a living if she hadn't met him during an FBI operation.

"They probably won't. I'm not local," he said. His eyes were restless. Did he want to get out of here? Yvonne looked better than she had when she'd first heard the news, although Kate wouldn't count on her friend feeling normal for a long time after the two recent deaths, Donna's practically on her doorstep.

Duval came into the dining room with a file in his hand, looked at Kate, Sean, and then Yvonne. "What?" he asked her.

"Annie," Yvonne said. "Annie Brady. You remember her?"

"I remember the name," Duval said. Kate had hoped he would comfort his wife, but he sounded impatient.

"Hey, Yvonne, will you be okay? I'm really beat," Kate said. "I've got to call it a day." She was just about holding it together herself, and she didn't need to watch one more person get the bad news.

"As okay as I'm going to get for a while." Yvonne sighed. "What a nightmare. I really liked Annie. It's very sad."

"It's terrible," Kate said. "Sorry, Duval, excuse us."

"What happened to Annie Brady?"

"Just a sec, hon." Yvonne followed Kate and Sean to the door. "How about we have coffee tomorrow afternoon, Kate? I've got a dental appointment in the morning. Sean, you're most welcome too, of course."

"Thanks," he said as he stepped outside.

"Funny you two know each other and ended up at the same campground."

"Yes, an amazing coincidence," Sean said with a straight face.

"Yvonne!" Duval shouted, and she shut the door.

Sean took a big breath, stretched his shoulders back, then relaxed them. "How about a nightcap?"

"Sounds good." Kate didn't drink much, especially now that she spent so much time alone. But a glass of wine could be relaxing, especially with someone she'd been through so much with, both in Maine and here. Someone whose eyes made her whole body smile. Even today. Today had been a confusing mixture of painful, sweet, funny, and sad.

"Your place or mine?"

Kate was curious about his camper. "Yours."

"Oh, so you want to meet my Tiger?"

She looked at him. "And here I took you for a wombat kind of guy.

219

He insisted on a detour to her camper first. "I really am embarrassed," he said. "I don't want you to report me as a stalker." Then he grinned. "Not to mention the Bureau wants its equipment back."

He lay on the ground beside the front wheel of Kate's camper, reached underneath and gave a tug. When he got to his feet he had a box in his hand. One side was black, the rest crusted with red and brown mud.

"Here's the electronic tattle-tale," he said. "Stool pigeon. Snitch."

"Looks kind of big for a bug," Kate said.

"In the Bureau, if we're gonna do bugs we do 'em big."

* * *

"Hey, Growly," Sean said, unlocking his Tiger. "I'd like you to meet a friend of mine." He opened the door, on the right side behind the crew cab, and stood back.

"Growly?" Kate gave him a look, then climbed aboard. The Tiger was similar in size to her truck camper, but the cab and the living space in the back of the van were connected. While she had to leave her truck and walk outside the camper to its rear door, a Tiger driver could turn, crawl between the front seats and over the crew seats, and be in the camper.

"A company named Provan makes these in South Carolina," Sean said. "They manufacture fiberglass camper bodies and put them on chassis from Ford and GMC. Most of them have diesel engines, and this one has only thirty thousand miles on it. It's barely reached puberty."

"A teenaged Tiger. Scary."

The fridge was smaller than the one on her camper. "Beer okay?" he asked.

"Sure."

He put a couple more bottles in the fridge and ripped open a bag of pretzels. "I don't like coincidences," he said as she sat beside him on the couch, the bag between them. "The woman you mentioned—Donna?—she died of CO poisoning here, and then two weeks later and only a mile away the same thing happens to another woman. Has to be a connection."

"I checked the Winnebago's heater, and so did John, the campground handyman, and then the police," Kate said. "Nobody could find anything wrong with it, but how else do you get carbon monoxide into an RV? Had to be an accident."

"I just don't like it."

"Me neither." She was hungry, and the pretzels were good, crisp and salty. She suspected they were going to be all the dinner either she or Sean felt like preparing. If you could call opening a bag preparing.

After a while she said, "The local police will tell you what they've found, won't they?" Almost the same question Yvonne had asked, but Yvonne didn't know Sean was FBI.

"I don't have any official connection to the case. And they don't want to risk some dude with a federal badge telling them what to do. Not that I would," he said. "I'll try to make that clear. I'm just interested in what's going on because you're here."

They sat in thought for a while, the only sound the crunch of pretzels.

Sean shook his head. "I can't connect things. Look at what's been going on: CO poisoning case number one, accident. You're set adrift. You find house where a guy is maybe doing something nasty with young girls. You're attacked. CO poisoning case number two, murder. Tell me how any of that fits together." He pulled on his beer. "Unless the first case wasn't an accident, and you're seen as a snooper who's likely to discover that it was murder, too. Then things fit together better."

"What's the connection between the two victims, Donna and Annie?" Kate asked. "They both stayed at Roll and Rest, but it has to be something more than that."

"Yeah, that's not enough." He drained his beer and sat with the empty bottle in his hand. After a minute he sighed and got to his feet. "I can't think any more. But will you do me a favor and make a list of everything strange that's happened? It might help me see a pattern."

He gave her a yellow pad and pen, then went outside. He said he was checking the oil in the generator, but Kate thought that was an excuse to leave her alone so she could concentrate.

Smart move. She found him a major distraction.

She worked on the list for five minutes. Looked it over for another five. Went outside.

"Done?" he asked. He was sitting on the rear bumper, oil long since checked.

She sat beside him. Late crickets chirped at long intervals. The evening had cooled, and Sean's body heat lapped against her like a tide.

"For your safety," Sean said, "I'd like you to stay with me. I'm really tired, it was a long day, and I'm not coming on to you. Really. I don't know what's going on here, and I want to protect you."

"We're in the same campground. My rig is as safe as yours."

"You can have the king-sized bed over the cab, or the couch, whichever suits you."

"Thanks, Sean, but I'll be fine in my camper." Staying with him in the role of bodyguard would be uncomfortable. Awkward, and frustrating. No thanks.

"I wish you'd stay," he said. "We might have a better grasp on the situation tomorrow."

"You want a chance to save my life again, don't you?" she teased.

"Of course, if it needs being saved."

"Greedy pig." She gave him something like a smile. "I'm going home. It's a shout away from you."

"Well, keep your cell phone charged and handy. Do you have it on you?"

She pulled it out of her back pocket and added him as a contact, typing in the numbers as he spoke them.

He got out a flashlight and walked her to the door of her camper. Touched her shoulder. "Maybe tomorrow we can go out to dinner? Or something?"

"Something normal for a change? Sounds good, Sean. Let's talk in the morning."

His eyes shifted and his face hardened. "Kate. What's that on your door?"

She turned. A couple of handprints, some spatters. "Looks like somebody came by while I was out. Somebody messy."

"Wait a minute." He fished a small object from his pocket, unfolded it into a magnifying lens. With his left hand holding the flashlight close to the door, he had a careful look at the smudges.

"Blood. Fresh enough that I can smell it." He stepped back from the camper.

She wanted to laugh. She didn't know why. It was just too much, Donna and Annie both dead and Steve out there somewhere, fighting for his life in a way nobody should have to, maybe driven mad by it all—it was too much.

She fought the laugh down. She didn't know Sean well enough to know if he'd understand, and she didn't want to confuse him.

"So will you come sleep on the Tiger?"

"Sean, my door is still locked. Whoever it was, he didn't get in. It's safe in there, as safe as your, um, Tiger." The laugh hadn't gone away completely. She looked away from him quickly.

"You're a hard case, Kate. Let me just have a look on board to make sure you're the sole occupant."

Sole occupant? Sometimes he sounded like a training manual. She unlocked the door and he climbed inside, looked around, and opened the door to the bathroom, which was the only space you couldn't see from the door.

He flashed his light up over the cab, and she winced as the beam hit her stuffed animals. A red fox from Maine, a loon from the Adirondacks.

The beam hesitated, swept on, and then she was inside too, behind him, and he turned. They were inches apart. Would he—

"You sure you're okay? Sure you want to stay here?"

If he was interested in her, if they were going to develop some kind of relationship, she wanted it to come from who they were. Putting him in the role of bodyguard would confuse the emotional signals between them. And she didn't need protection. At least not tonight.

"Yes. See you tomorrow?"

"Deal," he said, and was out the door. Only after she snapped the lock home did she hear his footsteps on the gravel. He was careful, wasn't he? By training and probably by temperament as well.

She sat at the dinette, tired but not ready for sleep. Sean had come back into her life, and she was drawn to him in a deep way she didn't fully understand. He had saved her life in Maine; that was of course a factor. But it was more than that.

Tate drifted into her mind, the handsome, affectionate man who'd been her companion in the Adirondacks as she struggled to uncover the truth about the death of his employer. They'd enjoyed each other's company so much that he'd been thinking about following her on the road in a camper of his own—until a job offer came along that was too good to pass up. It had been wrenching to leave him, and she hadn't shut the door on the relationship.

Instructive to compare how she felt about the two men. Being with Tate was fun. Being with Sean affected her on another level entirely, deep and compelling. He stirred her—with his eyes, his face, his voice.

She'd slept with Tate. Sean had barely touched her. After driving here to see her, why was he holding back? Was he waiting for a sign from her the way she was waiting for a sign from him?

Whatever was going on between them, Sean was suddenly the most important person in her life.

\* \* \*

She made sandwiches the next morning, and she and Sean drove to Keystone State Park for a hike. The conservation land along the Loyalhanna didn't appeal after what they'd seen there the previous day. Sean said he'd talked with the police in Union Hill and had been told the woods would be full of however many officers and volunteers the department could field, hunting for Steve and any clues to the murder.

Kate liked the Tiger's pass-through from cab to camper: if the weather was bad, or a rogue grizzly was on the loose, being able to drive away without getting out of the camper was in one case a convenience and in the other a life-saver. But these vans were expensive, way beyond what she could afford.

Using his GPS, Sean found a dirt road near Keystone "to feed the Tiger after too many highway miles." Kate hadn't known four-wheel drive had to be engaged at least a couple times a month to keep it in good shape mechanically, but it made sense. Use it or lose it, for both muscles and machines. "Keeps things lubricated," Sean said.

The good gravel on the road thinned after a mile, then petered out altogether. A dirt parking area on the right was empty, and after that the road narrowed, plain dirt with sandy patches. Curving to the left, it went higher, rough with rocks. The trees around them subsided to scrub.

Rocks took over the road. Then boulders. The Tiger tilted and lurched, and Kate found a handhold over the door. Sean steered with his hands loose, and she could see why: the wheel jerked unpredictably as the front tires responded to the uneven terrain of the boulder field. His thumbs stayed outside the steering wheel.

They didn't talk; he needed to concentrate.

The road flattened and ended. They were at the crest of a hill, the sharp drop ahead of them opening a vista of woods and farmland like one of Edna's quilts. Irrigation circles in some of the fields. A small lake.

Kate lowered her window. The air was clean and bright. "Landing strip?" She pointed.

He squinted. "Maybe." He took a pair of binoculars out of the center console and looked again. "Nope. Cars, not planes. Drag racing course." He put the binoculars away, flipped the lid shut and rested his hand on the lid. She wanted to put her hand on his, feel its warmth.

But she needed something from him first. A word. A sign.

Another minute. His hand beside her. Above, vultures tilted. Below, the wind made cat's-paws that flickered against the dark lake like tinsel.

He cranked the van around on the lip of the drop-off, so close that Kate held her breath. Then back: boulders to modest rocks, to dirt, to gravel. The turn onto pavement, which now felt as smooth as Shadow's fur.

"The Tiger's happy," Sean said. "The rest of us?"

"Hanging in there," Kate said. A knot filled her chest, and she tried to untie it for him. For herself. "I feel sad, but in such an odd way. I only knew Annie a few days, and Donna not much more than that. But God, Donna radiated kindness." How else to say it? She couldn't find the right words. "Annie I felt sorry for. She had such a huge burden in Steve, and her husband was divorcing her, and she was trying so hard to cope with all of it."

He turned into the state park, sunlight through the trees flickering on the windshield as the Tiger went down the long access road. In the parking lot an old couple got out of a station wagon, pulled fanny packs from the back and strapped them on. The woman had a tight gray cap of curls like Donna's. The man said something to her and she laughed.

Damn. Donna should be here, Donna and Richard.

Kate and Sean found a trail that wandered through oak trees to the top of a hill, where hemlocks surrounded the foundation of an old building. Not the elevation they'd reached in the Tiger, but still a pretty view.

"Great place to put a house," Kate said, standing on one of the stone blocks and looking at the undulating field of foliage below them, the harvest of color less vibrant than a few days ago. In a few days it would be November.

Sean scooped a handful of hemlock cones from the ground and popped them at her, one by one. Laughing, she helped herself to a similar supply of ammunition and chased him through the trees while they pelted each other with the tiny cones. Her left-handed aim was terrible, but it didn't matter. For a few minutes Kate didn't think about Annie or Steve, Donna or Richard.

But she and Sean were quiet as they ate the tuna-on-rye sandwiches she'd made, sitting on the stone foundation. The hemlock dropped a few cones on them, and Kate looked up. "We've got plenty, thanks," she told the tree.

\* \* \*

In the parking lot he used the remote to open the Tiger's doors, then got in the passenger seat. Kate smiled and climbed behind the wheel.

It had gotten late, and she had to turn down Sean's offer of a four-wheel-drive lesson. A glance at the dashboard clock told her she didn't have much time to get back for her coffee date with Yvonne. Probably just as well. She wasn't sure her sore arm would enjoy a 4x4 driving lesson as much as the rest of her would.

It was fun to pilot the Tiger even in two-wheel mode. The van was about the same length as her truck camper, but lower and more streamlined. She could feel the difference in how it handled. When sideways wind gusts buffeted them on the way back, the Tiger held the road like a true cat. Her camper would have lurched.

At Roll and Rest, Sean passed on coffee, saying he had paperwork to do. Kate backed the big van into his site and he got out to plug into shore power. When he got into the camper she looked back at him, expecting a smile. But his face said his mind was elsewhere, so she took her daypack and bailed. Left the pack on the picnic table by her truck and knocked on the door with the smiling cats.

The aroma of chocolate filled the dining room; Yvonne had made brownies. She poured coffee and slumped in her chair. "I thought we needed some cheering up. And I needed something to do."

"Yes. It's been a shock."

"I didn't know Annie very well," Yvonne said, tearing up. "She seemed troubled, but I liked her."

"She had a lot to deal with. Steve's condition was bad enough, but she was also in the middle of a divorce. Came here hoping to stay with her brother for a while and get a job." Kate looked around. Something was different. "I liked her too."

Yvonne bit her lip. "She was so young. I don't know about her brother, but she would have gotten over the divorce and discovered a whole new life on the other side. I've had friends who got divorced. It's bad, but it isn't the end of the world."

"Yes." Ah, no knitting. The room seemed awfully still without the needles flying on Yvonne's side of the table.

Kate took a brownie and ate it half-heartedly.

They sat, two friends. Drinking coffee, sharing losses. No words needed.

Shadow sprang into Yvonne's lap, startling her. Before the cat had time to do the falling-over trick, her owner grabbed her furry face and kissed it. "You are such a comfort, you."

Someone rapped on the door. Shadow dropped to the floor as Yvonne got up. "Just a sec, Kate," she said. "It's probably the heating guy. I'm having the furnace checked out for the winter."

"Good idea."

The technician was blonde and bouncy. *"Good* afternoon! I'm Brian, from Speedy Heating and Cooling. Lovely to see you ladies today." Kate wasn't sure which she preferred, this lay-it-on-thick good cheer or the monosyllabic style of most tradesmen she'd dealt with in the past. Given her mood, Brian's ebullience made him seem like an alien.

Yvonne showed him the basement door and flipped the light on for him.

"We'll have you ladies fixed up in a jiffy," he said, and trotted down the stairs, whistling.

"Speaking of fixing," Yvonne said, "has John gotten around to your generator yet?"

"Yes. Finally."

Yvonne rolled her eyes. "Hallelujah."

"Two days ago," Kate said. "After you brought me back from the hospital post-Zeus. I usually like to watch when people work on my rig, but I was in no shape to do that. I went back to sleep. I haven't seen him yet to pay him."

"He'd probably like cash instead of a check."

"I figured. I'd planned to take cash-back on my credit card when I got groceries, but I didn't have to. I made more than enough at the fair to cover what he's charging me."

"How do you manage without carrying a handbag?" Yvonne asked. "I sure couldn't."

"I have a system. Big bills in my left pocket, small bills in my right pocket along with chapstick and jackknife. Left back pocket, license and credit cards in a soft case. Back right, cell phone. And I comb my hair with my fingers. What would I put in a purse?"

Kate was happy to hear Yvonne laugh. The worry champion of southwest Pennsylvania needed the distraction of conversation.

"You'd be lost without five-pocket jeans," Yvonne said. "What's the little 'secret' pocket for?"

"Change. Except quarters. I take them out and hoard them to feed the machines at laundromats." Kate shook her head. "I used to carry a handbag, but I'd always forget and leave it hanging off a chair somewhere, have to go rushing back. Panic and inconvenience."

After a moment Yvonne said in a different voice, "With your generator taken care of, are you thinking of moving on?"

"Not right away. Not with what's happened."

"I'll miss you."

Kate looked up quickly. Yvonne's eyes had filled again. "I'll miss you too. You've been amazing. Thank you for everything you've done for me. All your help—yours and Edna's—getting me jump-started in the business side of my art. Not to mention taking care of me after the dog encounter and the near-death experience in my kayak."

"You're more than welcome, Kate. I hope we'll stay in touch after you move on. I've so enjoyed having you—"

Footsteps came up the stairs, and Brian popped into the kitchen. "All done, ma'am," he said. "I've tested your thermostat, verified ignition, cleaned the burners and lubed the blower. Everything's fine."

"Thanks so much," Yvonne said. "What do I owe you?"

He slipped a sheet of paper onto his metal clipboard and scribbled on it. "You don't owe a penny," he said. "It's included in the service contract. You're all set for a year. Please sign this, down at the bottom, saying I did the work." He handed her the clipboard. After Yvonne scribbled her signature, Brian took the clipboard back and saluted her with the pen. "Cheerio," he said, and turned toward the door.

Wait!" Kate said, more urgently than she meant to.

Yvonne looked at her, startled. Brian turned around.

"No, it's not—I mean—" she sputtered, then gathered herself. "Yvonne, wouldn't you like Brian to have a look at the heater in Savvy's room?"

Yvonne looked surprised. "Oh," she said, as if Kate had suggested something pleasant, like a movie or a drive in the country. "What a good idea. I'll show you the way, Brian." She stood up. "Now why didn't I think of that?"

"No problem. I'll leave my toolbag here," he said. "I just need a couple of things."

They went upstairs, Kate following with a cup in each hand, having snagged Yvonne's off the table. Her right arm was much better. She was glad she'd thought to ask Brian to do this. He wouldn't find anything unusual, of course, but she'd be able to put to rest the dark thought that had sprung into her mind a minute ago.

At the top of the stairs, she gave Yvonne her cup, and the two women stood in the hallway.

"So where are you going next?"

"Oh, you know me, Yvonne. I don't plan ahead. I'll look for someplace pretty, somewhere south of here. I'm migratory these days."

"Free as a bird, which isn't all that free. Weather pushes birds around."

"You're right. It pushes me too," Kate said. "I wouldn't want to live in my camper in a foot of snow."

"Ma'am?" Brian called, his tone puzzled. "Could I show you something here? It's kind of, um, odd."

"What is it?" Yvonne asked, going into Savvy's room. Kate stood in the doorway.

Kneeling by the heater, Brian held up what looked like an ordinary piece of cardboard as if it held great significance.

"What's that?" Yvonne said.

"It was behind this grate here," Brian said. He pointed with his screwdriver to a rectangular opening in the heater, near the floor, about the size of a page in Kate's eleven by twenty-four sketchbook. He'd removed the metal grate and leaned it next to the opening.

"It blocked a lot of the air coming through—that was supposed to come through—the vent, right?" Kate asked the technician.

"Yeah, that's right." Brian gave Kate a confused look.

"What? No, wait," Yvonne said. "That's just some old piece of paper that slipped down into the heater. That's all it is."

"No, ma'am," Brian said, glancing at Kate. "It's good stiff cardboard, not paper. And it was cut to just the right size. It had to be a tad bigger than the opening in the heater and a tad smaller than the grate covering it. On three sides, anyway. That way it wouldn't interfere with the screws, and the grate pressing on the edges—" he held the cardboard up against the opening—"would hold it in place."

Yvonne sat on the end of Savvy's bed. She looked confused.

"It couldn't just—be there? Fall there?"

"No, ma'am. What I'm trying to say is somebody had to unscrew four screws and put this carefully in place."

Yvonne looked helplessly at Kate.

"It's what's wrong with Savvy," Kate said, a sinking feeling in her chest. "Carbon monoxide. The same thing that happened to Donna."

Brian looked back and forth between the two women, frowning.

"Yvonne, would it be all right if I got Sean in here? He's— knowledgeable about, uh, things like this."

Yvonne nodded, but her eyes were somewhere else. Kate wondered if she'd really heard. If she knew what the cardboard meant.

Outside, she took a deep breath of crisp air. Rusty was sitting on the picnic table next to her boat and meowed a greeting, but for once she ignored him. She ran along the gravel path.

Sean opened the Tiger door, yawning. "Glad you're here. This report is putting me to sleep. C'mon in. Have time for a beer?"

"Actually, Sean, I think we have another crime scene."

He woke up in the space of a blink. From a yawny friend he turned into an alert professional. "Who?"

Had he jumped straight to murder? "No, nobody's dead." It was too complicated. She thought of saying "attempted murder" but she didn't think Carson wanted to kill his sister, just torment her. The same as he did with cats. "Would you come have a look?"

They went inside without speaking, and up the stairs. Brian hadn't put the grate back on. He was sitting cross-legged, writing on the clipboard on his lap.

Yvonne stopped pacing and shut the door behind them. "Shadow and Rusty," she said. "I don't want them going inside the heater."

Brian explained what he'd found, and Sean picked up the cardboard and studied it. "It's been blackened all over with a marker," he said. "It used to be a lighter color."

"He must have tried it out and realized the light color was visible through the grate," Kate said. She took the rectangle from Sean and weighed it in her hand. "This cardstock feels like hundred-pound cover. He used sturdy stuff."

"He? The husband?" Sean asked. He was looking around the room. Kate imagined his mind recording details like a camera with a motor drive.

Yvonne looked bewildered.

"The son," Kate said. "He's twelve."

Sean looked at her. His face gave away nothing. "He's not here? Where's his room? Let's check it out."

Carson's room was the same disaster it had been a few days ago—was it only a few days?—when Yvonne had taken a look after Savvy had shown off the canopy and curtains she'd made. This time Kate noticed cardstock tucked behind the boy's bureau. Pushing clothes and model planes aside with her foot, she pulled one of the light blue pieces out.

"Let me see that," Yvonne said. She ran a finger along an edge. "I was using this stuff for posters in the library, helping Edna out," she said. "And we used scraps of it for price tags at the fair, remember, Kate? It came in big sheets and Carson asked if he could have one to make wings for his planes. That's what he was using it for. That's why it's here."

Kate looked at the model planes on the floor. None of them had light blue wings.

Lying was the least of Carson's sins. Most kids lie once in a while. But most don't try to wreck their sister's health for the fun of it.

Sean gave Kate another cryptic look. He waded to the desk and tapped a finger next to several black marker pens. "I don't think the ink in these can be matched," he said. "But it won't be necessary in this case. It's obvious what's happened here."

"He's just a boy," Yvonne said. "He likes planes." She navigated her way to the bed, straightened the comforter, and sat. Folded her hands in her lap like a schoolgirl and looked straight ahead.

In the space behind the bureau where she'd seen the big piece of cardstock, Kate saw two other pieces, blackened with marker ink. She held them up to Sean. "Test pieces?"

"They're smaller than the one Brian has," Sean said. "Maybe your daughter's symptoms weren't severe enough—" he glanced at Yvonne—"and he went to a bigger piece."

Yvonne looked lost. "What are you saying?" She picked up a T-shirt from the floor and began folding it. "He's a boy. Lots of boys have rooms that look like this."

"Why didn't he just cut down the piece he had?" Kate asked. "Why make a new one?"

Sean pondered her question for a few seconds. "Because he was swapping them in and out," he said, "to control her level of distress."

"He's twelve," Yvonne said in her new, distant voice. "A baby. He didn't do it, what you're saying."

"He'll need a lot of help," Sean said quietly.

Kate pulled something else from the shadows behind the bureau. Another piece of cardboard? She flipped it over. Her drawing of the rock above the beach, where she'd been working the day she was set adrift, unconscious. "Holy cats," she said. "Look, Yvonne. Remember the girl at the fair who left the hundred dollar bill? She wasn't Gaston's go-for like I thought. She bought this for Carson. I wonder why."

Yvonne was folding another T-shirt and didn't look up.

"I think we need to contact Child Protective Services as well as the local police," Sean said.

Yvonne dropped the shirt on the floor and put her head on her folded arms. "Oh, God, no."

Kate sat next to her and touched her hand. "We can get help for him. For you. The whole family."

"Would you like me to make the call?" Sean asked.

The "yes" was barely audible.

"I'll use the landline," he said, picking his way across the floor.

Yvonne's head came up. "Kate, can I use your cell? I want to call Duval, tell him what's going on. I want him home."

She called, but her husband didn't answer. While she was leaving a message, Brian came down the hall and stood uncertainly at the door, the report on his clipboard filled with tiny writing. Kate wondered how much he'd heard. Not that it mattered: he must have long since figured out what Carson had been up to. "Ma'am?" he said after a moment. "Could you sign this for me? I had to rewrite it."

"Let's go downstairs," Kate said. Besides being depressing, the room was a crime scene.

Sean wasn't on the landline in the dining room; he was on the patio, on his cell phone, perhaps to spare Yvonne his side of the conversation. She and Kate sat at the kitchen table while Brian packed up his tools.

"The good news is Savvy's going to be getting better soon," Kate said.

"Yes," Yvonne said. "I can cancel her appointment with the neurologist."

Kate waited a couple of beats. "I wouldn't do that. Even though the CO source is gone, she's been exposed for weeks. You might want to have her assessed, just to be safe."

"Oh, God. You mean she could have permanent damage?"

"Probably not, but maybe. You'd want to know, wouldn't you?"

Finished with his tools, Brian gave Yvonne a copy of the report, a more subdued man than when he'd arrived. "I don't know what my boss will do—I've never seen anything like this. Maybe he'll report it to the police. I wrote up what I found, and the rest is up to him. But I want to make sure you know this is very dangerous."

"Yes," Yvonne said. Her face was wooden, her voice flat.

"I mean it *was* dangerous. I remedied the blockage. It's fine now. But don't let him—"

"Thank you," Kate said, opening the door for him. Sean was right outside. He waited for Brian to pass him and then came in, his face all business. "The police will be here soon, Yvonne," he said. "They'll talk to you, ask questions about your son. Then, when he gets home from school, they'll probably take him into custody, deliver him to the juvenile facility."

Yvonne's eyes widened. "They'll take him away?"

"Yes," Sean said. "You want them to. He's dangerous, and you or your husband could be next. Or any one of your campers." He turned to Kate. "Can I talk to you?"

He led the way to the Tiger and went to the far side of it. Out of sight of Yvonne's window.

"I've been called back in," he said. "I was hoping to get the whole week off, but the situation in Pittsburgh is heating up. They need me. It's urgent."

Kate felt a stab of disappointment. That's why he'd been on his cell. "Oh, damn," she said. "I'll miss you, Sean. Big-time."

His smile was pained. "Yeah, big-time." He opened his arms.

The hug didn't last long enough. Then he held her in front of him, hands on her shoulders. His gold eyes glowed.

"Stay in touch?" she said. "I mean, in some way I can appreciate. Not watching my camper blip its way across a computer screen."

He smiled. "You mean I should call you?"

"That's the preferred method. Texts, emails? Also acceptable."

"I wish—" His eyes were full of words, but he spoke only the two.

When he turned toward the Tiger, Kate went back to the house. Hearing the big diesel start up and fade down the driveway was going to be bad enough; she didn't have to watch.

She stepped inside. Despite its big window the dining room seemed dark.

# TWENTY

Yvonne's pain was palpable. Almost visible, like mist. She was pacing again, pausing for a hug from Kate and then continuing.

The door opened. Savvy. Her face changed when she saw her mother. "Mum, what's the matter?" She slipped out of her backpack and it thumped to the floor.

"Oh, honey." Yvonne took two steps and embraced her daughter.

"What's going on?"

Yvonne held Savvy's face in her hands. "I love you, you know."

"Mum—" Savvy made a face. "I love you too. Ugh! Enough already." She wriggled away from Yvonne, looked at Kate, then back at her mother. "You two are making me feel like a funeral."

"Where's Carson, Savvy?" Kate asked.

"Isn't he home? I stopped to talk to Daphne, and he said we were stupid girls and he wasn't going to listen to us blather."

"How long did you talk to her?"

"Maybe, I don't know, ten, fifteen minutes? She's made because somebody said she was fat, online. We're trying to figure out who."

Kate looked at Yvonne. "I wonder if Brian's truck—"

"Spooked him? Because it said Heating and Cooling on the side? Yeah," Yvonne said. She paced in a tight circle. "Where would he go?" Another circle. "I'm calling Duval again. At the office."

The buttons on the the land-line beeped under her mother's fingers as Savvy went upstairs, dragging her pack and muttering she wished someone would tell her what the heck was going on.

"Please tell him to come home right away," Yvonne said. "It's urgent. You'll tell him? Thank you." Clatter of plastic on plastic as she hung up.

"Kate, Would you stay with me? Until Duval gets home?" Yvonne wrung her hands, sat down, got up, paced. "I don't want to tell Savvy alone. And I don't want to talk to, to him alone, either."

She meant Carson. Kate hesitated. She had no idea how the boy would react to being found out, but she thought of Marjorie's warning that all was not well in this family. Could Carson become violent? Even if the answer was no, Yvonne needed support.

"Sure, I'll stay." She sat, turning her chair so she could see the door.

Even though the cups on the table were half full, Yvonne scooped grounds into the coffee machine. Something to do, like making brownies nobody ate. At least her voice had gotten more normal since she'd hugged her daughter.

She dropped into a chair, restlessness gone for the moment. The coffee-maker gurgled an gave off its aroma. She gave Kate a sad smile. "I love my children. Both of them. No matter what he's done."

"Of course you do." Kate couldn't imagine being a mother, feeling responsible for an infant, a toddler, a twelve-year-old. A boy who would torment cats and harm his sister. And worse.

She drained her cup as Duval's pick-up skidded to a stop in the driveway. He rushed in. "What is it? Are you all right? The children?"

As Yvonne threw herself into his arms, Kate slipped out the door.

She went around the back of her camper and was startled to see John slapping the door. His version of a knock. He jumped when he saw her.

"Hey, Kate, thought I'd stop by and see if you wanted to settle up."

"Sure, John." She was distracted, at least half her mind still wondering where Carson had gone. Who would get here first, him or the police? A police car would definitely scare him off. She took the roll of bills from her left pocket and counted out what she owed into John's palm, which glistened with dirt and sweat.

John stashed the bills in his jeans and said sheepishly. "Hey, I'm sorry about the mess I made."

"Mess?"

"I stopped over yesterday but you weren't home, and now I see I got some blood on your door. My buddy and me, we bagged ourselves a deer and I guess I didn't clean up enough after gutting it."

His palm had more than dirt and sweat on it, then. Kate tried not to notice as he ran his hand though his hair.

"I'll get some rags and clean up your door. Okay if I do it in the morning? I haven't had a chance to eat all day."

"I'd really appreciate it, John. Morning's fine. You got yourself a deer?"

"Sure did, a big one. It'll feed me all winter, and Yvonne's family, too. Glad you didn't see the mess. I didn't see it myself in the dark last night."

She hesitated, then went ahead and said it. "Actually, I did see it and I was a little scared." An experienced FBI agent was also alarmed, but she kept that to herself.

"Scared?" He seemed genuinely surprised.

"Yes. Bloody handprints? I didn't know it was deer's blood."

"Oh, gosh, I see," John said. He scratched his beard, but no crumbs fell out this time. "I'm really sorry. I didn't even think of that."

"Well, it's fine as long as you clean it up real well."

"You got it!" He almost fell over himself turning around and getting out of there.

He was okay. He was about as clean as a rat's ass, but he meant well. He'd been shocked to think he'd done something scary; she'd enlightened him because it might help him be more aware of his effect on other people. Judging only by his looks, he could easily get classified as one scary dude.

She climbed inside to get a couple of cotton balls, and felt her back pocket to make sure her cell phone was still there. She'd had some more dark thoughts, but before she passed them on to Yvonne and the police she wanted to test them.

The Millers' Winnebago looked like it needed a good wash. Autumn wind had showered it with dust, and twigs littered the hood. Kate moved down its side to the vent for the propane heater. She wanted to have a closer look at the rectangle of differing texture she'd noticed the morning Donna died.

Yes. The rectangle was a shade darker than the rest of the RV. The strong winds on the morning Zeus attacked her had put dust everywhere. It had landed on horizontal surfaces and stayed there. It had blown against vertical surfaces, and if they were sticky it stayed there, too.

She pulled a few wisps from the cotton ball and trailed them over the rectangle. They didn't stick the way she'd expected them to, the way that would confirm her suspicions. She pressed the whole cotton ball against the rectangle, and when she let go it stayed attached.

The innocent ball of fluff told her something not so innocent.

Good news and bad news. Good news for the police and for Donna's soul, she supposed. Bad news for the Chouinard family.

Carson had put duct tape over the Winnebago's heater vent. That's why he'd later tried to hide the roll of tape from Kate outside the shed when she went to get her bicycle.

After Brian's discovery, Kate had remembered Carson with the tape, claiming he was "not doing nothing." She wouldn't have thought anything at the time, or remembered it later, if he hadn't tried to hide, first himself, and then what he had in his hand. Because who would think twice about a boy carrying a roll of duct tape? A boy with model planes all over the floor of his room?

She wished she'd figured out sooner what the duct tape meant. She might have stopped Carson. Saved Annie.

But wait, Carson couldn't have put her in the kayak headed for the dam. That had to be someone a lot stronger. The guy with the attack dog? Steve had worked with dogs in the Army, but she'd never seen a dog out by Annie's van. Could Steve be keeping a dog somewhere else? Kate couldn't feature the reticent man she'd met trying to kill her, but then she couldn't imagine anybody committing murder. The only scenes of violence in her head came from movies and books.

Quick footsteps, and a small figure came around the front of the Winnebago.

"Carson," she said. "Your parents have been worried about you."

He looked at her, then the vent with the cotton ball still stuck next to it. Back to her. His eyes narrowed. "What are you looking at? You're going to spoil everything."

"What am I going to spoil, Carson?"

"Before you got here, you and those old people, things were good with me and Uncle Gassy. Then I told him about how I tried to get rid of the dog and he said I was stupid, stupid, *stupid!*" He leaned against the Winnebago, breathing hard. He'd run here. He must have gone somewhere after school.

Kate didn't know what to make of it. Get rid of what dog? She took a step toward him. "Hey, Carson, you need to talk to your parents, let them know you're—"

"Stay away from me!" He jumped back and came down in a fighting posture, knees bent, hands out and ready. He looked like a nerd, with his glasses and small stature, but this kid must have seen some schoolyard combat.

"I thought Uncle Gassy was my friend but he's not. So I'm going to tell on him. He takes pictures of girls without any clothes on. I don't know what the big deal is, but he said not to tell anybody. So I'm telling."

"Good move," Kate said. "Now let's go inside and tell your parents."

Carson didn't move. "He'll be mad at me," he said. "But I don't care. He's been a jerk ever since that stupid Donna woman died. I don't need him. I'm a big deal at school now. I've got lots of money. I've got a girl friend."

The boy was standing straighter. He didn't see her as an adversary. And she wasn't. She thought he was a screwed-up kid who needed help. She wanted to get him inside, to his parents, who would get him that help.

"Before you showed up, I could steal things and everybody blamed the hermit. I came and went whenever I wanted, out the window and down the tree. At first I just looked through people's windows. In RVs and houses. It was fun. And then you spoiled it all."

"Carson, it had nothing to do with me."

"You were snooping. Looking at the vent. I told Gassy. He said we had to make a plan about you. Back when he was my friend, before my girlfriend and I got together. She says he's a creep and a loser."

Kate swallowed hard. "He never was your friend, Carson," she said. "Your parents are your real friends. And I'll do what I can to help you too."

"You're a liar. It's all your fault," Carson said. "And I've got something to show you." The boy reached inside his jacket and pulled out a stubby revolver. It was a small gun, but it looked big in his hands.

Even a small gun is big enough to kill a person. Kate's scalp tingled. "Carson, be careful with that. Don't point it at me."

He looked at it as if it were a just a thing, a cup or bar of soap or roll of duct tape, not a deadly weapon. It was pointed right at her chest.

Come to think of it, in his hands a roll of duct tape was in fact a deadly weapon.

"This is Gassy's gun. He has a bunch. He keeps this one in his truck, under the seat. I told him I'm not gonna be his brother anymore and I stole his gun. And I'm going to shoot you for real. Because you ruined everything."

His brother? He'd lost her again. "Carson, if you shoot me, you'll go to jail. Think about what jail is like. No trees to climb, no woods to play in, no river. Just a small cement room with a toilet and a hard bed and no windows. Bars on one wall. Like you're an animal at the zoo." Her only hope was to keep him talking. Where were the police? They were supposed to be on their way. Her lousy luck Sean had to leave.

"I used to wish Uncle Gassy was my dad. We had tickle-fights and we wrestled. He taught me some karate moves and he showed me his thing and I showed him mine. We—we did things. We were brothers afterwards. He told me so."

245

Oh, poor Carson. Gaston was using him in even worse ways than she'd thought. "Carson, you have got to tell your father what you just told me. Gaston should never have done that."

Carson didn't seem to hear her. "I've been stealing from him so I could watch him go nuts looking for things. He never suspects me. I'm just a kid."

In Kate's mind Carson was getting older by the second. "You need to stay away from your uncle from now on, and not help him get pictures of girls. Or anything else he wants."

"Don't worry about that. He's a jerk."

"Good," Kate said. "Smart thinking." She kept her eyes on the revolver. Guns are heavy, especially to small hands, and the muzzle of this one was wavering, dropping. The short barrel gave her hope: accuracy would be poor.

She'd keep the boy talking until the police got there. It wasn't much of a plan, but it was the best she had.

Maybe she should talk him *into* his hostile impulses. The sound of a gunshot would certainly get her some help.

No, bad idea. Yvonne and Duval might come out to see what was going on and walk right into an ambush. If Carson shot at Kate, which he seemed about to do, there was no reason he wouldn't shoot at his parents. And he might not miss.

The pistol came up. Short barrel in her favor. Close range against her. "You're a jerk, too," he said.

She dived to her left as the night exploded with a roar and a flash of light. Rolled toward her camper, got her feet under her and scrambled behind it. Her mind was filled with an image of Carson a split second before he fired. Over his shoulder, a large black shape.

Why hadn't he fired again? She eased out for a careful look.

Carson was on the ground, and there was something on top of him, something large and dark. It growled.

Zeus.

Carson was crying. He sounded like a little boy for a change.

A tall figure stood over the boy and dog. "Alt." His voice was low and harsh. Like a dog's growl. "*Alt,* Zeus."

Walter Tremblay, the man with the black SUV. Zeus's master.

# TWENTY-ONE

The dog opened its jaws and Carson's arm dropped from it, limp.

"Ow, Uncle Gassy, it hurts," the boy wailed.

"You stupid shit," the man said. His boot caught Carson in the ribs with a solid thump.

"Hey!" Kate said. "Leave the kid alone." She moved toward him, toward the gun on the ground between them, but kept her eyes on his face.

"You stay out of this," the man said. "It's none of your damn business." He looked bigger than he had at the fairgrounds, and his eyes were small and bright under heavy black brows.

She dashed for the revolver, collided with Gaston. They both went down. She had her hand on the gun, but her arm was pinned under her, and with his weight on top of her she couldn't move. Her arm hurt like hell.

Stalemate. Good.

She heard a siren in the distance. Even better.

Gaston heard it, too. He was forcing his hand under her, wedging it along her arm toward the gun. She shoved her other elbow at him, but it didn't stop him. He was going to get the revolver away from her.

She squirmed, but she was pinned.

He laughed.

\* \* \*

A few years earlier, in Massachusetts, Kate had lost control of her motorcycle avoiding a dog that ran into the road. After the crash she'd picked the bike up, surprised she could. At home she looked up its weight: three hundred and fifty pounds.

"How was I able to do that?" she'd asked the big mechanic at the bike shop. With his huge tattooed biceps, his formidable triceps, he looked like he could pick up three motorcycles and juggle them.

"How were you feeling?"

"Angry," Kate said. "I'd asked those people nicely, three times, to keep their damn dog from running into the road."

"Adrenalin. That's how you picked the bike up."

\* \* \*

After Gaston laughed, Kate had a flash memory of righting the motorcycle. She arched her back, threw Gaston off, raised the gun and fired toward the woods, counting. Most revolvers have six chambers, but it didn't matter if it had more. She'd shoot until it was empty.

Carson had fired once. She squeezed the trigger. Two, three, four—

Gaston was on her again. He grabbed her wrist, pulled it down. Her next shot hit the Winnebago: the window splintered and showered them with bits of glass.

He was forcing her arm lower. She couldn't keep shooting because she didn't know where Carson was, or the dog. Or the cops, if they ever got here. She couldn't tell if the sirens were closer; the gunshots had wiped out her hearing.

The weight on her back disappeared and she was picked up and slammed face-first against the side of the Winnebago, her arms pulled behind her. Handcuffs clicked around her wrists, tight.

Over the buzz in her ears she heard someone say, "Search him," and hands ran along her legs and under her jacket.

"It's not a him, it's a her. She's clean."

The side of the Winnebago pulsed with blue light. Hands, more gentle than they'd been a minute earlier, turned her around, and the light bar on a cruiser swept instead across the house and the figures moving in front of it. The day was almost gone; the blue was bright, searing. A second police car pulled into the driveway.

"Ma'am?" The flashlight in her face was blinding; she turned her head away and closed her eyes.

"She's okay." That was Duval. "We'll vouch for her."

"She's the one who was shooting up a storm when we got here," the first voice said. "Looks like she took out the window of this RV. Anybody on board?"

"No," Duval said. "The owner's away."

"I was emptying the cylinder," Kate said. She turned toward the men. Duval's face, beyond the uniformed cop's shoulder, looked worried. "Using up the rounds so the gun would be useless."

"Is the weapon yours?" The uniform wasn't ready to take Duval's word that she was trustworthy.

"Kate!" Yvonne hurried from the house to join her husband. She touched the side of Kate's cheek. "You're bleeding." She looked around wildly. "Can't you release her? She's not the problem, she's our friend."

Nobody answered. The cop who'd handcuffed Kate had joined the others checking around the house and campground with flashlights, making sure there wasn't anyone else lurking near the crime scene.

Not much of a crime, in the end. Dog bites boy. Man and woman scuffle. Nobody gets shot. Kate looked around for Zeus and found him tied to a tree near the house. He sat at the end of the short rope and stared at his owner. Daylight was fading, but the flashing light from the cruiser lit the gray fur around his muzzle. A gray-haired old man of a dog.

Beyond Zeus, a paramedic knelt beside Carson, who was crying and hiccupping and crying again.

Duval glanced at Zeus's owner, standing cuffed like Kate against the Winnebago, and did a double-take. "Gaston!" He took a few steps toward his brother. "What's going on?"

"It's all a misunderstanding, bro," Gaston said.

The flashing lights made Kate feel dizzy, and her brain wasn't working right. The scene looked two-dimensional, patches of color like a kaleidoscope: Yvonne's face, hair backlit and haloed blue at its edges, blocks of pale blue that were Kate's camper and the house, bluish trees filigreed around the whole scene. It looked like a still from a movie.

Then, like a kaleidoscope, patches slid and the colors rearranged themselves. Motion returned to the scene.

The paramedic stood and helped Carson to his feet, his arm in a sling. A policeman in street clothes who'd been talking to the two brothers came over to Yvonne and Kate.

"We have to stop meeting like this," he said. It was Brandon. He had that grin. Even better, he had the keys to the handcuffs. He pulled her around, gently, and the pressure on her wrists went away.

Kate had never thought about it before, but when you're in handcuffs you can't do a thing if your nose itches.

Her nose had itched.

With apparent amusement, Brandon watched her give her nose a good scrub with the back of her hand. "Looks like you got yourself sprayed with shattered safety glass," he said. "Well, that's what they call it, anyway. I suppose it's safer than the untempered stuff, which can break into big pieces and slice you up. You've just got a couple of nicks."

"Sure," Kate said, although she wasn't following him all that well. Tempers? Safety? She rubbed her sore wrists.

"Hey, next time you take your boat out on the river, put your paddle together," Brandon said. "It works better that way."

"What?" Now she was sure her brain was suffering a major glitch, struggling to keep up with ordinary conversation. Must be the after-effects of the adrenaline rush of her struggle with Gaston over the gun.

"That pretty red carbon-fiber paddle of yours? Somebody found the two halves, downstream of the dam. Turned them in at the station. Your name was etched on the shaft, on both pieces."

"Oh, how great," Kate said. She knew the paddle was important to her, but she knew it in a distant way. As if her boat and paddle and the river were all from a story she'd been told a long time ago.

"She didn't forget to put her paddle together," Duval said. He'd come back from talking to Gaston, maybe waiting for Brandon to sort things out. "Somebody took it apart. The same guy who pushed her out there in her boat."

Thank you, Duval. She wasn't sure if she said it aloud or not.

"Whoever did it didn't want her to be able to paddle," Yvonne said. "He wanted her to go over the dam. We still don't know what the heck was going on."

"I'd never have launched without—" Kate couldn't find the rest of the sentence. She felt awfully tired.

"I think somebody else around here may have a few answers," Brandon said. He took a few steps along the Winnebago and leaned against it, arm extended, facing Gaston. "So, Uncle Gassy, how's it going?"

Gaston glanced at Duval and then looked back at Brandon from under bushy eyebrows. "I'd rather not talk right now."

"You just did," Brandon said, and laughed.

He enjoys being in a position of power, Kate thought. She didn't know whether to admire him or dislike him. "He saved my life," she said. "Carson would have had plenty of time to shoot me if Gaston hadn't showed up with Zeus to knock the kid over."

"When the guys in white hats came along," Brandon said, "you and Gaston were fighting over the gun and you were blazing away like you were in a cowboy movie. Want to explain?"

"I already told one of your guys. I was emptying the gun. Turning it into a paperweight."

"But you just said Gaston was on your side," Brandon said.

"I said he saved my life when Carson had the gun," Kate said. "I didn't say I trusted him not to shoot me himself."

"I wasn't going to shoot you," Gaston said in a tired voice. "Just scare you, like with the dog. I wanted you to get out of town."

"You two need to communicate better," Brandon said.

"I wanted the revolver back," Gaston said. "Carson stole it from me. He stole money, and phones, and the gun, and—and he did a lot of things he shouldn't have."

"Oh, yeah? Like what else?" Brandon asked.

Gaston looked at the ground.

Brandon pointed at the paramedic and waved him over, Carson with him. The boy was looking at the ground, too, and wincing as he walked.

Whatever Brandon had in mind to ask Carson, the first item on the agenda was going to be what Kate had figured out about the boy. "When Donna died," she said, "that was your fault, Carson, wasn't it?"

Yvonne gasped. Duval stared at Kate.

253

The boy's head came up and he looked at the adults around him and smirked. Then he shrugged. "I didn't know she was even in there. The Hyundai was gone. But the stupid dog barked, so I thought they'd gone off and left it behind. I wanted to nail the dog."

"Carson, did you put me in my boat and push it into the river?'

"No, Uncle Gassy did."

Gaston groaned. "Kid's making it up," he said.

"Am not." The boy gave his uncle a look both nasty and triumphant, and turned back to Kate. "I just dropped a rock on your stupid head so he could grab you."

"Whose idea was that? About the rock?"

"Mine," Carson said, and shrugged again. "It was such a good plan. But I should have found a bigger rock."

Gaston looked up. "You deserve everything you've got coming to you, kid."

"So do you, Gas Bag."

"All right, that's enough," Brandon said. "You both sound like children. Get the real kid to the hospital."

Gaston watched the paramedic take Carson toward the ambulance, then turned to his brother. "I tried to stay away from your family, you know? Safer for you. Since last summer, when I got into my new business. Making money like a damn mint. Wouldn't have gotten caught, either, if it weren't for Carson. He cost me big-time."

"Right, blame it on a twelve-year-old."

"Something wrong with him all along, bro. I don't know how you could've missed it. I'm no angel, okay, but I don't hold a candle to him. Your son's a vicious little shit."

It happened so fast all Kate saw was Gaston collapsing, and two officers pouncing on Duval and handcuffing him.

"That's pretty low, fella," one of the cops said. "Kicking a guy in the crotch when he can't fight back."

Duval smiled. "I hope it hurts for a year."

"A hell of a way to treat a brother," the other cop said.

"He ruined my son. Taught him evil things." Duval's voice cracked. "Carson killed Donna? Is that really true? And he tried to kill Kate?" Tears were streaming down his face and he looked not down at his brother but up at the sky.

Yvonne folded herself against him. "Oh, honey, now you're going to jail too," she wailed. "Everybody's going to jail but me and Savvy."

A heavy man in cords and a hooded sweatshirt made his way around the group to Brandon. "Chief, we found some stuff in the black SUV parked out on the road."

So Brandon was the chief of police. She'd rated a visit from the chief, twice, at the hospital? Well, it was a small town.

"Shoot," Brandon said, and looked at Kate with that grin of his.

The big man handed the chief some plastic cards. "Couple of spare IDs, for starters," he said. "Plus photos of little girls, buck naked."

Brandon was looking through the IDs, and laughed aloud at one. "A few photos of girls, or a lot?" he asked, looking up, handing the cards back.

The hooded cop had smiled when his chief laughed. "Tons. Plastic bins, some with eight-by-twelves, some with smaller prints. One with albums made up in sets. Maybe ten of those." He was still smiling; the bonanza of evidence must be making his day. "A laptop, too, like this was his office on wheels. And a shoebox full of those little drives, the ones so small you can give 'em away."

"Sell them, you mean. Oh, goody," Brandon said, rubbing his hands together. He was half-turned toward Kate, as if he were putting on a show for her. "Put tape around the vehicle and have the guys watch it tonight. We'll get the state to look at in the morning, tow it to their lab. Ha! A whole pile of evidence on wheels. Fingerprints show up real nice on photos and album covers."

"You got it, Chief," the cop said, and turned away.

Gaston was still lying on his side, his knees pulled up. "I won't," he said through a grimace of pain, "press charges."

"You want to trade?" Duval asked over his wife's shoulder. "You don't press charges, I don't press charges?"

Yvonne stepped away so the brothers could talk.

Gaston rolled slowly onto his knees. "You're sounding good, brother. Tell me more."

"Did Carson see the kind of pictures they found in your truck?"

"Who cares? They're just pictures. But listen, man, you assaulted me." Gaston looked up, hopeful. "I didn't have anything to do with this Donna person getting killed, that was totally your son's caper. And Kate here is alive and well. So I'm not front and center, you know what I mean? Maybe we can work something out. I won't press charges if you'll go easy on me."

Duval shook his head. "I can't believe what you've turned into. What you've done to my son. You've ruined his life. Go easy on you? I don't think so."

"It's not up to him anyway, Gaston," Brandon said. "Not up to me, either. The feds and the state are going to be fighting over you. You may luck out and be prosecuted by both." He smiled. "Thanks for delivering a whole truckload of evidence."

Duval took a step forward and spat on his brother.

The two officers who'd handcuffed Duval grabbed him by the elbows and pulled him farther away from Gaston, out of range.

Yvonne staggered away from her husband, and Kate caught her. She was sobbing.

I'd be crying too, Kate thought. Her son had killed a family friend and another woman, had tried to kill Kate, and had possibly caused brain damage to his sister. Not to mention Yvonne's normally calm husband was totally out of control.

"All right, that's it," Brandon said. "Let's get these two in the cruisers."

Yvonne left Kate with a wobbly smile and followed Duval as he was led away.

"I'm glad you asked Carson those pointed questions, Kate," the chief said. "You were a catalyst who got some reactions going."

"Before he started shooting, Carson told me a lot of interesting things about what he and his uncle have been doing recently," Kate said.

"I'd like you to tell me all of those interesting things, but tomorrow will be soon enough. You've had a long day. Ever been shot at before?" The amused look he gave her assumed she hadn't.

"As a matter of fact, I have," Kate said.

Startled, he turned away from her. Called out to his men, "All right, guys, let's wrap it up."

Wasn't it already wrapped? Night had overtaken Watkins Spur, and Loyalhanna Creek, and everything between them, under the dim lantern of a quarter moon hung aslant on an invisible peg in the sky. Carson, clutching his sling with his other arm, had been taken away in an ambulance; Gaston had walked, slowly and painfully, to one of the police cars, which had left with him; Duval was sitting in another cruiser, the light bar turned off, Yvonne at the back window talking to him. Only one officer was left to wrap anything up; at Brandon's shout he walked toward the remaining cruiser.

Yvonne trudged toward the house, and Brandon intercepted her. The two of them talked intently, Yvonne's head down, the chief's hand on her shoulder.

The door opened. A small figure ran to Yvonne, slipping between her and Brandon and grabbing her around the waist. Savvy. Her mother turned and swept her close.

Brandon stepped back, came over to Kate. "Doggone, I hate it when the circus leaves town," he said.

It really had been a show, at least to him.

"A useful technique, isn't it?" Rhetorical question. "Instead of hustling everybody into cruisers right off the bat, why not let 'em hang around and yell at each other? Bang their heads together? In the heat of the moment, Duval let loose with info he might not have given, otherwise. He'd have thought of the family's reputation."

"He let loose with something else, too," Kate said.

"You mess with his son, you take your chances. I get it."

Kate looked around. The circus had left town, but one of the animal acts had been left behind. "What's going to happen to Zeus?"

"Who?"

"The poor dog, who doesn't know his master is scum." She looked at the German shepherd. Zeus was lying down, head on paws, still tied to the tree. His tail thumped the ground in response to his name.

Yvonne, with Savvy close by her side, had heard Kate's question.

"We'll take him." She winced. "I'll take him. Until last summer, he and I were buddies." Her daughter followed as she went to Zeus, untied him, and led him back toward Kate and Brandon.

The chief kept his eyes on the dog. Zeus heeled nicely without a command, and sat when Yvonne stopped. Savvy rubbed the dog behind his ears. The chief relaxed.

"Zeus is a sweetie," Yvonne said. "I'll feed him when I get back from the police station. Or, honey, why don't you feed him now?" she asked her daughter. "You know where the kibble is, don't you?"

"Sure, Mum," Savvy said. "But I don't want to stay at the house alone. All that shooting was scary, so don't go get Daddy without me, okay? C'mon, Zeus."

"Course not, honey." Yvonne turned to the chief. "I always have some dog food around in case someone staying at the campground runs out." She glanced over her shoulder, waiting for Savvy to close the door. "She told me she hid under the bed, she was so scared."

"Your husband won't be held," Brandon said. "I'll give him a talking to. He probably won't even be charged with assault, unless Gaston insists, which I doubt. You can stay home and take care of your daughter and that elderly canine. Duval will be home after a while." Brandon turned to Kate. "We can go easy when we're aware of extenuating circumstances."

"Appreciate it," she said.

"Payback," Brandon said. "You told us something funny was going on at the house at the end of Watkins Spur. Wish we'd figured it out sooner. But all we found was a deaf old dear who said a guy named Walter Tremblay let her live there for peanuts. A room with some lights and a printer, what's the big deal? And then tonight Gaston has a couple of IDs on him, one of 'em in Tremblay's name."

"Oh, that's why you laughed at the ID."

"You think she'd have wondered about him showing up for a few hours on Wednesday nights, with girls."

"She knew," Kate said. How could the woman have been unaware of those bright flashes? She was deaf, not blind. And her saying Kate was too old made sense only if she'd been aware of what Gaston was doing. "I'll tell you why I'm sure she lied to you, but can I do it after I get some sleep?"

"Sure," the chief said. "I'm going to ask you all to come down to the station tomorrow." He took a few steps toward the cruiser Duval was in, then turned. "Thanks for outing the youngest murderer I've ever met," he said to Kate. "Given what Yvonne here told me he did to his sister, I'm sure we'll figure out what he did to the Winnebago to kill the Miller woman."

"I know how he did it," Kate said.

Yvonne had started toward the house, but she turned around, a startled look on her face.

"Oh, you do?" Brandon's tone was light but his eyes were intense. "And how long have you known that small piece of information?"

"About half an hour. I would have told you, but I was kind of busy."

Brandon yawned. "Shot at by small boys and tackled by large, irate men. All in a day's work for us. Maybe you should join the force."

"I'd rather not." More theatrics. Kate wondered if his yawn had been real. Hers was.

"So how did he do it?"

"He climbed down the tree from his room and put duct tape over the heater vent on the outside of the Winnebago. Thought he was doing in Juneau, the dog that always barked at him. Found out otherwise when the ambulances came. After they'd left, he came down and peeled the tape off. Duval and John and the officers you sent didn't check the Winnebago until the next day."

"The perfect crime," Brandon said, nodding.

260

"He didn't realize what he was doing," Yvonne said, mostly to herself. "Killing a dog is bad, but not as bad as—"

It wasn't a good time to remind her that Carson knew exactly what he was doing to Annie.

The back door opened and Savvy and Zeus came out. "I can't find the Purina," the girl said. Maybe she couldn't find it because she'd rather stay close to her mother. Kate wouldn't blame her one bit.

"Why don't you take care of these two?" Kate asked Yvonne. "It's been a hard night for everybody." Having something that needed doing might be therapeutic for a mother who'd just had a son taken away.

Savvy leaned against her mother's hip. Zeus sat in front of Yvonne and looked up at her expectantly.

"You bad dog, you broke Carson's arm," Yvonne said, her tone mild, even affectionate. Then, as if she'd heard what she'd just said, sadness swept into her face. "I should get down to the hospital to see him, but I'm still—I'm getting used to everything. He's not the son I thought I knew."

"He hid a lot from you," Kate said. "I bet that computer club didn't meet on Wednesdays. I bet that's when—"

"Computer club?" Brandon asked.

"Yes. You should ask Savvy about it," Kate said. "She said it met outdoors sometimes. Right, Savvy? Which I thought was strange. Maybe the club took field trips to a certain house on Watkins Spur. Maybe the members were mostly girls."

"A club at the school?" Brandon asked, looking from Kate to Savvy.

The girl nodded.

"We'll talk about it tomorrow, then," the chief said. "You can tell me all about your brother."

"He hid a lot from me, for sure," Yvonne said. She bent over Zeus, rubbing his big shoulders. "And so did Gaston—that

261

bastard—" Her tears fell and stood on Zeus' fur, catching the light from the back porch.

Kate put an arm around her friend and one around Savvy. Wished she'd had another arm for Zeus.

"Hey," she said. She didn't know what else to say to a woman who was facing so much difficulty in the weeks and months ahead, appalling disruptions to the family that had been the anchor for her life.

The anchor had dragged, but it would hold. Duval was not the source of Carson's troubles, despite Kate's occasional suspicions. Yvonne had him, and she had Savvy.

"Hey," Yvonne said back. She pulled her face out of Zeus's fur and gave Kate a weak smile, then looked at Savvy. "Let's go feed Zeus. Let's feed everybody. Including you, Kate. Come on."

Mother and daughter started toward the door. Kate looked around. Brandon had left them, gracefully, without a word. Halfway down the driveway, the taillights of the cruiser cast a red glow into the darkness.

* * *

Yvonne took a big pot out of the fridge. "I made some soup yesterday. I'll just heat it up." She put kibble down for Zeus first: he ate noisily and fast, as if he hadn't been fed in a week. "Zeus is a great dog, and Gaston won't be able to take care of him for a good long time. I like dogs. I keep thinking about Juneau and how she saved Richard's life.

"Juneau. It all started with her." Kate put bowls and spoons on the table and sat gratefully down. She was tired and her arm ached again. She'd been cold, but the warmth of the room fell around her like one of Yvonne's sweaters.

"What do you mean?" Savvy slid into a chair next to Kate, looking subdued.

"Carson didn't like Juneau because she barked at him. You ever notice? He was the only person she barked at, and he hated it," Kate said.

"Yeah, I noticed that," Savvy said.

"There was probably a reason. Your brother wasn't kind to animals. He might have hurt Juneau when nobody was looking."

"He shot rubber bands at Shadow," Savvy said. "I stopped him a bunch of times, but I couldn't watch him twenty-four seven."

"Juneau is one smart dog," Yvonne said. "If he was mean to her, she'd remember."

"Carson is pretty smart, too," Savvy said. "Isn't he, Mum?"

Yvonne didn't say anything for a minute. She turned the burner on low and found a lid for the pot. Then she sat down, looked at Savvy with red eyes. "Yes, he's smart, Savvy. But something's very wrong with your brother."

Kate reached across the table and gave Yvonne's hand a squeeze.

"He's smart but he uses it wrong," Savvy said.

Her mother, staring at the table, didn't answer.

"That's it exactly," Kate said to the girl. "Right, Yvonne?"

Her friend looked up, but she hadn't heard. "I don't feel like eating, but we should." she said. "Will you be okay with just soup? I could make a salad, I suppose."

"Soup is plenty," Kate said.

"Savvy?"

"Soup's awesome, Mum."

"I always wondered why he kept taking the screen out. He said the screen got in the way of the fresh air coming in." Yvonne closed her eyes. "What a liar. I wish I understood how he got that way." She got up heavily, brought the pot to the table, and ladled chicken soup into the bowls. Steam rose.

Kate quieted her vegetarian objections; this wasn't the time. And she had to admit it smelled good.

\* \* \*

Exhausted, they ate slowly. Savvy looked as if she might fall asleep over her bowl, and it was still half full when her mother took her upstairs to bed.

Yvonne came back sooner than Kate expected. "She fell asleep like a rock. She'll be full of questions in the morning, and I'll have to tell her everything. Gently. I'm glad I don't have to figure it all out tonight."

"Being a mother is so complicated. You have to filter the world for a kid. Rearrange reality, or the worst parts of reality."

"For Savvy I do. With Carson, it's the other way around. He's rearranged my reality." She ladled more soup into both bowls without asking Kate if she wanted more. Automatic mother mode. "I wish I understood him. I wish I understood how he could have done what he did."

"Carson didn't say this, so this is me imagining how Donna's death affected him," Kate said. "He waited, but nobody figured out that he was responsible. So that encouraged him."

Yvonne met Kate's eyes. "He'd done it by accident, but then he thought he'd gotten away with murder."

"Right. He knew about Steve hiding in the woods—the hermit—and then he saw Annie had moved her van out there and was living in it with her brother. So he saw a chance to get away with doing the same thing."

Yvonne wasn't eating. "Wait for one of them to start the van, stuff the exhaust pipe with rags, then sneak back later and remove them?"

Kate nodded. "But Sean and I came along too soon, and Carson didn't have a chance to take the rags out and hide that evidence."

"Oh, God. He didn't care whether his victim was Annie or Steve." Yvonne's face was etched with pain. "And he could have taken Savvy from us. He could have killed her."

"It was a close call," Kate said. "He was experimenting. He could have gotten it wrong."

Yvonne shuddered. "He must have lost his moral compass by hanging around with his uncle. I wish Duval and I had figured out sooner what a terrible influence Gaston was."

Kate was startled to see she'd finished her second helping. Somehow the soup was exactly what she'd needed.

She pushed the bowl away. "That was all just guesswork, about Annie," Kate said. "Carson said a lot to me before the police got here, partly to get his uncle in trouble, but he didn't talk about her. The police will look for evidence. I'll bet the rags in the exhaust pipe will be traced to this house."

"I wish I'd known. I could have gotten him some help."

"Yvonne, you really can't blame yourself. Or maybe even Gaston. A very few people are born without a conscience, and it's your bad luck Carson is one of them. It wasn't anything you did. Or didn't do."

Yvonne didn't answer. Kate looked up and saw her friend's soup was being salted with tears.

# TWENTY-TWO

"At least it's over," Savvy said. She sat cross-legged on a patio chair, drinking cocoa; her parents and Kate had mugs of hot cider.

"Oh, honey, it won't be over for a long time," Yvonne said. "Your brother needs so much help."

"But at least we know what happened," Duval said, his face only a shade less grim than it had been during his confrontation with his brother.

"Amen," Yvonne said.

The four had spent hours at the police station that morning, being interviewed and re-interviewed. One of the blessings of a small town: you gave evidence at a civilized hour. Brandon could have dragged them all in the night before, but he hadn't. Even Duval had slept in his own bed after a cruiser dropped him off, late. The first thing he'd done that morning was to set up a large wooden CLOSED sign at the campground entrance. "We need a day off," he said, and called his office to take a vacation day. He'd spent the most time being questioned, but Kate had gone over her statement with three different officers and so had Yvonne, who must be grateful not to have to deal with incoming RVers.

Except for an occasional cricket chirp, the autumn afternoon was quiet. Roll and Rest was host to only three rigs: Kate's camper, John's van and Richard's big RV. Yellow CRIME SCENE DO NOT CROSS tape ran around the Winnebago's site, and the shot-out window was covered in black plastic.

"Hear anything from Richard?" Kate asked.

"He's staying with his son in Pittsburgh until he feels up to traveling," Yvonne said. "Then he'll fly straight to Florida. The police are impounding his RV, and when they're through with it Duval and I will sell it for him. Richard doesn't want it. He doesn't even want to to see it again."

If she overlooked the Winnebago's window and crime scene tape, Kate could imagine it had all been a wild dream: gunshots, an attack dog, a broken arm, a broken boy, animosity between brothers, the scenes lit by the unreal, pulsing blue of police cruisers.

All was calm now, the attack dog snoring at their feet. "Last night seems like a dream, doesn't it?" Kate asked. "Or is it just me?"

Savvy said quickly, "It's just you, Kate. Last night was definitely not a dream. I felt like I was waking up." She'd spent less time talking to the police than her parents and Kate had; after a talk with a woman officer, she'd curled up in a chair in Brandon's office with a school workbook.

"No wonder," her mother said. "Last night, for the first time in a month, your room wasn't being gassed with carbon monoxide."

"Yeah, but I was awake because of the shoot-out," Savvy said. "Sounded like a small war starting up right outside the house." She looked scared. "I got under my bed."

"Oh, honey." Yvonne leaned forward to stroke her daughter's hair. "You're safe now. And no more getting lost and forgetting things and being cranky."

"I can't believe my own brother did that to me." Savvy sounded more sad than angry. "I'm so far behind in school."

"You'll catch up, sugar," Yvonne said. She sat back heavily. "I wish I could have protected you. But I didn't know Carson was seeing Gaston, and—all that." She bit her lip.

"I didn't know he was running around at night whenever he pleased," Duval said. "No wonder he begged us not to cut down the tree next to the house. He claimed he loved having a 'big green friend' outside his window. What a line."

"We fell for it," Yvonne said.

"I should have ratted him out," Savvy said. "But I thought he was just hanging out in the woods, playing, like we used to do together. At school? He was popular all of a sudden. With girls I didn't like. So I ignored him, like he wasn't even my brother."

Zeus groaned in his sleep and rolled over onto his back, paws tucked. The girl smiled and slipped down beside him, rubbing the tan fur on his belly.

"Why don't you take him for a walk, Savvy?" Yvonne asked. "I bet you could find a good stick to throw for him."

At the word *walk,* Zeus scrambled to his feet and stared at Yvonne.

Savvy rolled her eyes. "You said the magic word, Mum. Now I have to take him." But she didn't sound unhappy. She stood and said "C'mon, Zeus." The big dog's interest in Yvonne vanished, and Savvy laughed.

She led her canine friend across the empty sites toward the woods at the back of the campground.

"It's a good thing Carson and Gaston had a falling out," Kate said when Savvy was out of earshot. "The phones I found were the first sign something fishy was going on around here, and it turns out Carson tossed them just to aggravate his uncle. A way to rebel. And he had his first girlfriend to impress."

"Gaston getting some of his own back," Duval said, sour.

"Man, I got some creepy messages on those phones," Kate said. "I'm not sure if they were from Gaston doing business, or from Carson trying to scare me. If it was Carson he may have deliberately left the phones where I'd find them."

She thought a moment. "Maybe it was both of them, because a man phoned me in the middle of the night and called me by name. The voice wasn't a boy's. That had to be Gaston."

Duval gave her a sympathetic look. "That's unnerving. How did he know your name?"

"It took me a while to figure that out," Kate said. "The tag at my campground site. Full name, and number of days reserved."

Yvonne and Duval looked at each other. "We'll use initials from now on," he said.

At the back of the campground, Zeus barked. Arm raised, Savvy was poised to throw a stick. The big dog crouched, ready for action.

"The whole thing started with a bark," Kate said.

"Right," Duval said. "Carson got mad at Juneau for barking at him, and that's why he taped the vent, and things went to hell from there."

Tears sparkled in Yvonne's lashes. "I always thought Gaston had too much money for what he did. He never had a career, only jobs here and there, selling cars or RVs. Or real estate."

"He showed houses," Duval said. "He wasn't a broker. He would have had to study to get a license. Too much work, that's how he thought. He was only interested in easy money."

"You were hurt when he dropped us last summer," Yvonne said, "but now you know the whole story aren't you glad he wasn't around?"

"Yeah. But Carson was still seeing him. And by last summer the damage was done. It was years in the making." Duval's voice was dull. He swirled the cider in his cup. "Don't know if I'll ever see my brother again. Ever want to see him."

"Don't think about that now, honey," Yvonne said.

Kate wondered if he'd be called upon to testify at Gaston's trial. Maybe not. He'd been immersed in his insurance job and hadn't communicated with his brother in months. And he certainly wouldn't be a good choice as a character witness.

"Last night he said he was staying away to keep us safe," Duval said. "Bull feathers. He didn't want me to figure out what he was up to. Safe? He made Carson his apprentice. A fledgling criminal."

"Gaston took advantage of people," Yvonne said. "Like the girls at the school." She frowned into her cup.

"And a veteran with PTSD," Kate said.

"Yes." Yvonne closed her eyes for a moment. "Gaston was Steve's last chance for a job, but it turned out to be a job that cost him dearly."

"What kind of work did he do?" Duval asked. "Now that you've told the police everything, tell me."

"The police are the ones who told me," Kate said. "He started training a puppy to replace Zeus. He tuned up the SUV. He took care of the house out there he used to own, cleaned the gutters, did handyman chores. But then he found out Gaston was taking nasty pictures of little girls and selling them, and he quit."

"Quit" was an understatement. Brandon had told Kate and Yvonne that Steve had suffered a meltdown when he saw a flash from one of the photo sessions at the house. He'd dropped a bag of groceries in the driveway and bolted for the woods. Climbed a tree and stayed there for two days. When he came down, he figured out what the photo shoots were all about.

"He got bullied into one last job, cutting the wires in the breaker box." Kate nodded toward the corner of the house. "Gaston was jealous because of your family and your business, the stable life you'd built, the respect you'd earned—everything he wanted and wasn't willing to work for."

"I've missed so much," Duval said. "Been working too hard."

"I didn't tell anyone I found Annie's van in the woods," Kate said. "At first I thought she was the hermit, which tickled me—a woman, how about that. But then I met her brother, the real hermit, and he said he'd worked for a bad guy who told him to damage the box," Kate said. "I figured the baddest guy around was the one connected to the old house on Watkins Spur. I thought his name was Walter Tremblay. I didn't know Walter was Gaston until last night."

"And today, Duval, while you were explaining to a couple of detectives why you kicked your brother," Yvonne said, "I got lots of the missing pieces to this story from Brandon, the police chief."

"Oh, yeah," Duval said. "The guy who thinks he's so funny. Mr. Comic Cop."

"Steve overheard enough when the police came down on Annie's van to know his sister's death was murder," Yvonne said. "He figured he'd be suspect number one, and he saw how many people were looking for him. So he turned himself in late last night. Brandon said the poor guy was a wreck, shaking and crying. He could barely talk."

"Poor Steve," Kate said. "He ended his hermit days for the worst possible reason. He'll be a wreck about Annie, all right, and about losing the only way of life he was comfortable with."

"Brandon said he found him a bed at a VA hospital near Pittsburgh. Steve will get counseling," Yvonne said.

"Enough about that guy," Duval said. "Get back to Carson and my brother."

"Carson was finding girls for Gaston to take those horrible pictures of," Yvonne said. "When Donna died Gaston wanted to make sure Carson didn't get questioned, because he might spill the beans about what his uncle was up to." Her voice trembled. "He's just a little kid."

"Then Carson saw me checking the vent on the Winnebago," Kate said. "He and Gaston thought I'd figured out Donna's death wasn't an accident. So the two of them ambushed me: Carson dropped a rock on my head and Gaston threw me in the river."

"What a couple of—" Duval put his hands over his face. "My brother. My *son.*"

"Gaston's life is ruined. He'll be in prison for decades," Yvonne said. "We'll have to work hard to keep Carson from going down that road."

They were quiet, absorbing the intertwined stories. Three pairs of siblings, one of each pair in dire trouble. As the news spread, distress would radiate outward from Gaston, and Carson, and poor Steve. To the Chouinards in Quebec and Yvonne's parents in Maine, for starters. To Steve and Annie's family in Wisconsin.

And onward from there. Not only families, but friends and associates. Steve's veteran friend John. The girls in the Union Hill school tainted by Gaston's depravity, and their parents and grandparents and friends. All the other residents of Union Hill. And the Millers and their connections. Society was a human version of the Internet, news propagating along lines that branched like neurons.

A bark from a border collie like a spark in tinder. The tinder a sick man, a vulnerable boy. He'd killed twice, and Kate had almost been the third victim.

"You know that drawing I did of the rock where I was sitting the day I got set adrift? Yvonne and I found it in Carson's room," Kate said. "He got a friend to buy it for him at the fair. He must have seen it as a trophy."

"You can have it back," Duval said. "A different kind of trophy, of having survived my son's madness."

Yvonne put a hand on his knee.

One squirrel chased another across the gravel and under the Winnebago. Kate closed her eyes against the image of the maimed squirrel at Gaston's house. Opened them. These two energetic animals were alive and well. Carson couldn't hurt them.

"I guess squirrels can't read police tape," Duval said.

Yvonne's laugh was quiet, but Kate found her vision blurring with tears. Under the circumstances, a joke was a gift. And a laugh was a treasure. Her two friends would be okay. They would rise above the dark forces that had threatened their small family.

Kate's thoughts returned to all the people damaged by Gaston's greedy scheme. "Did Brandon say anything about the old woman at the house?" Kate asked. "Who she was?"

"No," Yvonne said. "Probably somebody poor, who couldn't afford to be curious about what he was up to. In trade for a place to stay, and free food."

"I bet he trolled for her outside the welfare office in Pittsburgh," Duval said. "He needed somebody to be a caretaker at the house, right? And to tell him if anybody showed up asking questions."

"Like me," Kate said. "Taking the phone to the house must have made Gaston suspicious. And I parked my camper pretty close to the house a few times, including the night I gave Sharon a ride to town. She might have told him I was hanging around."

"I am so glad all those girls will get counseling," Yvonne said. "Thank goodness Savvy wasn't involved."

"Gaston had to be careful not to be seen on the school grounds," Duval said. "He used Carson as a recruiter."

The conversation stopped as Savvy came back with a panting Zeus. "I could have thrown the stick a ton more times, Mum. But he was only good for like, five minutes?" she said. "He's kind of old."

Yvonne laughed. "He was doing all the work, honey. You were supervising."

"Yeah." The girl dropped into a chair. "Is Uncle Gassy the devil?"

Kate heard Yvonne's breath catch.

"Close enough," Duval said. "When we were younger he was happy-go-lucky. You couldn't count on him for anything except being up for a party. Later, though, all these schemes—" He shook his head.

"The devil got Carson," Savvy said.

Kate leaned forward. "Your brother has a brain abnormality," she said. She'd had a good talk with Marjorie early that morning. "He had some wires crossed before he was even born. It isn't anything your parents should feel bad about, Savvy. Carson's just the way he is." She stopped. She'd told Yvonne about the dead squirrels she'd found, including the mutilated one, and she'd told the police. But Savvy didn't need to hear about her brother's gruesome entertainment.

Yvonne and Duval were quiet, looking down at their empty cups. Kate took it as a sign she could say a little more.

"He didn't choose to be the way he is, and he can't help it. But with some professional care, some training, he can learn how to live a nearly-normal life.

"I should have figured it out," Yvonne said. "The way he was making you sick, Savvy."

"I should have." Duval put his hand over his wife's, on the arm of her chair. "I'm going to be careful, from now on, not to focus completely on work. I lost sight of my family."

"Mum, Dad." Savvy slid out of her chair and hugged Yvonne, and then Duval. "I wish *I'd* figured it out."

Kate looked away, across the campground, giving the family some time. Rusty patrolled at a slow, majestic pace. He found a patch of sunlight and sat, smiling. His coat glowed. Eyes like headlights.

Savvy was back in her chair. Yvonne's eyes were wet, Duval's face flushed.

"All the bad things, like Donna dying and Savvy's forgetfulness and me almost going over the dam, they were all connected," Kate said. "And now they're history."

"That's a good way to look at it," Yvonne said. "A big chunk of bad stuff is in the past. Now we can look forward to some peace." She wiped her eyes.

They're water over the dam?" Kate smiled. "And I'm really happy it was only water."

# TWENTY-THREE

She'd had coffee with Yvonne, going early so she could see Duval and Savvy, too. Duval had given her a big goodbye hug. "You saved my family, Kate," he said. "I'll be grateful forever." He gave her a quick kiss on the cheek and then stepped away, looking embarrassed.

"You saved my life, Kate," Savvy said. "If Carson had made a mistake with the size of those pieces of cardboard, I could have been toast."

"Oh, please don't say that," Yvonne said. "It makes me crazy just to think about it."

"Kids at school will probably say things about your brother," Kate said. "My advice? Don't listen. And for sure don't answer."

"I've already talked to some friends, now I'm allowed a cell phone," Savvy said, flashing a sideways smile at her mother. "They've been great, and I haven't even known them very long. I have good friends."

"Something you can appreciate now that you can think again," Yvonne said.

Savvy laughed. "The last month was one weirdo trip, let me tell you. Not having enough oxygen makes you stupider than dirt."

"C'mon, Savvy, you'll be late," Duval said. "Hop in the truck."

Savvy slung her pink backpack over a shoulder and gave Kate a one-armed hug. "School first," she said. "It's my new mantra."

"School first," Kate said. "Way to go, girl."

"It was her old mantra, too, before all this happened," Yvonne said. She and Kate stood at the front door and watched the truck go down the driveway. "I'm keeping the neurologist's appointment for her, but I'm thrilled at how much her old self she seems."

"She's going to be fine," Kate said. "You know, it was Carson's bad luck—and Donna's and Annie's—that he killed either one of them. If the carbon monoxide detector on the Winnebago had worked, and if the engine cover in Annie's van hadn't leaked, both of them would still be alive. And Carson wouldn't be locked up in a juvie facility."

"True," Yvonne said. "He had evil intent, though."

"It's the thought that counts?" Bad joke, and Kate wished she hadn't said it. It sounded flippant, which wasn't how she felt.

"It'll take me a while to feel like his mother again. I'm so glad you were here, Kate. I don't know what would have happened next if you hadn't figured things out."

"You would have managed," Kate said. "The police were about to bust Gaston, and they would have discovered what happened to Annie, too." She followed Yvonne to the dining room, and picked up her cup. On more swallow of coffee left, and she drank it. Carried her cup to the kitchen.

"Just leave it beside the sink," Yvonne said. "I don't know. Managed? Maybe I would have. But such a lot of things were happening all at once." She gave Kate a sad smile. "Last night Duval said we have some wild stories to tell people. Not about Carson—I won't be talking about him much. No, about you. Nearly going over the dam, letting an eighty-pound German shepherd dangle off your arm in a windstorm—"

"And thereby hangs a tale?" The question was out of her mouth before Kate recognized it as something her father used to say.

"Yes. Oh! Speaking of tails, here comes one now," Yvonne said, beaming at Shadow as the cat rubbed against her ankles. "We have long tails around here, don't we, honey?" She scooped up the cat and stroked her, then let her jump down to a chair.

"So do roadrunners. And scissor-tailed flycatchers," Kate said.

"Those are birds?"

"Or wait, like a magpie," Kate said. She thought of Annie, fondling the green necklace, repeating the old story about magpies collecting bright things. Not something she wanted to share with Yvonne: too sad. "The magpie's tail is as long as the whole rest of the bird."

They went to the back door together, and Kate collected her third hug of the morning. It was the longest one, and Kate saw tears in Yvonne's eyes before the door with the smiling cats closed.

She started the generator and let it run while she double-checked her site. Camper unplugged from shore power, check. Electrical cord stowed: check. Kayak unlocked from picnic table, strapped to roof rack: check. Nothing left on the ground or table: check.

Inside the camper, she made sure the coffeemaker was stowed in a cabinet and books were tucked on the shelf with the bungee cord across the row of spines. Shipshape. Secure.

It had been an intense month. Kate was glad to have made friends with the Chouinards, but even so she was ready to put southwestern Pennsylvania behind her.

The strongest tug at her heart came when she thought of Sean. Smart, tough, funny Sean. She'd sent him an email describing what had happened in Union Hill after he left, with no idea when he might have time to respond: being an agent on an FBI task force had to be as demanding as any job could be, right up there with being a soldier on the front lines. Her thoughts skittered away from how much the jobs had in common.

She turned off the generator and locked the camper door. In the cab, she opened an atlas on the passenger seat, excited to see a whole string of National Forests running along the Appalachians. She could follow the string southwest, going first to the Monongahela, then the George Washington and Jefferson, then Cherokee and Pisgah. Holy cats, there were thousands of square miles waiting for her boots, her binoculars and sketchbook, her rescued red paddle, her grateful eyes and ears.

Monongahela National Forest was the first, and it wasn't far, only an hour and half to its northern edge. Kate started the engine.

A slap on the driver's window stopped her. It was John, grinning.

She smiled back and pushed the button. The window slid down, but John dropped from sight. What the heck?

He stood back up with an armful of orange fur and two imperious yellow eyes.

"Didn't think you were leaving without saying goodbye, did you?"

Kate didn't know if he meant himself or Rusty, but she laughed and stroked the rough fur, along with a few of John's fingers.

"You be good," she said. "If you can." She didn't know which one of them she meant.

John laughed. "I'll just take this big bad kitty to the patio, away from your truck. He's used to cars and trucks and RVs, but gosh he was hanging around pretty close to your site. He must like you."

"The feeling's mutual," Kate said, and waved. As she gave the truck some gas and turned the wheel, the atlas slid off the passenger seat and flipped itself closed on the floor.

It didn't matter. She would find her way.

If you enjoyed this book, look for others in the Art of Murder series: *Drawing Fire*, Book 1, and *Boat Camp Killer*, Book 2, available now on Amazon.

See www.PamFoxAuthor.com for updates.

Comments? I'd enjoy hearing from you! Email me at PamFoxAuthor@gmail.com or follow me on Twitter at @PamFoxAuthor.

www.ingramcontent.com/pod-product-compliance
Lightning Source LLC
Chambersburg PA
CBHW030321200626
46816CB00006BA/1880